The Antelope Wife

Also by Louise Erdrich

Tales of Burning Love

Love Medicine

The Beet Queen

Tracks

The Bingo Palace

The Blue Jay's Dance

The Crown of Columbus (with Michael Dorris)

Jacklight (poetry)

Baptism of Desire (poetry)

THE ANTELOPE WIFE

A NOVEL

LOUISE ERDRICH

HarperPerennial
A Division of HarperCollins*Publishers*

A hardcover edition of this book was published in 1998 by HarperFlamingo, an imprint of HarperCollins Publishers.

First HarperPerennial edition published 1999.

Designed by Claudyne Bedell

The Library of Congress has catalogued the hardcover edition as follows:

Erdrich, Louise.
The antelope wife : a novel / Louise Erdrich.
p. cm.
ISBN 0-06-018726-3
1. Ojibwa Indians—Fiction. I. Title.
PS3555.R42A8 1998
813' .54—dc21 97-48894

ISBN 0-06-093007-1 (pbk.)

99 00 01 02 03 ❖/RRD 10 9 8 7 6 5 4 3 2 1

This book was written before the death of my husband. He is remembered with love by all of his family.

To my children,

Persia, Aza,

Pallas, Birdie,

and Sava

Acknowledgments

As always, my family is first in my thanks. My brother, Louis, has kept a strict eye on environmental engineering at several reservations. Dad copyedited and John Burke gave me Wing Chun. Marian Moore gave me blueness. My sisters and brothers held my hand in theirs all year. Don, my heart. Thanks to Diane Reverand, my gifted editor at HarperCollins, and thanks to Trent Duffy for his coherent view. Jay Redhawk for the name "Almost Soup." Thanks to Joyce Kittson, one of the country's finest beadwork artists; to Mom, Barb Nagle, the whole beading table, and Anishinabemowin Dopowin. Lisa Record, thank you. Regina Thunderhawk. Tish, Chad, Cleo—Megwitch, mino aya sana onishisin abinojeen. Last and first, Jim Clark, Nauwigeezis, gekinoamadaywinini. Apijigo megwitch. Any mistakes are mine.

Contents

Part One

Bayzhig

Ever since the beginning these twins are sewing. One sews with light and one with dark. The first twin's beads are cut-glass whites and pales, and the other twin's beads are glittering deep red and blue-black indigo. One twin uses an awl made of an otter's sharpened penis bone, the other uses that of a bear. They sew with a single sinew thread, in, out, fast and furious, each trying to set one more bead into the pattern than her sister, each trying to upset the balance of the world.

1

Father's Milk

Scranton Roy

Deep in the past during a spectacular cruel raid upon an isolated Ojibwa village mistaken for hostile during the scare over the starving Sioux, a dog bearing upon its back a frame-board tikinagun enclosing a child in moss, velvet, embroideries of beads, was frightened into the vast carcass of the world west of the Otter Tail River. A cavalry soldier, spurred to human response by the sight of the dog, the strapped-on child, vanishing into the distance, followed and did not return.

What happened to him lives on, though fading in the larger memory, and I relate it here in order that it not be lost.

Private Scranton Teodorus Roy was the youngest son of a Quaker father and a reclusive poet mother who established a small Pennsylvania community based on intelligent conversation. One day into his view a member of a traveling drama troupe appeared.

Unmasked, the woman's stage glance broke across Roy's brow like fire. She was tall, stunningly slender, pale, and paler haired, resolute in her character, and simple in her amused scorn of Roy—so young, bright-faced, obedient. To prove himself, he made a rendezvous promise and then took his way west following her glare. An icicle, it drove into his heart and melted there, leaving a trail of ice and blood. The way was long. She glided like a snake beneath his footsteps in fevered dreams. When he finally got to the place they had agreed upon, she was not there, of course. Angry and at odds, he went against the radiant ways of his father and enlisted in the U.S. Cavalry at Fort Sibley on the banks of the Mississippi in St. Paul, Minnesota.

There, he was trained to the rifle, learned to darn his socks using a wooden egg, ate many an ill-cooked bean, and polished his officers' harness leather until one day, in a state of uneasy resignation, he put on the dark blue uniform, fixed his bayonet, set off marching due west.

The village his company encountered was peaceful, then not.

In chaos of groaning horses, dogs screaming, rifle and pistol reports, and the smoke of errant cooking fires, Scranton Roy was most disturbed not by the death yells of old men and the few warriors shocked naked from their robes, but by the feral quiet of the children. And the sudden contempt he felt for them all. Unexpected, the frigid hate. The pleasure in raising, aiming. They ran fleet as their mothers, heading for a brush-thick gully and a slough of grass beyond. Two fell. Roy whirled, not knowing whom to shoot next. Eager, he bayoneted an old woman who set upon him with no other weapon but a stone picked from the ground.

She was built like the broken sacks of hay he'd used for practice, but her body closed fast around the instrument. He braced himself against her to pull free, set his boot between her legs to tug the blade from her stomach, and as he did so tried to avoid her eyes but did not manage. His gaze was drawn into hers and he sank with it into the dark unaccompanied moment before his birth. There was a word she uttered in her language. Daashkikaa. Daashkikaa. A groan of heat and blood. He saw his mother, yanked the bayonet out with a huge cry, and began to run.

That was when he saw the dog, a loping dirt-brown cur, circle the camp twice with the child on its back and set off into open space. As much to escape the evil confusion of this village and his own dark act as out of any sympathy for the baby, though he glimpsed its face—mystified and calm—Scranton Roy started running after the two. Within moments, the ruckus of death was behind him. The farther away the village got, the farther behind he wanted it. He kept on, running, walking, managing to keep the dog in view only because it was spring and the new grass, after a burn of lightning, was just beginning its thrust, which would take it to well over a full-grown man's height.

From time to time, as the day went on, the dog paused to rest, stretched patient beneath its burden. Grinning and panting, she allowed Roy to approach, just so far. A necklace of blue beads hung from the brow guard of the cradle board. It swayed, clattered lightly. The child's hands were bound in the wrappings. She could not reach for the beads but stared at them as though mesmerized. The sun grew razor-hot. Tiny blackflies settled at the corners of her eyes. Sipped moisture from along her lids until, toward late afternoon, the heat died. A cold wind boomed against Scranton Roy in a steady rush. Still, into the emptiness, the three infinitesimally pushed.

The world darkened. Afraid of losing the trail, Roy gave his utmost. As night fixed upon them, man and dog were close enough to hear each other breathing and so, in that rhythm, both slept. Next morning, the dog stayed near, grinning for scraps. Afraid to frighten him with a rifle shot, Roy hadn't brought down game although he'd seen plenty. He managed to snare a rabbit. Then, with his tinderbox and steel, he started a fire and began to roast it, at which smell the dog dragged itself belly-down through the dirt, edging close. The baby made its first sound, a murmuring whimper. Accepting tidbits and bones, the dog was alert, suspicious. Roy could not touch it until the next day when he'd thought to wash himself all over and approach naked to diminish his whiteman's scent.

So he was able at last to remove the child from its wrappings and bathe it, a girl, and to hold her. He'd never done such a thing before.

First he tried to feed her a tiny piece of the rabbit. She was too young to manage. He dripped water into her mouth, made sure it trickled down, but was perplexed at what to feed her, then alarmed when, after a night of deprivation, her tiny face crumpled in need. She peered at him in expectation and, at last, violently squalled. Her cries filled a vastness that nothing else could. They resounded, took over everything, and brought his heart clean to the surface. Scranton Roy cradled the baby, sang lewd camp tunes, then stalwart hymns, and at last remembered his own mother's lullabies. Nothing helped. It seemed, when he held her close upon his heart as women did, that the child grew angry with longing and desperately clung, rooted with its mouth, roared in frustration, until at last, moved to near insanity, Roy opened his shirt and put her to his nipple.

She seized him. Inhaled him. Her suck was fierce. His whole body was astonished, most of all the inoffensive nipple he'd never noticed or appreciated until, in spite of the pain, it served to gain him peace. As he sat there, the child holding part of him in its mouth, he looked around just in case there should be any witness to this act which seemed to him strange as anything that had happened in this sky-filled land. Of course, there was only the dog. Contented, freed, it lolled appreciatively near. So the evening passed and then the night. Scranton Roy was obliged to change nipples, the first one hurt so, and he fell asleep with the baby tucked beside him on his useless teat.

She was still there in the morning, stuck, though he pulled her off to slingshot a partridge, roasted that too, and smeared its grease on his two sore spots. That made her wild for him. He couldn't remove her then and commenced to walk, holding her, attached, toward a stand of cottonwood that wavered in the distance. A river. A place to camp. He'd settle there for a day or two, he thought, and try to teach the baby to eat something, for he feared she'd starve to death although she seemed, except for the times he removed her from his chest, surprisingly contented.

He slung the blue beads around the baby's neck. Tied the cradle board onto his own back. Then the man, child, and the dog struck farther into the wilderness. They reached hills of sand, oak covered, shelter. Nearby, sod he cut painstakingly with the length of his bayonet and piled into a square, lightless but secure, and warm. Hoarding his shots, he managed to bring down a buffalo bull fat-loaded with the summer grass. He fleshed the hide, dried the meat, seared the brains, stored the pounded fat and berries in the gut, made use of every bone and scrap of flesh even to the horns, carved into spoons, and the eyeballs, tossed to the dog. The tongue, cooked tender and mashed in his own mouth, he coaxed the baby to accept. She still much preferred him. As he was now past civilized judgment, her loyalty filled him with a foolish, tender joy.

He bathed each morning at the river. Once, he killed a beaver and greased himself all over against mosquitoes with its fat. The baby continued to nurse and he made a sling for her from his shirt. He lounged in the doorway of his sod hut, dreaming and exhausted, fearing that a fever was coming upon him. The situation was confusing. He did not know what course to take, how to start back, wondered if there'd be a party sent to search for him and then realized if they did find him he'd be court-martialed. The baby kept nursing and refused to stop. His nipples toughened. Pity scorched him, she sucked so blindly, so forcefully, and with such immense faith. It occurred to him one slow dusk as he looked down at her, upon his breast, that she was teaching him something.

This notion seemed absurd when he first considered it, and then, as insights do when we have the solitude to absorb them, he eventually grew used to the idea and paid attention to the lesson. The word *faith* hooked him. She had it in such pure supply. She nursed with utter simplicity and trust, as though the act itself would produce her wish. Half asleep one early morning, her beside him, he felt a slight warmth, then a rush in one side of his chest, a pleasurable burning. He thought it was an odd dream and fell asleep again only to wake to a huge burp from the baby, whose lips curled back from her dark gums in bliss, whose tiny fists were unclenched in sleep for the first time, who looked, impossibly, well fed.

Ask and ye shall receive. Ask and ye shall receive. The words ran through him like a clear stream. He put his hand to his chest and then tasted a thin blue drop of his own watery, appalling, God-given milk.

MISS PEACE MCKNIGHT

Family duty was deeply planted in Miss Peace McKnight, also the knowledge that if she did not nobody else would—do the duty, that is, of seeing to the future of the McKnights. Her father's Aberdeen button-cart business failed after he ran out of dead sheep—his own, whose bones he cleverly thought to use after a spring disaster. He sawed buttons with an instrument devised of soldered steel, ground them to a luster with a polisher of fine sand glued to cloth, made holes with a bore and punch that he had self-invented. It was the absence, then, of sheep carcasses that forced his daughter to do battle with the spirit of ignorance.

Peace McKnight. She was sturdily made as a captain's chair, yet drew water with graceful wrists and ran dancing across the rutted road on curved white ankles. Hale, Scots, full-breasted as a pouter pigeon, and dusted all over like an egg with freckles, wavy brown-black hair secured with her father's gift—three pins of carved bone—she came to the Great Plains with enough education to apply for and win a teaching certificate.

Her class was piddling at first, all near grown, too. Three consumptive Swedish sisters not long for life, one boy abrupt and full of anger. A German. Even though she spoke plainly and slowly as humanly possible, her students fixed her with stares of tongueless suspicion and were incapable of following a single direction. She had to start from the beginning, teach the alphabet, the numbers, and had just reached the letter *v*, the word *cat*, subtraction, which they were naturally better at than addition, when she noticed someone standing at the back of her classroom. Quietly alert, observant, she had been there for some time. The girl stepped forward from the darkness.

She had roan coppery skin and wore a necklace of bright indigo beads. She was slender, with a pliable long waist, graceful neck, and she was about six years old.

Miss McKnight blushed pink-gold with interest. She was charmed, first by the confidence of the child's smile and next by her immediate assumption of a place to sit, study, organize herself, and at last by her listening intelligence. The girl, though silent, had a hungry, curious quality. Miss McKnight had a teaching gift to match it. Although they were fourteen years apart, they became, inevitably, friends.

Then sisters. Until fall, Miss McKnight slept in the school cloakroom and bathed in the river nearby. Once the river iced over at the edges, an argument developed among the few and far between homesteads as to which had enough room and who could afford her. No one. Matilda Roy stepped in and pestered her father, known as a strange and reclusive fellow, until he gave in and agreed that the new teacher could share the small trunk bed he had made for his daughter, so long as she helped with the poultry.

Mainly, they raised guinea fowl from keets that Scranton Roy had bought from a Polish widow. The speckled purple-black vulturine birds were half wild, clever. Matilda's task was to spy on, hunt down, and follow the hens to their hidden nests. The girls, for Peace McKnight was half girl around Matilda, laughed at the birds' tricks and hid to catch them. Fat, speckled, furious with shrill guinea pride, they acted as house watchdogs and scolded in the oak trees. Then from the pole shed where they wintered. In lard from a neighbor's pig, Scranton Roy fried strips of late squash, dried sand-dune morels, inky caps, field and oyster mushrooms, crushed acorns, the guinea eggs. He baked sweet bannock, dribbled on it wild aster honey aged in the bole of an oak, dark and pungent as mead.

The small sod and plank house was whitewashed inside and the deep sills of small bold windows held geraniums and started seeds. At night, the kerosene lamplight in trembling rings and halos, Miss Peace McKnight felt the eyes of Scranton Roy carve her in space. His gaze was a heat running up and down her throat, pausing elsewhere with the effect of a soft blow.

SCRANTON ROY

He is peculiar the way his mother was peculiar—writing poetry on the margins of bits of newspaper, tatters of cloth. His mother burned her life work and died soon after, comforted by the ashes of her words yet still in mourning for her son, who never did make his survival known but named his daughter for her. Matilda. One poem survived. A fragment. It goes like this. *Come to me, thou dark inviolate.* Scranton Roy prays to an unparticular god, communes with the spirit headlong each morning in a rush of ardor that carries him through each difficult day. He is lithe, nearly brown as his daughter, bearded, strong, and serene. He owns more than one dozen books and subscribes to periodicals that he lends to Miss McKnight.

He wants to be delivered of the burden of his solitude. A wife would help.

Peace tosses her sandy hair, feels the eyes of Scranton Roy upon her, appreciates their fire, and smiles into the eyes of his daughter. Technically, Miss McKnight soon becomes a stepmother. Whatever the term, the two women behave as though they've always known this closeness. Holding hands, they walk to school, kick dust, and tickle each other's necks with long stems of grama grass. They cook for Scranton Roy but also roll their eyes from time to time at him and break into fits of suppressed and impolite laughter.

MATILDA ROY

Emotions unreel in her like spools of cotton.

When he rocks her, Matilda remembers the taste of his milk—hot and bitter as dandelion juice. Once, he holds her foot in the cradle of his palm and with the adept point of his hunting knife painlessly delivers a splinter, long and pale and bloody. Teaches her to round her *c*'s and put tiny teakettle handles on her *a*'s. Crooks stray hairs behind her ears. Washes her face with the rough palm of his hand, but gently, scrubbing at her smooth chin with his callus.

He is a man, though he nourished her. Sometimes across the room, at night, in his sleep, her father gasps as though stabbed, dies into himself. She is jolted awake, frightened, and thinks to check his breath with her hand, but then his ragged snore lulls her. In the fresh daylight, staring up at the patches of mildew on the ceiling, Matilda watches him proudly from the corners of her eyes as he cracks the ice in the washing pail, feeds a spurt of hidden stove flame, talks to himself. She loves him like nothing else. He is her father, her human. Still, sometimes, afflicted by an anxious sorrow, she holds her breath to see what will happen, if he will save her. Heat flows up the sides of her face and she opens her lips but before her mouth can form a word she sees yellow, passes out, and is flooded by blueness, sheer blueness, intimate and strange, the color of her necklace of beads.

KISS

Have you ever fallen from a severe height and had your wind knocked forth so that, in the strict jolt's sway, you did experience stopped time? Matilda Roy did when she saw her father kiss the teacher. The world halted. There sounded a great gong made of sky. A gasp. Silence. Then the leaves ticked again, the guineas scornfully gossiped, the burly black hound that had replaced the Indian dog pawed a cool ditch in the sand for itself. Sliding back from the casual window to the bench behind the house where she sat afternoons to shell peas, shuck corn, peel dinner's potatoes, pluck guinea hens, and dream, Matilda Roy looked at the gold-brown skin on her arms, turned her arms over, turned them back, flexed her pretty, agile hands.

The kiss had been long, slow, and of growing interest and intensity, more educational than any lesson yet given her by Miss Peace McKnight. Matilda shut her eyes. Within herself at all times a silent darkness sifted up and down. A pure emptiness fizzing and gliding.

Now, along with the puzzling development between her friend and father, something else. It took a long concentration on her stillness to grasp the elusive new sensation of freedom, of relief.

OZHAWASHKWAMASHKODEYKWAY / BLUE PRAIRIE WOMAN

The child lost in the raid was still nameless, still a half spirit, yet her mother mourned her for a solid year's time and nearly died of the sorrow. A haunting uncertainty dragged the time out. Ozhawashkwamashkodekway might be picking blueberries and she feared she would come across her daughter's bones. In the wind at night, pakuks, she heard them wailing, black twig skeletons. Stirring the fire, a cleft of flame reminded her of the evil day itself, the massed piles of meat put to the torch, their robes and blankets smoldering, the stinking singe of hair, and the hot iron of the rifle barrels. At night, for the first month after that day, her breasts grew pale and hard and her milk impacted, spoiling in her, leaking out under her burnt clothes so that she smelled of sour milk and fire. An old midwife gave her a new puppy and she put it to her breasts. Holding to her nipple the tiny wet muzzle, cradling the needy bit of fur, she cried. All that night the tiny dog mercifully drew off the shooting pains in her breasts and at dawn, drowsy and comfortable, she finally cuddled the sweet-fleshed puppy to her, breathed its salty odor, and slept.

Wet ash when the puppy weaned itself. Blood. Her moons began and nothing she pressed between her legs could stop the rush of life. Her body wanting to get rid of itself. She ate white clay, scratched herself with bull thorns for relief, cut her hair, grew it long, cut it short again, scored her arms to the bone, tied the skull of a buffalo around her neck, and for six moons ate nothing but dirt and leaves. It must have been a rich dirt, said her grandmother, for although she slept little and looked tired, Blue Prairie Woman was healthy as a buffalo cow. When Shawano the younger returned from his family's wild rice beds, she gave her husband such a night of sexual pleasure that his eyes followed her constantly after that, narrow and hot. He grew molten when she passed near other men, and at night they made their own shaking tent. They got teased too much and moved farther off, into the brush, into the nesting ground of shy and holy loons. There, no one could hear them. In solitude they made love until they became gaunt and hungry, pale windigos with aching eyes, tongues of flame.

Twins are born of such immoderation.

By the time her husband left again with his sled of traps, she was pregnant and calm. During that winter, life turned more brutal. The tribe's stores had been burned by order, and many times in starving sleep Blue Prairie Woman dreamed the memory of buffalo fat running in rivulets across the ground, soaking into the earth, fat gold from piles of burning meat. She still dreamed, too, with wide-eyed clarity of the young, fleet brown dog, the cradle board bound to its body. Even carrying two, she dreamed of her first baby bewildered, then howling, then at last riding black as leather, mouth stretched wide underneath a waterless sky. She dreamed its bones rattled in the careful stitching of black velvet, clacked in the moss padding, grown thin. She heard their rhythm and saw the dog, the small pakuk flying. She howled and scratched herself half blind and at last so viciously took leave of her mind that the old ones got together and decided to change her name.

On a cool day in spring in the bud-popping moon the elders held a pitiful feast—only nothing seems pitiful to survivors. In weak sunlight they chewed spring-risen mud-turtle meat, roasted coot, gopher, the remaining sweet grains of manomin, acorns, puckoons from a squirrel's cache, and the fresh spears of dandelion. Blue Prairie Woman's name was covered with blood, burned with fire. Her name was old and exquisite and had belonged to many powerful mothers. Yet the woman who had fit inside of it had walked off. She couldn't stop following the child and the dog. Someone else had taken her place. Who, as yet, was unclear. But the old ones did know, agreed between them, that the wrong name would kill what was in there and it had to go—like a husk dried off and scattered. Like a shell to a nut. Hair grown long and sacrificed to sorrow. They had to give her another name if they wanted her to return to the living.

The name they gave her had to be unused. New. Oshkay. They

asked the strongest of the namers, the one who dreamed original names. This namer was nameless and was neither a man nor a woman, and so took power from the in-between. This namer had long, thick braids and a sweet shy smile, charming ways but arms tough with roped muscle. The namer walked like a woman, spoke in a man's deep voice. Hid coy behind a fan and yet agreed to dream a name to fit the new thing inside Blue Prairie Woman. But what name would help a woman who could only be calmed by gazing into the arrowing distance? The namer went away, starved and sang and dreamed, until it was clear that the only name that made any sense at all was the name of the place where the old Blue Prairie Woman had gone to fetch back her child.

OTHER SIDE OF THE EARTH

Once she was named for the place toward which she traveled, the young mother was able to be in both places at once—she was following her child into the sun and also pounding the weyass between rocks to dried scruffs of pemmican. She was searching the thick underbrush of her own mind. She was punching holes to sew tough new soles on old moccasins and also sew new ones, tiny, the soles pierced before she beaded the tops. She starved and wandered, tracking the faint marks the dog left as he passed into the blue distance. At the same time, she knocked rice. She parched and stored the grains. Sugared. Killed birds. Tamed horses. Her mind was present because she was always gone. Her hands were filled because they grasped the meaning of empty. Life was simple. Her husband returned and she served him with indifferent patience this time. When he asked what had happened to her heat for him, she gestured to the west.

The sun was setting. The sky was a body of fire.

In the deep quiet of her blood the two babies were forming, creating themselves just as the first twin gods did at the beginning. As yet, no one had asked what might happen next. What would happen to the woman called Other Side of the Earth when Blue Prairie Woman found Matilda Roy?

A DOG NAMED SORROW

The dog nursed on human milk grew up coyote gray and clever, a light-boned, loping bitch who followed Blue Prairie Woman everywhere. Became her second thought, lay outside the door when she slept, just within the outer flap when it rained, though not in. Not ever actually inside a human dwelling. Huge with pups or thin from feeding them, teats dragging, the dog still followed. Close and quiet as her shadow, it lived within touch of her, although they never did touch after the dog drew from Blue Prairie Woman's soaked and swollen nipples the heat, the night milk, the overpowering sorrow.

Always there, looking up alert at the approach of a stranger, guarding her in the dusk, waiting for a handout, living patiently on bits of hide, guts, offal, the dog waited. And was ready when Blue Prairie Woman set down her babies with their grandmother and started walking west, following at long last the endless invisible trail of her daughter's flight.

She walked for hours, she walked for years. She walked until she heard about them. The man. The young girl and the blue beads she wore. Where they were living. She heard the story. The twins, two girls, she left behind to the chances of baptism. They were named Mary, of course, for the good blue-robed woman, and Josephette, for the good husband. Only the Ojibwa tongue made Zosie of the latter name. Zosie. Mary. Their grandmother, Midass, who had survived the blue-coat massacre, would raise them as her own.

When she reached the place they lived, Blue Prairie Woman settled on a nearby rise, the dog near. From that distance, the two watched the house—small, immaculate, scent of a hearth fire made of crackling oak twigs. Illness. There was sickness in the house, she could sense it—the silence, then the flurries of motion. Rags hung out. Water to haul.

One shrill cry. Silence again. All day in thin grass, the dog, the woman, sunlight brave on them, breathed each other's air, slept by turns, waited.

MATILDA ROY

She heard the gentle approach that night, the scrawl of leaves, the sighing resonance of discovery. She sat up in her crazy quilt, knowing. Next to her, held in the hot vise of fever, Peace muttered endlessly of buttons and sheep bones. Sounds—a slight tap. The clatter of her beads. In the morning, there was no Matilda Roy in the trunk bed. There was only a note, folded twice, penned in the same exquisite, though feminized, handwriting of her father.

She came for me. I went with her.

SCRANTON ROY

Peace McKnight was never devout, so there was no intimacy of prayer between the newlyweds. Their physical passion suffered, as well, because of the shortness of his bed. There was, after all, very little space inside the sod house. Scranton Roy had slept in a tiny berth on one side of the room, his daughter on the other. Both slept curled like snails, like babies in the wombs of their mothers. More difficult with an extra person in the bedding. It wasn't long before, in order to get any rest at all, Peace slipped outside to sleep with the guineas, took up nightly residence apart from her husband.

Still, there were evenings when Scranton was inflicted with ardor and arranged them both, before she could leave, in the cramped and absurd postures of love. If only he had thought to use the armless rocking chair before the fire! Peace's mind flashed on the possibility, but she was too stubborn to mention it. Even the floor, packed dirt covered with skins, would have been preferable. Again, she didn't care to introduce that possibility into his mind. Anyway, as it happened she had every right to turn her back when the tiny knock of new life began in the cradle of her hipbones. And he retreated, missed the rasp of her breath, wondered about Matilda, and imagined the new life to come all at once. Prayed. Wrote poems in his head. *Come to me, thou dark inviolate.*

After her deliverance from the mottled skin sickness, the gasping and fever that made her bones ache, Peace was in her weakness even warier of her new husband. For the rest of her pregnancy, she made him sleep alone. Her labor began on a snowy morning. Scranton Roy set out for the Swedish housewife's in a swallowing blizzard that would have cost him his life but for his good sense in turning back. He reached the door. Smote, rattled, fell into the heat of a bloody scene in which Peace McKnight implored her neglected God in begging futility. For two days, then three, her labor shook her in its jaws. Her howls were louder than the wind. Hoarser. Then her voice was lost, a scrape of bone. A whisper. Her face bloated, dark red, then white, then gray. Her eyes rolled back to the whites, so she stared mystified with agony into her own thoughts when at last the child tore its way from her. A boy, plump and dead blue. Marked with cloudy spots like her earlier disease. There was no pulse in the birth cord but Scranton Roy thought to puff his own air into the baby's lungs. It answered with a startled bawl.

Augustus. She had already named her baby. Known that it would be a boy.

Scranton wrapped the baby in the skin of a dog and kissed the smoothed, ravaged temples of Peace with tender horror at the pains of his own mother, and of all mothers, and of the unfair limitations of our bodies, of the hopeless settlement of our life tasks, and finally, of the boundless iniquity of the God to whom she had so uselessly shrieked. *Look at her*, he called the unseen witness. And perhaps God did or Peace McKnight's mind, pitilessly wracked, finally came out of hiding and told her heart to beat twice more. A stab of fainting gold heeled through a scrap of window. Peace saw the wanton gleam, breathed out, gazed out. And then, as she stepped from her ripped body into the utter calm of her new soul, Peace McKnight saw her husband put his son to his breast.

BLUE PRAIRIE WOMAN

All that's in a name is a puff of sound, a lungful of wind, and yet it is an airy enclosure. How is it that the gist, the spirit, the complicated web of bone, hair, brain, gets stuffed into a syllable or two? How do you shrink the genie of human complexity? How the personality? Unless, that is, your mother gives you her name, Other Side of the Earth.

Who came from nowhere and from lucky chance. Whose mother bore her in shit and fire. She is huge as half the sky. In the milk from her rescuer's breasts she has tasted his disconcerting hatred of her kind and also protection, so that when she falls into the fever, she doesn't suffer of it the way Peace did. Although they stop, make camp, and Blue Prairie Woman speaks to her in worried susurrations, the child is in no real danger.

The two camp on the trail of a river cart. The sky opens brilliantly and the grass is hemmed, rife with berries. Blue Prairie Woman picks with swift grace and fills a new-made makuk. She dries the berries on sheaves of bark, in the sun, so they'll be easy to carry. Lying with her head on her mother's lap, before the fire, Matilda asks what her name was as a little baby. The two talk on and on, mainly by signs.

Does the older woman understand the question? Her face burns. As she sinks dizzily onto the earth beside her daughter, she feels compelled to give her the name that brought her back. Other Side of the Earth, she says, teeth tapping. Hotter, hotter, first confused and then dreadfully clear when she sees, opening before her, the western door.

She must act at once if her daughter is to survive her.

The clouds are pure stratus. The sky is a raft of milk. The coyote gray dog sits patiently near.

Blue Prairie Woman, sick to death and knowing it, reaches swiftly to her left and sets her grip without looking on the nape of the dog's neck. First time she has touched the dog since it drank from her the milk of sorrow. She drags the dog to her. Soft bones, soft muzzle then. Tough old thing now. Blue Prairie Woman holds the dog close underneath one arm and then, knife in hand, draws her clever blade across the beating throat. Slices its stiff moan in half and collects in the berry-filled makuk its gurgle of dark blood. Blue Prairie Woman then stretches the dog out, skins and guts her, cuts off her head, and lowers the chopped carcass into a deep birch-bark container. Suspended over flames, just right, she knows how to heat water the old way in that makuk. Tending the fire carefully, weakening, she boils the dog.

When it is done, the meat softened, shredding off the bones, she tips the gray meat, brown meat, onto a birch tray. Steam rises, the fragrance of the meat is faintly sweet. Quietly, she gestures to her daughter. Prods the cracked oval pads off the cooked paws. Offers them to her.

It takes sixteen hours for Blue Prairie Woman to contract the fever and only eight more to die of it. All that time, as she is dying, she sings. Her song is wistful, peculiar, soft, questing. It doesn't sound like a death song; rather, there is in it the tenderness and intimacy of seduction addressed to the blue distance.

Never exposed, healthy, defenseless, her body is an eager receptacle for the virus. She seizes, her skin goes purple, she vomits a brilliant flash of blood. Passionate, surprised, she dies when her chest fills, kicking and drumming her heels on the hollow earth. At last she is still, gazing west. That is the direction her daughter sits facing all the next day and the next. She sings her mother's song, holding her mother's hand in one hand and seriously, absently, eating the dog with the other hand—until in that spinning cloud light and across rich level earth, pale reddish curious creatures, slashed with white on the chest and face, deep-eyed, curious, pause in passing.

The antelope emerge from the band of the light at the world's edge.

A small herd of sixteen or twenty flickers into view. Fascinated, they poise to watch the girl's hand in its white sleeve dip. Feed herself. Dip. They step closer. Hooves of polished metal. Ears like tuning forks. Black prongs and velvet. They watch Matilda. Blue Prairie Woman's daughter. Other Side of the Earth. Nameless.

She is seven years old, tough from chasing poultry and lean from the fever. She doesn't know what they are, the beings, dreamlike, summoned by her mother's song, her dipping hand. They come closer, closer, grazing near, folding their legs under them to warily rest. The young nurse their mothers on the run or stare at the girl in fascinated hilarity, springing off if she catches their wheeling flirtation. In the morning when she wakens, still holding her mother's hand, they are standing all around. They bend to her, huff in excitement when she rises and stands among them quiet and wondering. Easy with their dainty precision, she wanders along in their company. Always on the move. At night she makes herself a nest of willow. Sleeps there. Moves on. Eats bird's eggs. A snared rabbit. Roots. She remembers fire and cooks a handful of grouse chicks. The herd flows in steps and spurting gallops deeper into the west. When they walk, she walks, following, dried berries in a sack made of her dress. When they run, she runs with them. Naked, graceful, the blue beads around her neck.

2

The Antelope Wife

Klaus Shawano

I used to make the circuit as a trader at the western powwows, though I am an urban Indian myself, a sanitation engineer. I'd hit Arlee, Montana. Elmo, Missoula, swing over Rocky Boy, and then head on down to Crow Fair. I liked it out there in all that dry space; at first that is, and up until last year. It was restful, a comfort to let my brain wander across the mystery where sky meets earth.

Now, that line disturbs me with its lie.

Earth and sky touch everywhere and nowhere, like sex between two strangers. There is no definition and no union for sure. If you chase that line, it will retreat from you at the same pace you set. Heart pounding, air burning in your chest, you'll pursue. Only humans see that line as an actual place. But like love, you'll never get there. You'll never catch it. You'll never know.

Open space plays such tricks on the brain. There and gone. I suppose it is no surprise that it was on the plains that I met my wife, my sweetheart rose, Ninimoshe, kissing cousin, lover girl, the only one I'll ever call my own. I take no credit for what happened, nor blame, nor do I care what people presently think of me—avoiding my eyes, trying not to step in the tracks I've left.

I only want to be with her, or be dead.

You wouldn't think a man as ordinary as myself could win a woman who turns the heads of others in the streets. Yet there are circumstances and daughters that do prevail and certain ways. And, too, maybe I have some talents.

I was sitting underneath my striped awning there in Elmo—selling carved turtles. You never know what will be the ticket or the score. Sometimes they're buying baby moccasins, little beaded ones the size of your big toe. Or the fad is cheap neckerchiefs, bolo slides, jingles. I can sell out before noon if I misjudge my stock, while someone else set up next to me who took on a truckload is raking the money in with both hands. At those times, all I can do is watch. But that day, I had the turtles. And those people were crazy for turtles. One lady bought three—a jade, a malachite, a turquoise. One went for seven—small. Another bought the turtle ring. It was the women who bought turtles—the women who bought anything.

I had traded for macaw feathers also, and I got a good price on those. I had a case of beautiful old Navajo pawn which I got blessed, because the people who wore that turquoise seem to haunt the jewelry, so I believe. A piece gets sold on a sad drunk for gas money, or it's outright stolen—what I mean is that it comes into the hands of traders in bad ways and should be watched close. I have a rare piece I never did sell, an old cast-silver bracelet with a glacier-green turquoise the shape of a wing. I have to tell you, I can hold that piece only a moment, for when I polish the pattern on some days it seems to start in my hands with a secret life, a secret pain.

I am just putting that old piece away when they pass. Four women eating snow cones as they stroll the powwow grounds.

Who wouldn't notice them? They float above everyone else on springy, tireless legs. It's hard to tell what tribe people are anymore, we're so mixed—I've got a Buffalo Soldier in my own blood, I'm sure, and on the other side I am all Ojibwa. All Shawano, though my name is Klaus, a story in itself. These ladies are definitely not from anywhere that I can place. Their dance clothes are simple—tanned hide dresses, bone jewelry, white doeskin down the front and two white doeskin panels behind. Classy, elegant, they set a new standard of simplicity. They make everyone else around them look gaudy or bold, a little foolish in their attempts to catch the eyes of the judges.

I watch these women put their mouths on ice. They tip their faces down, half smiling, and delicately kiss the frozen grains. Sipping the sweet lime and blueberry juice, their black, melting eyes never leave the crowd, and still they move along. Effortless. Easy. The lack of trying is what makes them lovely. We all try too hard. Striving wears down our edges, dulls the best of us.

I take those women in like air. I breathe hard. My heart is squeezing shut. Something about them is like the bracelets of old turquoise. In spite of the secrets of those stones, there are times that I cannot stop touching and stroking their light. I must be near those women and know more. I cannot let them alone. I look at my setup—van, tent, awning, beads, chairs, scarves, jewelry, folding tables, a cashbox, a turtle or two—and I sit as calmly as I can at my trading booth among these things. I wait. But when they don't notice me, I decide I must act bold. I trade store-minding with my neighbor, a family from Saskatoon, and then I follow the women.

Tiptoeing just behind at first, then trotting faster, I almost lose them, but I am afraid to get too close and be noticed. They finish circling the arbor, enter during the middle of an intertribal song, and dance out into the circle together. I lean against a pole to watch. Some dancers, you see them sweating, hear their feet pound the sawdust or grass or the Astroturf or gym floor, what have you. Some dancers swelter and their faces darken with the effort. Others, you never understand how they are moving, where it comes from. They're at one with their effort. Those, you lose your heart to and that's what happens to me—I sink down on a bench to watch these women and where usually I begin to drift off in my thoughts, this morning I am made of smoothest wood. They dance together in a line, murmuring in swift, low voices, smiling carefully as they are too proud to give away their beauty. They are light steppers with a gravity of sure grace.

Their hair is fixed in different ways. The oldest daughter pulls hers back in a simple braid. The next one ties hers in a fancy woven French knot. The hair of the youngest is fastened into a smooth tail with a round shell hairpiece. Their mother—for I can tell she is their mother mainly by the way she moves with a sense of all their consolidated grace—her hair hangs long and free.

Dark as heaven, with roan highlights and arroyos of brown, waves deep as currents, a river of scented nightfall. In her right hand she holds a fan of the feathers of a red-tailed hawk. Those birds follow the antelope to fall on field mice the moving herd stirs up. Suddenly, as she raises the fan high, my throat chills. I hear in the distance and in my own mind and heart the high keer of the stooping hawk—a lonely sound, coldhearted, intimate.

Back at my tables, later, I place every item enticingly just so. I get provisions of iced tea and soda and I sit down to wait. To scout. Attract, too, if I can manage, but there isn't much I can do about my looks. I'm broad from sitting in my foldable chair, and too cheerful to be considered dangerously handsome. My hair, I'm proud of that—it's curly and dark and I wear it in a tail or braid. But my hands are thick and clumsy. Their only exercise is taking in and counting money. My eyes are too lonesome, my lips too eager to stretch and smile, my heart too hot to please.

No matter. The women come walking across the trampled grass and again they never notice me, anyway. They go by the other booths and ponder some tapes and point at beaded belt buckles and Harley Tshirts. They order soft drinks, eat Indian tacos, get huckleberry muffins at a lunch stand. They come by again to stand and watch the Indian gambling, the stick games. They disappear and suddenly appear. The mother is examining her daughter's foot. Is she hurt? No, it's just a piece of chewing gum that's stuck. All day I follow them with my eyes. All day I have no success, but I do decide which one I want.

Some might go for the sprig, the sprout, the lovely offshoot, the younger and flashier, the darker-hooded eyes. Me, I'm strong enough, or so I think, to go for the source: the mother. She is all of them rolled up in one person, I figure. She is the undiluted vision of their separate loveliness. The mother is the one I will try for. As I am falling into sleep I imagine holding her, the delicate power. My eyes shut, but that night I am troubled in my dreams.

I'm running, running, and still must run—I'm jolted awake, breathing hard. The camp is dark. All I've got is easily packed and I think maybe I should take the omen. Break camp right this minute. Leave. Go home. Back to the city, Minneapolis, Gakahbekong we call it, where everything is set out clear in lines and neatly labeled, where you can hide from the great sky, forget. I consider it and then I hear the sounds of one lonely passionate stick game song still rising, an old man's voice pouring out merciless irony, no catch in his throat.

I walk to the edge of the rising moon.

I stand listening to the song until I feel better and am ready to settle myself and rest. Making my way through the sleeping camp, I see the four women walking again—straight past me, very quickly and softly now, laughing. They move like a wave, dressed in pale folds of calico. Their pace quickens, quickens some more. I break into a jog and then I find that I am running after them, at a normal speed at first, and then straining, putting my heart into the chase, my whole body pedaling forward, although they do not seem to have broken into a run themselves. Their supple gait takes them to the edge of the camp, all brush and sage, weeds and grazed-down pastures, and from there to alive hills. A plan forms in my mind. I'll find their camping place and mark it! Go by with coffees in the morning, take them off guard. But they pass the margin of the camp, the last tent. I pass too. We keep looping into the moonlighted spaces, faster, faster, but it's no use. They outdistance me. They pass into the darkness, into the night.

My heart is squeezing, racing, crowded with longing, and I need help. It must be near the hour that will gray to dawn. Summer nights in high country are so short that the birds hardly stop singing. Still, at dawn the air goes light and fresh. Now the old man whose high, cracked voice was joyfully gathering in money at the gambling tent finally stops. I know him, Jimmy Badger, or know *of* him anyway as an old medicine person spoken about with hushed respect. I can tell his side has won, because the others are folding their chairs with clangs and leaving with soft grumbles. Jimmy is leaning on a grandson. The boy supports him as he walks along. Jimmy's body is twisted with arthritis and age. He's panting for breath. They pause, I come up to him, shake hands, and tell him I need advice.

He motions to his tired grandson to go to bed. I take the medicine man's arm and lead him over tough ground to where my van is parked. I pull out a lawn chair, set it up, lower him into it. Reaching into my stores, I find an old-time twist of tobacco, and I give it to him. Then I add some hanks of cut beads and about eight feet of licorice for his grandkids. A blanket, too, I give him that. I take out another blanket and settle it around his back, and I pour a thermos cap of coffee, still warm. He drinks, looking at me with shrewd care. He's a small man with waiting intrigue in his eyes, and his gambler's hands are gnarled to clever shapes. He has a poker-playing mouth, a head of handsome iron-gray hair that stretches down behind. He wears a beat-up bead-trimmed fedora with a silver headband and a brand-new denim jacket he's probably won in the blackjack tents.

I'm an Ojibwa, I say to him, so I don't know about the plains much. I am more a woods Indian, a city-bred guy. I tell Jimmy Badger that I've got a hunting lottery permit and I'm going to get me an antelope. I need some antelope medicine, I say. Their habits confuse me. I need advice on how to catch them. He listens with close attention, then smiles a little crack-toothed pleasant smile.

"You're talking the old days," he says. "There's some who still hunt the antelope, but of course the antelope don't jump fences. They're easy to catch now. Just follow until they reach a fence. They don't jump over high, see, they only know how to jump wide."

"They'll get the better of me then," I say, "I'm going to hunt them in an open spot."

"Oh, then," he says. "Then, that's different."

At that point, he gets out his pipe, lets me light it, and for a long time after that he sits and smokes.

"See here." He slowly untwists his crushed body. "The antelope are a curious kind of people. They'll come to check anything that they don't understand. You flick a piece of cloth into the air where you're hiding, a flag. But only every once in a while, not regular. They're curious, they'll stop, they'll notice. Pretty soon they'll investigate."

Next day, then, I set up my booth just exactly the same as the day before, except I keep out a piece of sweetheart calico, white with little pink roses. When the women come near, circling the stands again, I flicker the cloth out. Just once. It catches the eye of the youngest and she glances back at me. They pass by. They pass by again. I think I've failed. I wave the cloth. The oldest daughter, she turns. She looks at me once over her shoulders for the longest time. I flick the cloth. Her eyes are deep and watchful. Then she leans back, laughing to her mother, and she tugs on her sleeve.

In a flash, they're with me.

They browse my store. I'm invisible at first, but not for long. Once I get near enough I begin to fence them with my trader's talk—it's a thing I'm good at, the chatter that encourages a customer's interest. My goods are all top-quality. My stories have stories. My beadwork is made by relatives and friends whose tales branch off in an ever more complicated set of barriers. I talk to each of the women, make pleasant comments, set up a series of fences and gates. They're very modest and polite women, shy, stiff maybe. The girls talk just a little and the mother not at all. When they don't get a joke they lower their lashes and glance at one another with a secret understanding. When they do laugh they cover their lovely calm mouths with their hands. Their eyes light with wonder when I give them each a few tubes of glittering cut beads, some horn buttons, a round-dance tape.

They try to melt away. I keep talking. I ask them if they've eaten, tell them I've got food and show them my stash of baked beans, corn, fry bread, molasses cookies. I make them up heaped plates and I play a little music on the car radio. I keep on talking and smiling and telling my jokes until the girls yawn once. I catch them yawning, and so I open my tent, pitched right near, so nice and inviting. I tell them they are welcome to lie down on the soft heap of blankets and sleeping bags. Their dark eyes flare, they look toward their mother, wary, but I fend off their worry and wave them inside, smiling the trader's smile.

Alone together. Me and her. Their mother listens to me nice and gentle. I let my look linger just a little, closer, until I find her eyes. And when our eyes do meet, we stare, we stare, we cannot stop looking. Hers are so black, full of steep light and wary. Mine are brown, searching, anxious, I am sure. But we hold on and I can only say that for what happens next I have no adequate excuse.

We get into the van while she is still caught by the talk, the look. I think she is confused by the way I want her, which is like nobody else. I know this deep down. I want her in a new way, a way she's never been told about, a way that wasn't the way of the girls' father. Sure, maybe desperate. Maybe even wrong, but she doesn't know how to resist. Like I say, I get her in my van. I start to play a soft music she acts like she never heard before. She smiles a little, nervous, and although she doesn't speak, uses no words anyway, I understand her looks and gestures. I put back the seat so it's pleasant to recline and watch the dusky sky and then I pamper her.

"You're tired, sleep," I say, giving her a cup of hot tea. "Everything's all right with your daughters. They'll be fine."

She sips the tea and looks at me with dreaming apprehension, as though I'm a new thing on earth. Her eyes soften, her lips part.

Suddenly, she leans back and falls hard asleep. Something that I forgot to tell—us Ojibwas have a few teas we brew for very special occasions. This is one. A sleep tea, a love tea. Oh yes, there's more. There's more that Jimmy Badger told me.

"You're shifty like all those woods Indians," Jimmy Badger said. "I see that trader's deception. If you're thinking about those women, don't do it," he said. "Long time ago, we had a girl who lived summers with the antelope. In the winters she brought her human daughters to the camp. They could not keep up with her people as they moved on in the bitter cold, the frozen pastures, scattering across the plains. Don't go near them if that is what you're thinking of doing. We had a man who did once. Followed them, wrestled one down. Made love to her and was never the same. Few men can handle their love ways. Besides, they're ours. We need them and we take care of these women. Descendants."

"They might be," I said. "Or they might just be different."

"Oh, different," agreed Jimmy. "For sure."

He looked at me keenly, grabbed me with his eyes, kept talking. His voice was remote and commanding.

"Our old women say they appear and disappear. Some men follow the antelope and lose their minds."

I was stubborn. "Or maybe they're just a family that's a little unusual, or wild."

"Leave," said Jimmy Badger. "Leave now."

But in my heart, I knew I was already caught. The best hunter allows his prey to lead, not the other way around. That hunter doesn't force himself to figure and track, just lets himself be drawn to the meeting. That's what I did.

Suddenly I have her there with me in the van, and she is fast asleep. I sit and watch her for a long time. I am witched. Her eyelashes are so long that, when the light from the outdoor flood lamps com on, they cast faint shadows on her cheeks. Her breath has the scent of grass and her hair of sage. I want to kiss her forever. My heart's a panic on my sleeve.

I drive off. Yes, I do. I drive off with this woman while her daughters are breathing softly, there in the tent, unconscious. I leave the girls all of my trade beads and fancy pawn and jewelry, everything that was stored in the corner of the tent. The miles go by, the roads empty. The Missions rear before us, throwing fire off sheer rock faces. Then we're past those mountains into more open country. My sweetheart wakes up, confused and tired. I tell her jokes and stories, list for her strange or valuable things people throw away. Trading is my second nature, but garbage supports me. I'm in the waste haul business. Work for the tribe, the city even, big companies, little ones. I drive through the day. I drive through the night. Only when I am so exhausted that I'm seeing double, do I finally stop.

Bismarck, North Dakota, center of the universe. Locus of space and time for me and my Ninimoshe. We turn in, take a room at the motel's end. I lead her in first and I close the door behind and then she turns to me—suddenly, she knows she is caught. *Where are my girls,* her eyes say, their fear sharp as bone, *I want my girls!* When she lunges, I'm ready, but she's so fast I cannot keep her from running at the window, falling back. She twists, strong and lithe, for the door, but I block and try to ease her down. She pounds at me with hard fists and launches straight into the bathroom, pulling down the mirror, breaking her teeth on the tub's edge.

What can I do? I have those yards of sweetheart calico. I go back. I tear them carefully and with great gentleness I bandage her cuts. I don't know what else to do—I tie her up. I pull one strip gently through her bleeding mouth. Lastly, I tie our wrists together and then, beside her, in an agony of feeling, I sleep.

r. I'll do anything for her. Anything except let her go. Once I city, things are better anyway. She seems to forget her daughters, their wanting eyes, the grand space, the air. And besides, I tell her that we'll send for her daughters by airplane. They can come and live with me and go to school right here.

She nods, but there is something hopeless in her look. She dials and dials long-distance numbers, there are phone calls all over the whole state of Montana, all of these 406 numbers are on the bill. She never speaks, though sometimes I imagine I hear her whispering. I try the numbers, but every time I dial one that she's used I get an out-of-service signal. Does she even understand the phone? And anyway, one night she smiles into my face—we're just the same height. I look deep and full into her eyes. She loves me the way I love her, I can tell. I want to hold her and hold her—for good, for bad. After that, our nights are something I can't address in the day, as though we're wearing other bodies, other people's flaming skins, as though we're from another time and place. Our love is a hurting delicacy, an old killer whiskey, a curse, and too beautiful for words.

I get so I don't want to leave her to go to work. In the morning she sits at her spot before the television, watching in still fascination, jumping a little at the car chases, sympathizing with the love scenes. I catch her looking into the mirror I've hung in the living room and she is mimicking the faces of the women on the soap operas, their love looks, their pouting expressions. Their clothes. She opens my wallet, takes all my money. I'd give her anything. "Here," I say, "take my checkbook too." But she just throws it on the floor. She leaves off her old skins and buys new, tight and covered with bold designs. She laughs harder, but her laugh is silent, shaking her like a tree in a storm. She drinks wine. In a pair of black jeans in a bar she is approached by men whenever I turn aside, so I don't turn aside. I stick to her, cleave to her, won't let her go, and in the nights sometimes I still tie her to me with sweetheart calico.

Weeping, weeping, she cries the whole day away. Sometimes I find her in the corner, drunk, marvelous in frothy negligees, laughing and lip-synching love scenes to the mirror again. I think I'll find a mir doctor, things cannot go on. She's crazy. But if they lock her up, th have to lock me up too. She'll rage at me for days with her eyes, bare her teeth, stamp on my feet with her heeled boot if I get near enough to try for a kiss. Then just as suddenly, she'll change. She'll turn herself into the most loving companion. We'll sit at night watching television, touching our knees together while I check the next day's schedule. Her eyes speak. Her long complicated looks tell me stories—of the old days, of her people. The antelope are the only creatures swift enough to catch the distance, her sweeping looks say. *We live there. We live there in the place where sky meets earth.*

I bring her sweet grass, tie it into her hair, and then we make love and we don't stop until we're sleeping on each other's pillows.

Winter, and the daylight dwindles. She starts to eat and eat and puffs up before my eyes devouring potato chips and drinking wine until I swear at her, say she's ugly, tell her to get a job, to lose weight, to be the person she was when I first met her. Those teeth are still cracked off, and when she smiles her smile is jagged with hatred but her eyes are still dark with love, with amusement. She lifts into the air in a dance and spins, spins away so I can't catch her and once again she is in my arms and we're moving, moving together. She's so fantastically plump I can't bear it all, her breasts round and pointed, and that night I drown, I go down in the depth of her. I'm lost as I never was and next morning, next afternoon, she drags me back into bed. I can't stop although I'm exhausted. She keeps on and she keeps on. Day after day. Until I know she is trying to kill me.

That night, while she's asleep, I sneak into the kitchen. I call Jimmy Badger, get his phone through a series of other people.

"It's her or me," I say.

"Well, finally."

"What should I do?"

"Bring her back to us, you fool."

urn behind my eyes. If you see one you are lost forever. d disappear like shadows on the plains, say the old women. Some men follow them and do not return. Even if you do return, you will never be right in the head. Her daughters are pouting mad. They don't have much patience, Jimmy says. He keeps talking, talking. They never did, that family. Our luck is changing. Our houses caved in with the winter's snow and our work is going for grabs. Nobody's stopping at the gas pump. Bring her back to us! says Jimmy. There's misery in the air. The fish are mushy inside—some disease. Her girls are mad at us.

Bring her back, you fool!

I'm just a city boy, I answer him, slow, stark, confused. I don't know what you people do, out there, living on the plains where there are no trees, no woods, no place to hide except the distances. You can see too much.

You fool, bring her back to us!

But how can I? Her lying next to me in deepest night, breathing quiet in love, in trust. Her hand in mine, her wicked hoof.

3

Seaweed Marshmallows

Rozina Whiteheart Beads

When she first came here with Klaus we all wondered, couldn't help it. Why she made so much sense and none at all. His sweetheart calico. Why she seemed one of us and different, wholly other and yet familiar. Klaus brought her back but she proceeded to drive him crazy, to drive him out and away so we didn't see him for a year, then two years, then three altogether and at last four. During that time we were left with her, taming her, containing her, his antelope wife, his sweetheart calico.

Let me explain us, first of all.

The women in my family are the kind to argue with the spirits. Short, tough-minded, sinuous of thought and bold, we daughters of the granddaughters of Blue Prairie Woman are wavy haired and lightened by the Roy blood. We're twins of twins, going back through the floating lines of time. Descended of the three-fires people and of an

Ivory Coast slave, who crawled under the bark of an Ojibwa house and struck a match by which he looked into the eyes of the daughter of Everlasting, Magid, who blew the match out and opened to him her robes.

The bastard son of a bastard daughter of a French marquis entered the next generation via voyageur trails. Henri Laventure stole ten gold louis from the sock of a bishop, shoved the money up his ass in order to board ship in Calais. Stripped naked and doused with lye to discourage lice, the demi-royal ancestor then reclothed himself, shat the coins out one by one in pain, and stitched them into his jacket, which he then sewed onto himself and did not remove until Montreal. Hauling knives, guns, kettles, dressed in skins and velvet, he showed up in the raw territory of the wolf and married six Ojibwa women of whom the oldest, who was sixteen years older than he was, took care of him best and stayed with him the longest.

She was the sister of the court-convicted windigo, bear-walker, bad holy dream-man, Shesheeb, who was of those people from the north. After he was caught, they moved on south. Walking, walking, always in that direction, they were soon known as those people who had just left for the south. Shawano. One Shawano man stopped with a Pillager woman. He was lost. The others made a hunting camp, finally stayed put, became leaders who signed away land in treaty after desperate treaty. Midassbaupayikway, Ten Stripe Woman, Midass, the mother of Blue Prairie Woman, married into these south-looking people but her daughter was not one of them, for she went west.

Supposedly this Blue Prairie Woman, before she disappeared, had twins who had twins. Zosie. Mary. They were the first set of twins and the second too. The twins were named Zosie and Mary until me, Rozin, and my sister, Aurora, who died from diphtheria and was pried from my five-year-old arms. I named my girls Cally and Deanna. Bad choice. I broke more continuity, and they suffered for it, too. Should have kept the protection. Should have kept the names that gave the protection. Should have kept the old ways just as much as I could, and the tradition that guarded us. Should have rode horses. Kept dogs. Stayed away from Richard Whiteheart Beads, Frank Shawano, or maybe Klaus's woman with the flashy walk and broken teeth.

I would go back, if I could, unweave the pattern of destruction. Take it all apart occurrence by slow event. But how can you pick out the strands of all you might have changed and all you couldn't? How could I not have noticed Sweetheart Calico?

I was married to Richard Whiteheart Beads. Our twins were five years old. From that old-time connection, I had always known the Shawanos as a good family, big and numerous with relations all over the place, in every walk of life, but I didn't know a single one individually until I bought a loaf of bread from Frank. That was shortly after we came here, to the city. He ran his own storefront bakery. It was his calling. I entered for one reason and only this—her. Sweetheart Calico sat on the sidewalk just outside the shop. A beautiful woman in ripped black tights, shoeless. In her hand, a fragrant, tawny, puffed-up ball of dough with a saddle of lemon jelly that quivered when she bit.

She stuck out her hand for some change, held me with her bold eyes, tore again and again into the pastry like a wolf.

"Where did you get that?" I asked as I dug into my pocket.

She took my change and gestured at the doors beside us. So I went through, stood before the bank of glass display cases. I looked at the trays of bismarks and long johns and cinnamon rolls, craved only plain bread, made my choice. Told the baker. Frank reached behind him, selected from the case, then turned on the slicing machine, and sliced it all up for sandwiches. Gathered the slices into a tight transparent bag and held the loaf out, a loaf of white so fresh it sagged between his hands like an accordion.

"You're a Roy," he said.

"Whiteheart Beads." I was surprised, though. "I'm married now."

He smiled. "That should stop me, I know."

I took the loaf.

"It's so fresh and soft," he advised, "you should eat it as soon as you get home."

I walked out, looking for the woman. She was gone. I opened the bag and had a piece as I walked—salty, tender, porous, a flaking brown crust.

The first time Frank and I took a walk together, he fed me bits of a cinnamon roll from his bare fingers and then bent over and tied my shoe. Bent over in the middle of nowhere, by a rock. I sat. He put my foot down and he tied my shoe—it wasn't an attractive shoe, either, a track shoe, an old shoe. Frank unrolled the soft crush of bread in his fingers, shared. Toward the middle the taste intensified. Delicious spice. Talking of something else he fed the syrupy, fresh central bud to me from his fingers.

One week later, we met and had coffee and at that time as we talked he touched my knuckle, then the skin between my fingers. Frank's face is a loving declension, the skin smoothed by his work with butter, puckered delicately around eyes of sharply tuned brown. His mouth is plush and, back then, before he got sick, his lips fit around jokes with a goofy twist, his grin turned back and sudden, the laugh low, his eyebrows flaring, handsome, and slightly bashful.

That same day. That afternoon.

"Little dog, little dog, where did you come from?" I ask Cally.

"Not the circus this time."

"Where then, far away?"

"Yes, from devil land." Her face is careful, solemn.

"What's it like there?"

"Not too bad." It is her sister who shrugs with little-girl toughness. "They tried to burn me with fire."

I lie in our bed like a stunned animal, tears slowly leaking from the corners of my eyes. Nothing good can come of this love, I know, but I am in it so deeply I can only hear the waves crashing far away and overhead on the vault of the shore. I am afraid for my daughters. Cally is playing next to me with small toys of molded plastic. Horses. Lions. Dogs.

"I hate killer bees. They have a poison stuff around their waist," Deanna tells me. "I hope you'll never dream about them."

The twins are now eating raw sliced apples in bed. I've set the peel down on the carpet. Deanna is floating the white moon slices in the sheets.

"Mama, there's a wet spot in your bed."

Oh great. Another one. Tears. Tears. My sheets are turning in the dryer.

"Why do you have fur on your vagina?"

I've taught my girls to call everything by its correct name, the way they tell you to in parenting magazines. Sometimes Cally or Deanna surprise people in their nursery school with the directness of their questions, their clinical exactitude. I'm glad, but they aren't easy, these questions. Yet, at a time like this, what better subject?

"All grown-up women have it." I make myself sound important.

"What's it for?" Both are listening, intent.

"It's to keep my vagina warm." I think that up with surprising ease, then realize I'm on a roll. I keep talking. "While I'm growing a baby in there, it's to keep the baby warm, too."

"Is there a baby in you now?"

"No. You and Deanna are the last babies."

Tears fill my eyes and spill out again. Just two nights before, my husband, their father, had stroked my vagina, my labia, my clitoris, with his right hand. I always move to his left side when I want him to, of course, because he's right-handed, his hand is heavy, and I love him too. His fingers are square with square nails and even as I think of them I'm thinking of Frank's palms, a tiny wedge of broken muscle in the center, because he works great mounds of dough with his hands. Imagining him knead butter into pastry dough I melt too. He slaps the rye dough on the stainless-steel counter with a thwack that jolts me into lust.

"Mama, I'm going to be a teacher when I grow up."

I can't answer. I'm stuck on Frank's wrists.

"Mama, do teachers have a lot?"

"Of what, fur?"

"No, toys."

I turn to the girls, stroke their hands, speak with too much passion.

"Oh yes, yes, oh honeys, they have so many toys!"

Cally asks me, "Do you want a seaweed marshmallow?"

"Sure," I say, of course. And with great dignity, compassion, seriousness, and pleasure, my twins feed me from their clever fingers. From unseen buckets and cups and baskets, they draw out the seaweed marshmallows. One by one, they pinch from their imaginary store. One by one, they put their fingertips gently to my lips. And I eat every airsweet they give me, every single one until I'm filled with an invisible, light happiness.

I've borne this lovely child and her sister who have marked me through and through. I love them more than I thought was possible—my boundaries stretched. Other stretch marks, the ones on my lower stomach, never did turn to silvery lines, as the pregnancy books said they would. They stayed violet and jagged, but I don't care. They are real. I was broken open. I should have some sign to remember, some minor stripe that shows the inner shift, my tectonics. I was solid, before my children. Now I'm subject to earthquakes.

"Let's read," I say, filled to the lips.

Grandfather Twilight. Catkin. Seuss.

My girls are napping soon. I put them to sleep with my droning voice. Our little house yawns, its careful air plays through the walls, and I'm restless. Richard is at a meeting with environmental engineers, a planning commission that he says will make or break his schemes. Far up north on reservation land, there's money to be made in garbage. Disposal space. Landfill. I should be grading my students' papers, but I open a bottle of wine, take from beside the sink the same glass my husband drank from, the one still smudged from his fingerprints.

I never asked for this.

I put my lips on the edge, in panic, as though the ghost print of his kiss can save me. I fill the glass, drink from it. Decide not to believe in what is happening to me, or to wonder how I'll live with this flood. I haven't eaten actual food for two days, now. A box of Cheez-It crackers floats on the counter before me, perfect little squares. I open the box and begin to eat, holding the crackers between my teeth, mashing them into a salty paste, licking them until they disintegrate. I am impatient. I shove a whole handful in. The taste is cheap, false, distressing.

Out behind the bakery down the back alley to a playground field on a path barely hidden in a fringe of woods I suddenly lay down before him and he knelt between my legs unbuckling his belt. As he entered me, his face was distant in concentration and I wrapped my legs around him. I was wearing a long skirt. I wrapped that around us too. I could hear the cries of children in the field, excited with some triumph, and our own breathing. He stopped looking at me. I thought there was someone coming down the path, and smiled. It began to rain then, spattering at first lightly through the leaves.

The children's cries grew shrill and a plane passed overhead, a temporary ceiling, a hushed roar. After that there were no cries, only the increasing momentum of the drops, now hissing through the plants around us, wetting us very slowly even though the skies were pouring water now, the clouds open, drawing out the scents of plants, faint wintergreen, balsam, a sweetly rotting mushroom funk, the spongy cakes of moss, a wildly fruited berry, crushed, some deeper, browner, older scent of leaf, and then our own bodies, also of the woods.

Sometimes we moved very quickly and strenuously, straining to get inside each other, and then at other times we seemed to have forgotten that we were making love at all and even in the dripping undergrowth found ourselves talking, or touching, abstracted, so close inside each other we were somewhere else. I don't remember anything about coming or climaxing or about the finish of the episode because it seems even now to me that once it started, the closeness, it became continual and I at once lived within him just as he came alive in me so that wherever I go and whatever I do I am making love to him. It may seem that I am doing a mundane thing, for instance, buying groceries or reading to my daughters. But as I speak the words or pass my hands over the apples in the bin or as I shake cereal or pick a green cardboard box of pasta, rattling, from its shelf, I am every bit as passionate toward him as when he is within me, moving, or simply hard and still, looking at me through that gulf between our bodies, that inch of joyous, magnetic space.

4

Why I Am No Longer Friends with Whiteheart Beads

Klaus Shawano

When people ask me why I am no longer friends with Whiteheart Beads, I hedge around and come up with a neutral type of explanation. I say something innocuous, to keep things going on the surface. I have to do that. The reason is I'm afraid. My fear is this—if I ever begin to tell the story it will all flood out of me. It will be gone, unfixed, into the mouths of others. I'm afraid the story might stop being mine. Which would be dangerous. I rely on the story, you see. I keep it inside me because without it I might forget or dismiss the reason I no longer trust him. And once I did that, there is no telling what could happen.

Richard Whiteheart Beads, I've thought so often, foe or friend? I decided on the first because he cost me everything I had. I did manage to keep my life, but aside from that—my clothes, my savings, my house, my boat, and even, yes, my wife, Sweetheart Calico. My Antelope Girl. Gone. Due to Whiteheart.

Now you'll say to yourself there is no human on this earth with power of that magnitude. None. You wouldn't believe it surely if you did meet him. He has a handsome, bland, forgettable face. Forgettable unless of course he has ripped out your heart. So me, I remember his face just fine.

Some things happen easy, and you feel like they were meant to be. And some things, oh God, they come so hard. The party we attended together, put on by our trash collection concern, that was the easy part that led to the impossible.

I am standing before the salads and cheeses and deli meat with Richard Whiteheart Beads. We start loading our plates. While we are selecting food, he tells me about the new truck he is thinking of buying—he's always thinking of what he can acquire. This truck, it is just another example of Whiteheart's imaginary surround. I know that. But I listen as though I believe in its pinstripes and refurbished engine, its Thirstbuster cup holders.

"Wish I could get an automatic sunroof, too," Whiteheart Beads is saying. "Then you could travel with the wind in your hair."

"What hair?"

I'm an Indian with a buzz cut now. I got it when she left the first time. I cut my hair for sorrow. She left again. More sorrow. And again. Yet shorter. Anyway, now that she's back my hair says to her, I hope, what I believe. Plain living. Hard work. The simple life, unadorned, ridding the world of waste. "People You Can Count On." Our motto in garbage management. My belief.

"You should grow it out again. Live. Women love it."

Whiteheart Beads is referring to his own ponytail, a serious thick rope reaching halfway down his suit-jacket back. We, the two of us, present a very different image and I must admit that his is probably the more selling look in terms of women. And for sure, since from our company he has been given two Appreciation Top Prize all-expense-paid tickets to Maui, a fact revealed shortly after the soda pop stops flowing at this lunch, he does what he does in the high-end waste disposal business as well as it can be done.

We mill around. We eat more. Used to be us Indians had nothing to throw away—we used it all up to the last scrap. Now we have a lot of casino trash, of course, and used diapers, disposable and yet eternal, like the rest of the country. Keep this up and we'll all one day be a landfill of diapers, living as adults right on top of our own baby shit. Makes sense in some way. Makes sense to me. Of course, our main business is that we deal with other people's garbage. We're now the first Native-owned waste disposal company in the whole U.S. and proud of it. Proud of our management expertise and good old-fashioned ability to haul shit. Not mention stabilize it. That's the real question.

A cake is wheeled in and it is shaped like one of our new vehicles with company colors of thick frosting, the lard and sugar kind, heart-stopping artery paste.

"You want 'em?"

Whiteheart holds the tickets out casually in the presentation envelope. I take the envelope: pictures of windsurfing Barbies and Kens, a couple of sea turtles winging through the gloom. Native Hawaiians dressed in flowers, holding torches, paddling this huge wooden canoe.

"Right," I say, reluctant to hand the envelope back. I notice it's not transferable, his name is filled in the blanks.

Whiteheart waves his hands at me, fanning out his fingers.

"Keep 'em. Keep. My wedding present."

"No shit?"

Whiteheart looks at me and shrugs, very modest, as though any gratitude will just embarrass him, as though it makes him very nervous, which I notice he has been all along, that day, through the cheese and crackers, fruit, cold meats, the cake. He's been looking over his shoulder, staring into corners, behaving in this distracted and jumpy fashion I know so well. Woman trouble.

"Whiteheart, Whiteheart my friend." I put my hand on his shoulder. "Who is she? You can tell me."

His smile snaps across his face like a banner pulled tight.

"Not a woman. Not a woman. You take those tickets, Klaus. You can borrow my I.D. You have a good time—hey, I mean it."

Then, with surprisingly little fuss or bother, Whiteheart exits through a side door, disappears almost. Unlike him until the eleventh hour.

Next thing I know, my lady and me are getting ready for the trip. Maui. Glorious. Tropical. Hotel on the beach. We decide to go immediately in case Whiteheart's mind changes or he comes along, a thing he is fond of doing on our dates. I was always the one who minded those lopsided occasions worse than Sweetheart. I think back on that now. I should have known from the beginning, but love blinded me the way it does. She probably would have rather been with Whiteheart even then! But no, no. Don't get ahead of the next event.

It all happens bang right out of the gates. These guys. Two guys at the airport looking us over in that special way I am familiar with from being in the army. Big guys. In suits. Four words to cause concern. *Big guys in suits*. I'll never look at life the same.

We check in.

Apparently there is some sort of seating arrangement that goes with these tickets, and it involves my wife and I split up in separate seats. Not only that, but the middle row seats.

"Hey, this can't be right. We're together, on our honeymoon," I tell the check-in personnel—exotic-looking woman, nails to here.

She chews her lip and fiddles with the keyboard, scowls at what blips up on the screen, and then looks at us with a blank, closed expression. Lots of purple eye shadow.

"I can't do a thing about it." Her declaration is such that I don't even think to argue. She stamps our tickets, asks us if anyone had given us anything to carry on board the plane, waves us on.

"We'll switch once we're on the plane," I say to my lady love, reassuring her. "Someone will be glad to change places with a couple newlyweds."

I like your faith in human nature, her look tells me. I am proud of her pessimism, read it as an answer. And she is right about those guys. One of them sits next to each of us. I ask, politely, explaining. "We're newlyweds. Our seats got screwed up. Would one of you fellows mind switching?"

Like asking a favor of a set of bowling balls. These guys are muscle-bound and thick of neck, ponytailed like Whiteheart. One with a gold ring in the chunky lobe of his ear. The seatmate I address is the color of a Hereford, too, reddish and whitish. Dull eyes of a slab of meat. And you know what it's like in the middle seat of an airplane anyway, that stuffed-in-a-cat-carrier feeling, claustrophobic. I am directly behind my wife and to take my mind off my panic, I watch with longing the only part of her that I can see—top of her head and dark hair ponytailed in something I've heard called a scrunchie, a purple satin cloth band thing that bobs and slides up and down as she nervously mimics the flight attendant's demonstration.

It concerns me, her sitting next to that guy.

Quite apart from the weirdness in the first place, she's that sort of taut-bodied, fine-boned woman who arouses instant lust. From the back, especially, one of her most attractive angles. She has a sloping deer-haunch bottom. I am glad it is pressed against the seat. Her mouth now that her teeth are broken always looks as though she's just bit into a sweet tart candy, pursed together like her scrunchie. When she smiles, though, it looks real witchy. I find her broken teeth something to adore, though I admit it is not to every man's taste. Anyway, what I'm trying to say, politely, is that her front side, grinning, though lovely to me, is not her most attractive to the less discerning. I hoped she wouldn't have to rise, say, to visit the bathroom, putting that lovely rear of hers within a handsbreadth of that ape.

No chance of that, I later find.

I was in perfect agony, she communicates, slumping against me once we have deplaned, *and do you think they would so much as let me stir? Pretended to speak another sign language, or not understand me. I ended up pointing you know where and hissing.* I wince. *They didn't get it.* She shrugs. *Pretended not to. What's going on?*

This is at the car rental place, Maui herself, where we find ourselves waiting a mere ten hours after boarding that plane. We are standing in the patient headlights of those guys in suits.

"Something odd about those guys," I mutter, tired, fed by a prescient insight. "Something that has to do with Whiteheart."

Sweetheart always perks up when his name drops from my lips. She peers at me now through her tattered hair. Whiteheart. These burly types in suits. I keep not getting it even as we drive through the booming night air, light and sugary, blowing a pale salt through the windows of the car. They are going along the same road, it appears. I still don't get it when they make the turnoff, directly behind us. When they park, next space. When they emerge just as we do and form an escort phalanx around us like Roman guards. Then, as we march into the huge waterfall-running Bird of Paradise lounge and check-in desk, I do get it. They're going to kill us. They're assassins.

Once I understand that, I'm okay. My mind is clear.

The hallways of this big elaborate jungle hotel lobby contrast with the long white light tunnels to the stacks of rooms. Walking toward our number we are of course accompanied off the elevator by the big guys in suits, whom I am tired of seeing at every turn. So tired of it all, in fact, so clear in my read, that without thinking or caring about the consequences I confront them.

I whirl, annoyed to the point where I do not have fear. I face them with stony resistance. They sweep right past, whereas I thought they'd halt, we'd speak, have words. No words. At least an exchange where I could ask who on earth they thought Klaus Shawano was—a man worth pursuing and killing? How come?

"Hey," I take on the smaller, bullnecked one, "what's the rush?"

Both stop and look, eyes like marbles.

"You're sent to kill, I know," I say amiable. "Obvious. So why not enjoy yourself first?"

"We're not here to hurt you," says the shorter one after a pause. "It's nothing like that."

The bigger one laughs. "Worse."

My heart thumps. My voice comes out scratchy and small.

"IRS?"

"Not exactly. We're here because of dumping practices. You're part of a major sweep. It's okay to tell you, we just got the word."

"Might as well do the honors," says the big guy.

"You're under arrest." It is the smaller one who shows his badge.

"You have to say his name," the larger guy prompts, underneath his breath.

"Oh yeah," says the newer cop, officer, whatever.

"Whiteheart. Richard Whiteheart."

"Beads."

"No! I'm not him!" A sudden wave of relief gushes through me. I start to laugh, to explain. "He gave these tickets to me for my honeymoon. He sent us here, made us a gift, changed our lives."

"Oh, right." They both grin little tight shark smiles and remind me that I'm on an island. We'll leave in the morning. They'll accompany me to the airport.

"Really, though. I'm not Whiteheart. *Look.*"

I take out my wallet, open it, slip my license from the interior of its pocket, and to my complete sincere suddenly remembering shock I find that I am carrying the I.D. pictures of Whiteheart—he gave them to me, of course, to present for the tickets. We look enough alike, I guess, being both the real thing Anishinabe men.

"Wait," I say, digging for the real me, which I can't find. Where is it and where am I and worst of all who?

So that is about the extent of our honeymoon, me and Sweetheart. I decide, since we've got one night in paradise, to make the most of it. I purchase my babe mai tais in a big plastic cup. We go down the elevator to the tile whirlpool hot tub, a hidden glade unit surrounded by flowers. Of course, the big guys follow.

We get in, her and me. She's wearing a suit covered with blue hibiscus flowers. Something I bought her back in Gakahbekong. And oh man, but is it ever good, this whirlpool bath of heat and chlorine. The hot jets rumble up and down my spine and the presence of my lady is all but too much for me. I'll never forget this, never, I think, her face in the rushing blue lights. Her hair in smooth snakes and curlicues floating and drifting on the surface of the medicinal waters. The booze, which I suck down in order to enjoy the present moment, disremember the past, meet the stupid future, both knocks me down and buoys me up. The night progresses and the heat intensifies. Of course, there is a certain restraining factor in the presence of the gorilla.

"You have to sit there in that suit?" I say at last to the big boy in the shadows. "How come you don't just hop in here?"

"Yeah, wish I could." The most genuine response I've heard yet.

"Why don't you guys pretend not to catch me for a while and stay here, I mean, hang out and absorb some rays. Snorkel. Beachcomb. Hot tub. Swim."

"Oh, shut the fuck up," he says, but in a wistful tone.

My dear one and me stay up all night, and I tell you it is a night to remember. A night I won't forget. Sensations abound that haunt me even now in the underpasses and the park undergrowth and old abandoned boat shacks of Gakahbekong. There is something very pure and old that happens when we're on, together, moving like we're running over distances, floating like swift clouds. The next morning, breakfast, and by nine o'clock we're hustled off. We're boarding. We're gone. It's like we dreamed the night. I can't tell you with what a sense of desolation and purpose I look down on that green beauty and blue sea from on high.

Maybe I know then, and maybe I'm just starting to understand, that life will always be like this around Richard Whiteheart. One minute high in Maui and the next minute yanked from bliss. I'm heading back now to tell my story before the judge, and I don't even know what my story is. I don't know what it's all about, but I do know it has to do with Whiteheart. I decide, right then, as we pass into a cloud, whatever else happens I won't take the blame I can sense waiting at the terminal. No, that will be Richard. Whatever he has done, and it is big from the looks of it, I won't pay. Will not be held responsible. I'll rat. I'll speak. Things get dumped, terrible poisons in endless old wells. Nothing's endless, though. Every place has limits. Everybody. Toxins. Resins. Old batteries. Lead. Mercury. And Whiteheart. And Whiteheart.

5

Sweetheart Calico

A ball of heat flung her through the window, dragging melted plastic shower curtains that in snow hardened to the shape of her body as she loped crazily through the park. In the lighted shelter where the street people dragged her, she put her feet into wool pants, a silken blouse off a rich lady's back, and a heavy padded jacket. All of the beds were taken, so she curled up on a flea pallet in the corner and she slept for ten days, forgetting all of her children or taking them back into her body and holding them.

At night, she remembered running beside her mother.

Her daughters danced out of black mist in the shimmering caves of their hair.

When she touched their faces, they poured all their love through their eyes at her. Klaus, she never dreamed about or remembered. He was just the one she was tied to, who brought her here. Thongs of fabric, his need, tied to a stake and driven deep into the Minnesota earth. She found that no matter how fast or how far she walked, she couldn't get out of the city. The lights and car panic tangled her. Streets opened onto streets and the highways roared hungry as swollen rivers, bearing in their rush dangerous bright junk.

6

The Girl and the Deer Husband

Cally

I

I was small, woven of my parents and tied to my sister's arm, when my father took the two of us to the city park. He held my hand in the late afternoon. The air was pink and golden, smelling of fresh rain. Our canvas high-top shoes soaked through as we ran over wet grass to the time tunnels and the monkey bars and the fenced plain of deer. Late spring. Early June. The iris were blooming, their furred tongues flimsy, trembling, floppy velvet ears and throats open. Their beauty a knocking harangue. We saw a woman in a purple-blue iris dress just like our mother's. She was walking across the garden with a man.

I didn't know him at first. Like a cutout from a cereal box, like nobody, like Mr. Circus Buttons, dream of a deer man. Deer head on his shoulders. Body of an athlete. Hooves striking flames from the tree roots. This woman was with him and as they got closer, we saw that she was our mother. Rozin. We grabbed our father by the wrist, brought him to the iris beds. We pointed across the grass to make him understand that it was her. He only returned our excitement with a calm gaze, chin tipped down. From underneath his brows his eyes clouded and hardened.

"No, that isn't her."

"Look!" We pulled on his sleeves.

"No"—he spoke indifferently—"that isn't your mother. I know she looks like your mother."

"She is! She does!"

"I know she does."

"But Daddy"—we were together in this now, persuading him—"she has the same *dress*."

"I know." He spoke with deliberate and now forceful gravity. "Still, that is not your mother."

It was only when the two walking people got close enough for us to clearly see her face, laughter fading in our mouths, that we decided, as she bent forward to the other man, touching his chest with the flat of her hand, that our father was right. We were looking at some other woman whose face, alight and radiant and still with anticipation, we had never seen before.

II

When he kneeled over her, she saw the kind hunger in his eyes. Moody grays and yellows. A haunting of bees. His hands were callused and careful in touching her. He had shaken off his old winter coat and the dun patches lay all around them in strips and singleton hairs. Magnetic warmth. Riches of gentle trusting sleep. Making love, their hearts were sunk deep in earth and yet alert to the strangeness of who we are as human animals, as people reaching desperately through the wounds and synchronicities, as furtive unfortunates half drunk on the message of our mortality.

Drink from the clear stream. Drink slow. Drink deep. For when you reach the other side, you will forget you ever dreamed this beautiful life.

III

Later, she was the very same mother. Calmer. Irritable. But in the old familiar ways. Once again she drove off with father on certain evenings and they stayed away for the weekend while our grandmothers babysat. Our grandmothers were both round-shouldered powerful small women with eyes of deep brown sunk narrow in their faces. Their hands were tough and splayed, but delicate. Grandma Zosie pricked up beads and sewed calmly. Grandma Mary wore moccasins. They lived up north. One day Grandma Zosie told us it was no wonder we threw our clothes off and danced for each other, naked in the rainy yard. We were part deer and there was nothing to be done.

It happened a long time ago.

IV

Our grandmother many greats past counting was a peculiar girl known for her tremendous appetite though she stayed thin as a handful of twigs. During berry season, she went picking many times a day, filling her bucket over but eating it empty before she ever made it to the house. Not only that, but she couldn't keep her hands off mushrooms, food of the dead, or wild carrots. She robbed the wild rice caches. Ate all the boiled meat. It worried people to see that she was always eating, always hungry, but never full.

A voice.

I've been watching this girl. Maybe she's a windigo.

No, said her mother. She's only that hungry. Nothing wrong with her.

Still, the other people ignored her or gave her shaming looks when she approached a food pot. Hungrier than ever, she took to the woods. More and more time, days even, passed with her gathering and cooking out there in the heart of the dense bush. You could smell the steam, the good smells, you could smell the smoke rising.

She's cooking out there. Wonder what she's making? Wonder if a little child disappeared, we would find it in the cooking pot? Great-Great-Grandmother ate the whole rabbit. Ears too. She wanted to eat her own arm. So Hungry. That's finally what they named her. So Hungry. Apijigo Bakaday.

And then she was joined out in the woods.

As her own mother tells it, and she would know, Apijigo was cooking up a fine pot of stew when a deer approached, stood by the edge of her camp. Just waiting. Apijigo thought, Should I eat him or should I share with him? Which? She picked up her killing hatchet but when she finally advanced toward the deer and looked him in the eye, she felt ashamed. She knew hunger when she saw it. Just walked past the deer and chopped a little more wood for the fire. Finished that stew.

She put the stew onto the plate, set the plate down in front of the deer, got her own plate full, and ate sitting before him. He never moved. She ate the whole stew, mopped up every trace of it with bannock, pikwayzhigun, then sat quietly looking at him, crescent of horns, waiting. Unafraid. She had this feeling. Full. So this was what other people felt. She looked over at the deer. His eyes were steady and warm with a deep black light. His heart shone right out of his eyes.

He loves me, she thought. He loves me and I love him back. Right down to the ground. Who he is. No different. Of course, too bad that he's a deer. Still, she made a bed out of young hemlock branches and curled against his short, stiff pelt. She began to live with him, stayed with him out in the woods, and traveled with him on into the open spaces. Became beloved by his family, too. Got so that she knew how to call the hooved ones toward her. They came when she stood in the open. Her song was peculiar, soft, questing.

V

Who will ever understand the misery love causes?

"What did it mean, Grandmother, what?"

"Enough for now," she growled, baring her strong white teeth.

So we ran out the door and threw off our clothes. The grandmas stayed inside, lighted their small red-bowl kinnikinnick pipes. They sat in the corner, smoking and brooding.

Who will ever understand?

VI

He came to our house once. We knew it was him because there was sugar on his pants and flour in his hair. There was in his hands a large box and in the box, between layers of wax paper, an assortment of fancy sugar cookies cut into the shapes of carrots, trees, dolphins, stars, moons, dogs, and flowers. Each type of cutout was decorated with a different color of hard icing trimmed with a rickrack of frosting, studded with edible foil-sugar beads and blue-black raisins. I put the head of a pink dog into my mouth and bit it completely off. As the crumbly cookie dissolved grain by grain between my tongue and the roof of my mouth, I glanced over at the man who brought the box and at my mother. They were standing in the doorway, staring at each other. They were not talking. They did not say one word.

VII

She didn't want to leave her deer husband, but her brothers came to get her one brilliant spring. Shot her man with three arrows, one bullet. Brought her back to her family, her village, her people. She was not hungry anymore, and she was grown. They named her for the flowers that stretched past her shielding arms and were spattered with deer's blood, blue flowers scraped from patches of sky. Blue Prairie Woman.

She married one of the Shawano brothers, even though that family was said to be descended of windigos. She lived winters on the traplines with his father and brothers. Spring through late fall they stayed in a village where she could be with her woman relatives, talk all night, cook, laugh. She never used her medicine to attract the hooved ones. Never. But everyone knew what she could do.

Sometimes the deer people came to her, anyway.

One slender doe did on the morning of the big knives. Told Blue

Prairie Woman to leave, go now, tie her baby on the back of the dog, and run. Too late, though. Just as she started out a tornado of bluecoat men. Everything scattered, lost, burned, murdered. Strange. She saw the same man who killed her grandmother leap forward suddenly and run, uttering inhuman cries of loss, from the swirl of death into the distance. He was following her baby. Her baby tied in the tikinagun. Riding on the back of the dog-mother of six fat, fine puppies. One, Blue Prairie Woman would nurse with her own milk. The others grew too weak to save.

VIII

Rozin didn't want to lie to her husband, but he was touchy on all subjects. His love was deep clawed, hungry. He frightened her with his false candor. While they were together, he told her things, raw things, private things. Tender things. He kissed her, put his muscular tongue in her mouth, searching for the honey. But then he stung her with his lips, raked at her breasts. She was never sure how she stood because his mood changed with no reference to anything she did.

So when she lied she could at least control his anger by keeping him satisfied at the appearance of his world.

The lie became her nature.

Soon she could lie so well no truth stood in her way. She could make up a story on the spot and tell it with the light of calm veracity. Soon, nothing mattered enough. She couldn't see the real picture. One day, Richard came home and stepped into the house very quietly, stood still with his nose testing air.

"Frank's been here."

"Yes," she said, her voice light. "He brought me the hide he tanned. I'm beading again."

He believed her. The next day, however, he again asked if Frank had been there. This time she told him something else. Again, he said nothing. But when on the third day he once again wondered, she happened to be out in the backyard cutting the grass. So he decided to search the house. One of Frank's eyelashes was caught in the old deerhide. His baker's fingerprints were on the lard can. Cookies were in the cookie jar. The towel he might have used was balled up on the floor. Richard raised the sharp ax of his voice and called Rozin.

"Your lover is dead," said Richard, when she came in the house.

She started, her heart broke like a stick.

"Stay away from him," said Richard.

IX

She returned in the soft sorrow of her familiar skin, and collapsed on the pillows, switched on the television, which was broken. I curled against her on the mold-smelling couch and held on, and held on, and held her. Static flickered. Sound went backwards. Ribbons of ash scrolled over and over the screen. She was crying in my arms, my child arms, my deer mother.

I retrieved her in the slanted velocity of light, but her head felt so heavy and round with her iron sadness of mind that I let her fall against a pillow.

Let her sleep. She's too much trouble.

And the tattered leaves closed over her.

All of our actions have in their doing the seed of their undoing. So with my mother's heart. And I marvel: That it should be a heart of rag wool knit and unknit by one same needle. That it should be a cloth first woven and then unraveled by its own loomed strength. That in her creation of her children there should be the unspeakable promise of their death, for by their birth she had created mortal beings. That in her love there should be failure to love. That in the sudden hatred she developed toward our father there should be the split cotyledon, the tongue, the trembling shoot of a sunless white passion.

7

Yellow Pickup Truck

One of those heartbreaking snows that falls after a week of false spring. The buds caught half open, fooled. The walks dry, grass dusty and weak. Then it snows. Weightless, drifting, soon heavy enough to break the stressed limbs of oak. The flakes pile onto each branch, twig, and needle until at last in the windless morning the pines and soaring elms flare white. The more supple trees bend, the honey locusts nearly double. The streets narrow to dream tunnels and to either side the houses gather frosting until they are arranged like sugar wedding cakes in the white, white world.

Rozin waits for the school bus alongside her daughters. They stand close together on the street corner, watching traffic. Her hand brushes down Deanna's, down Cally's slippery brown hair. The bus bumbles to a stop and the doors sigh open.

"Don't worry," says Rozin. "It will be all right. It will be okay."

"What will?" asks Deanna, hopping past her, casual, grinning.

Rozin watches until the bus turns down the street and then she walks into the kitchen and puts the old blue kettle on to boil. Standing tall in her lavender robe, hands pressed on the pale tiles of the counter, unsmiling, she gazes out the window into the festooned yard. She leans forward and frowns as though looking for something hidden in the supernal light.

When her husband steps into the kitchen, yawning, rubbing his chest, and pulling down a thick sweatshirt, she drops her gaze. Unspeaking, she sets out spoons, milk, slices a grapefruit, rattles a cereal box, takes down a pair of white lotus bowls. Richard pours the steaming water into the plunger coffeepot and then he stands with her in a drowsy suspension.

The snow light, after the warm bleakness of early March, is unsettling.

"It'll melt by this afternoon," he pronounces.

She nods, but does not answer.

As always, she pours the coffee into his pottery cup. As always, he takes his first grateful drink as she turns away, but as he shakes out the morning paper Rozin sits beside him. Instead of reaching for a section of the paper, she puts her hand upon his hand, and tells him that she has something to say.

Later, he thinks of his indulgent grin and listening expression with humiliated rancor. But as she is speaking, her voice betrays none of the strain appropriate to the magnitude of what she is about to tell him. So how can he prepare to absorb from the beginning the blow she is about to deal? How blame himself for looking the fool, for his stupid, increasingly stupefied grin? Wrenched onto his face, it seems stuck there. He can't properly react to wipe it off even after she informs him that her old lover, Frank Shawano, is dying of cancer, has been given a five to ten percent chance of surviving the next nine months, and that she is going to him now, leaving their marriage, to be with this man until he dies because after all she truly loves him. Loves him, she says.

Three times during their marriage, Rozin had tried to leave Richard Whiteheart Beads. Twice he threatened, cajoled, persuaded, and horrified her into staying. Once there was a surprise pregnancy. Twins. She had stayed, too, wild about her babies, happy.

"You've got Cally and Deanna," he says, looks at her, and bites his words back.

"You can stay here, in the house. I'll go." Her voice is calm but there is an undertone he knows, a shaking undertone that he gropes for.

"Am I so terrible?" he asks, his voice piteous. "You want to get away that badly, that you'd leave?"

"I'm taking Cally and Deanna," she continues as though walking out on a suspension bridge.

"No you're not," he tries.

She holds her breath, lets it out explosively. "I won't stay."

He raises his eyes to change her mind, to see for himself another truth, but she's been to therapy, he thinks, and some fucking pseudoshrink has put these cold lines in her mouth. Black as river silt, her eyes swell with tears, but for the first time he cannot see himself in their mirror-flat depth.

School is good that day for Deanna because there is a pizza party for the readers, and Deanna is a top winner for the words she recognizes in the vocabulary list. Cally just one word behind. They were born that way, minutes apart. Deanna first. Decisive. Maternal. Volatile. Specific. They are slim, energetic, soft-spoken girls with a keen edge to their quiet. Observers, they both have smiles that start slow at the edges of their oval faces and then take over until the smiles practically come out their ears. Also there is the snow, fluffy enough to kick up clouds when they go in the school door. By noon it is perfect rolling material so that the teachers all warn about iceballs putting out eyes before they let the children shouting into the playground. There are snow people. Girls making, boys wrecking. And there is enough snow left to sled down the little hill just on the edge of the school grounds. It is the last sliding of the year, say the teachers, and so everyone gets fifteen extra minutes of recess and takes a bright plastic school sled—electric blue, hot pink, orange, or lime green. Holding them up like goofy shields, the eager phalanx of children trudge. Cally hauls part of the long toboggan with a friend. Deanna's is a yellow saucer. She whirls as she slides downhill and pops off, rolling over and over until she reaches the bottom.

Richard has the sense that this awful bubble will pop if he only takes a deep enough breath, and laughs, but when he does try to breathe no air enters. He can't fill his chest. And then, just as he stops trying, he empties inside, knowing what she says is going to happen. The way her eyes accept whatever he should do now, his fury, his hurt, his wish to hurt her in return. Her eyes tell him that this was one of her implacable statements. *No funeral*, had been one, for her own grandmother, a traditional Ojibwa, when she died. *No abortion*, even though when the pregnancy occurred they were separating. *We're moving*, when his job became dangerous and the reservation life too political. And now, directed to him, *I am leaving*.

He drives to work, sits in his office, moves paper and makes phone calls. Everything seems normal again. Then he remembers. There should be scenes, great explosions, ripping noise, crashing of a marriage like a vigorous tree charged in a blue-white storm, but because her lover is dying, after all, that does not happen. Will not. Jealous, he is jealous, but of a dying man! Maybe that Frank is the other brand of love medicine Ojibwa, damn rabbit choker, draws her to him. What can he do about that? White-hot lights pop behind his eyes, flashes of self-pity. He has been an idealistic student, so proud of marrying this girl with the old Roy blood. Now that blood calls to someone else, he thinks, and then laughs at how ridiculous that sounds. He tries for perspective. Frank Shawano is a man shot through with cancer-killing chemicals, hanging on by sheer terror, by the tips of his nails, a man doomed, going to old-time ceremonies. Pathetic. Shawano is a man facing his mortality daily, a man who has finalized his will, a man in anguish and crazy confidence. But a man who will see Rozin every morning of every day. If I get ill, wonders Richard, deadly ill, will she come back to me? How about when Shawano finally dies? Then?

Rozin Whiteheart Beads is a slim woman with a youthful tight-waisted figure, thick gray hair, long and piled often in a beaded clip. Her skin is rough, her mouth a passionate pink, her eyes sad even when she smiles. Reserved smile, bashful. The fervor of her laugh is always a surprise. Now he wishes there was all along something crooked or tainted or mistaken or deeply wrong. Having that affair, that love, that is deeply wrong. He frowns at his hands, scribbles on his calendar. Lying to him. All one big lie. Inside, he knows that if she didn't love him, too, didn't feel for him, she would not have lied and therefore not have stayed. Some of their best times even occurred during those same years she was with Shawano, apparently, but when? No block of time, not even a weekend, no mysterious vacations, no standing appointment unaccounted for, can he recall. Only that one sighting, in the park. Nothing else. Nothing. Part of him is shot with pity, even a little guilt—those furtive, stolen moments, so shabby, so unsatisfactory—she really deserves better even from a rival, a lover, even from this man with the stupid name Shawano.

He comes home early because the phone is busy and he can't stand thinking she might be talking to her lover. He hears Cally upstairs, crooning to her crocodile, a stuffed green creature with yellow eyes. A gift from her grandmothers. Huge. Takes up half her bed. She sleeps between its furry claws. He sits in one corner of the house, sprawled rigid in his chair. Rozin is still on the phone making calls beyond his hearing. Who else can she be calling? Unbearably, his heart grips and he starts to tremble, first his hands then his arms, and then the shaking moves into the core of his body so that his foot jerks out as though a nerve is cut. He grabs the chair's plaid armrests, leans into the dense atmosphere.

He sees it all.

"You slept with him the time I went to Albuquerque, didn't you?" Richard gathers himself and pitches his voice into the living room. "I just want to know. I have the right to know!"

There is an echo after the ugly shock of his yell, an alert stillness from upstairs. The walls around him are a beige and brown checkered material and the furniture Rozin chose and kept spot-free so carefully is a velvety putty color. He hears the phone tap into the cradle. She stands in the corridor gazing into the living room.

"Don't scare the girls," she says.

"I want to know," he insists.

"No, you don't."

He opens his mouth but then the thing is, he doesn't. Truly, he doesn't want to know. The knowledge that he can refuse something strikes him and he marvels. It is a little string of thought but there is integrity in it.

"You're right," he says, and dignity comes over him. "I don't want to know."

Rozin turns to go upstairs. Then she speaks. Her back to him.

"This is hard. The two of us here. Why don't you leave," she says, "go somewhere? Just for tonight. Then I'll be gone. I have to pack the girls' things, too."

His mouth opens wide, wider.

"Some of them," she says. "Of course, they'll be back here and of course they'll want to keep lots of things here."

She retreats into her office. A drawer squeaks, the phone rings again. Tap water runs and he hears the quick rustle of papers. After a few minutes, she walks past him, her heels solid on the wood floor. Her hair streams down her back, a simple fall of darkness.

"You leave," he shouts at her. His voice comes out a ragged yap. "You leave. Not me. I'm staying. I want to stay."

She walks near enough to hand him a business card and he lunges at her, flings himself down like a dancer, grabs her around the knees. Toppling backwards, she twists and the card spins from her fingers and strikes him in the face. He crawls on top of her and she goes stony with disdainful patience. Directly under his nose the card's face glares bold type up at him. Dr. Fry, lots of initials, probably another psychiatrist. He begins to cry into the rope of hair at her neck. Firmly, she puts him away from her, raises herself.

"It's okay, honey," she says in a reassuring voice, not to him. Deanna stands in the doorway, her face intense and still. Rozin walks up to her and takes her by the shoulders and leads her upstairs. He puts out his hands after them, claws air to grasp Rozin's fading scent, sees himself a crablike thing in his mind's eye but doesn't care. No. Not at all. Or maybe yes, he does. He should. He quiets himself. Lies on the floor listening again to them move about. Reckons up Rozin's actions all this past week. Her prized Navajo jewelry in a safe-deposit box. Piles and divisions of her possessions. A remoteness when he touches her and a sorrow in the wine they share every evening as the sun fails. He gets to his feet and fetches the wine from the refrigerator, a tall white bottle of Spanish wine.

"Tell me what to do. Tell me!"

There is no answer, although he speaks in a normal tone of voice and believes she heard him as she came back down the stairs.

He pours a full glass, drinks it fast, pours another and walks back to his chair by the window. He watches the late snow incrementally soften and disappear so that by the time the sun sinks that day earth again shows in patches and the trees, sere and black and all shades of brown, stand nearly stripped against the sky.

Something is wrong and Deanna knows and doesn't know it, but her stuffed animals do and her little china dogs and the walls of the room she shares with her twin sister, even, have a sense that there is something wrong. Her father's voice is a scratchy roar, loud as a zoo animal. Her mother is too quiet. Deanna and Cally brush their teeth exactly as they were taught, spit, rinse, and come down to say good night.

Cally, however, leaves when she sees her father.

Richard is sleeping already and his wineglass is spilled beside him. Deanna walks up to him and touches his shoulder, damp with tears, sweat, wine. She has heard things. She knows. For the first time ever, she can't tell Cally, either. She is afraid for how sad this would make her sister. Doesn't want her to cry. Maybe, she thinks, she can do something. Change her mother's mind. *I will. I will.* She tells her father. Fiercely promising, she looks into his sleeping face, watching the way he breathes in and out through his mouth, the air hissing through his clenched teeth.

Richard wakes in the chair, lights out, and sits looking into the dark air. Hopeless. Tastes a flat suspense in his mouth. Ahead, the whole night looms, packed with beams of adrenaline. He stares into the dark lake of his ceiling. The house is utterly quiet. The phone doesn't even chirp. He feels that to be anchored by his bones and held inside his body by a sheet of skin is unbearable. Snow slips off the trees. He can hear it, piece by piece.

Around one o'clock in the morning he dresses himself carefully from socks to tie, all in basic colors. Sober colors. Sober. The word perversely makes him want to drink some of that old whiskey Rozin saves for special guests. He pours a juice glass full, sets it down and shrugs on his topcoat, walks out to the garage.

A fresh wind booms and stirs, the night is vacant, cold, but with a springlike ardor in the atmosphere. He smells the snow of yesterday, new dirt, a tremulous promise of warmth in the big wind's blue edge. He takes a deep breath and walks directly into the garage, shutting the door behind. It is a small old well-built garage—he loves the challenge of easing the pickup along the walls of tools and paint. He stuffs a towel under the crack in the door. A rag in the tiny broken corner of a window. After he checks the yellow pickup truck's tailpipe, he slides into the cab and closes his eyes a moment before he starts the engine, drops it to an idle. Sighing deeply, groaning out loud, he leans back into the seat.

Toothman wakes her. The white tooth has a red grin and round black eyes. A stuffed tooth. Dentist's prize. Deanna hears the back door shut, looks out of her bedroom window and sees her dad, outside in the backyard. He unlocks the side garage door and then disappears into the dark rectangle. The door shuts. She waits. Waits. He does not come out. A dizzy warmth overcomes her. She almost falls asleep, but starts dreaming she is in school again. Yellow saucer sled. Knows she isn't. He is leaving, then, she wakes with a start understanding that her dad is leaving and without a good-bye.

Careful not to wake Cally or her mother, Deanna slips out of her bedroom, takes hesitant tiny steps down the carpeted stairway. There is her winter jacket. Her boots. She pulls on her big white snow boots with furry tops, listens for him. Lifts her puffy winter parka off its hook and slides her arms into the slick, soft sleeves. Then she sneaks out the door and edges toward the garage.

—

Just as he gets comfortable, Richard realizes that he has forgotten his glass of whiskey on the kitchen table—he'd planned to sip it slowly. Fire, slow fire to send him out easy. He has to have that whiskey, and so he clumps back into the house to fetch it.

Deanna steps into the shadow of their dry old broken Christmas tree and her father doesn't see her, passes her by. Inside the garage, the truck's motor is running. So she knows she's right and that he is really going to leave. Quickly, quietly, before he comes back, Deanna pulls herself into the space behind the seat, just right for a child. She curls into her coat, small as she can. It has been such a long day, in many ways a good day, with all that snow. And the inside of the truck is cozy with the heater on, blowing warm air, and she is suddenly so comfortable. In the winter her mama and dad always carry extra coats and sleeping bags in the back space, so it is easy to crawl into the heap, bury herself, and it is dark in there like a little animal's hideout. And he will be surprised, won't he, when he reaches wherever he is going and he turns around and she is sitting in the back jump seat very quietly and in her seat belt. She worries about the seat belt. The rule is, she buckles in at all times. She decides she'll put down the seat and connect the buckle when the garage door opens and he is preoccupied with backing out or maybe, better, once they're on the road and he has to look out for cars coming at him right and left, their lamps beaming out, their eyes shining like the deep crocodiles—emerald, blue, all jewel colors, and then the sled flipping high in the air.

Inside the house, looking for the glass of whiskey. The phone rings, or at least Richard thinks he hears it ring.

Richard picks up the receiver and says, "Fuck you, Shawano." He finds the glass, drinks a sip, walks back out the door with it and lets himself into the garage, then swings into the truck's front seat. He wraps his coat tightly around himself and positions his feet once again. He takes a gulp of the whiskey and then feels the plush sleepy noise of drunkenness roll over him.

He has planned and resisted his own death so often that these moments feel rehearsed, as though he is acting. He cannot even summon up an emotion that convinces him. No fear and no regret. In a swoon of incapacity, in the first swirl of alcohol, he reviews his efforts with Rozin over the years. As he totals up and ticks off the gifts, the trips, the many daily small kindnesses and large ardors, he is comforted by the thought that once he is gone and later, when Frank dies, she will be lonely. And then, she will miss him, sure, but he will not take her back. He is much too tired.

He wakes with a tremendous headache, the air in the garage still dark. Tries not to move his pin-stuck pincushion head. Gropes for the whiskey but the glass is empty. Notices he hasn't latched the door. He hasn't closed the actual garage side door tight enough and it blew open. Great. Open. He gets out of the truck painfully disoriented and automatically hits the lock switch as he slams the door shut behind him and then starts across the concrete floor to the garage door, which he's left half ajar when he returned from getting the drink and answering the telephone. He shuts the garage door, makes his way back to the truck with a swimming motion, determined to asphyxiate now except he's locked himself out of the truck and left it running with his keys inside. And his head! He turns to leave the garage, go back to the house, get another key. Across the tense little plot of a yard. He's locked the house, too. The keys including the one for the house are locked in the truck. His head swims with a thrilling agony. Around to the front door. Calmly breaks a pane of glass with his topcoat-covered fist, and reaches in. Turns the deadbolt. As soon as he enters all ambition to do harm to himself evaporates. And what is he doing anyway? What kind of father? He will always be a father. Deanna. Cally. And Rozin might come back and he will take her back without a word. That is love. Twenty years.

Who can know. So for now he will be brave. Besides, he seems too much trouble, even to himself, to kill. Let the snow slide off, he thinks, rolling onto the couch, pulling an afghan over his shoulders. Let the shit come down. Let truck run out of gas. Let it go. Let the truck run all night.

PART TWO

NEEJ

THE PATTERN GLITTERS WITH CRUELTY. The blue beads are colored with fish blood, the reds with powdered heart. The beads collect in borders of mercy. The yellows are dyed with the ocher of silence. There is no telling which twin will fall asleep first, allowing the other's colors to dominate, for how long. The design grows, the overlay deepens. The beaders have no other order at the heart of their being. Do you know that the beads are sewn onto the fabric of the earth with endless strands of human muscle, human sinew, human hair? We are as crucial to this making as other animals. No more and no less important than the deer.

8

Almost Soup

Windigo Dog

You will end up puppy soup if you're born a pure white dog on the reservation, unless you're one who is extra clever, like me. I survived into my old age through dog magic. That's right. You see me, you see the result of dog wit. Dog skill. Medicine ways I learned from my elders, and want to pass on now to my relatives. You. So listen up, animoshug. You're only going to get this knowledge from the real dog's mouth once.

There is a little of a coyote in me, just a touch here in my paws, bigger than a dog's paws. My jaw, too, strong to snap rabbit bones. Prairie-dog bones as well. That's right. Prairie. I don't mind saying to you that I'm not a full-blood Ojibwa reservation dog. I'm part Dakota, born out in Bwaanakeeng, transported here. I still remember all that sky, all that pure space, all that blowing dirt of land where I got my name, which has since become legendary.

Here's how it happened.

I was underneath the house one hot slow day panting in the dirt. I was a young thing. Just chubby, too, and like I said white all over. That worried my mother. Every morning she scratched dirt on me, threw me in the mud, rolled me in garbage to disguise my purity. Her words to me were this—My son, you won't survive if you lick your paws. Don't be respectable. Us Indian dogs have got to look as unappetizing as we can! Slink a little, won't you? Stick your ears out. Grow ticks. Fleas. Bite your fur here and there. Strive for a disreputable appearance, my boy. Above all, don't be clean!

Like I say, born pure white you usually don't stand a chance, but me, I took my mama's advice. After all, I was the son of a blend of dogs stretching back to the beginning of time on this continent. We sprang up here. We had no need to cross on any land bridge. We know who we are. Us, we are descended of Original Dog.

I think about her lots, and also about my ancestor, from way way back, the dog named Sorrow who drank a human's milk. I think about her because I know it was the first dog's mercy and the hand-me-down wit of the second that saved my life that time they were boiling the soup.

I hear these words—Get under the house, Melvin, fetch that white puppy now. Bam! My mama throws me in the farthest house corner and sits down on me. I cover up with her but once Melvin is in play distance I can't help it. I've got that curious streak of all the Indian dogs. I peek right around my mother's tail and whoops, he's got me. He drags me out and gives me to a grandma, who stuffs me in a gunnysack and slings me down beside the fire.

I fight the bag there for a while but it's warm and cozy and I go to sleep. I don't think much of it. Just another human habit I'll get used to, this stuffing dogs in sacks. Then I hear them talking.

Sharpen up the knife. Grandma's voice.

That's a nice fat white puppy. Someone else.

He'll make a good soup, but do you think enough to go around? Should we kill another one?

Then, right above me, they start arguing about whether or not I'll feed twenty. Me, just a little chunk of a guy, *owah!* No! I bark. No! No! I'm not enough for even five of your big strong warrior sons. Not me. What am I saying? I'm not enough for any of you! Anybody! No! I'm sour meat. I don't want to be eaten! In response, I get this tap from a grandma shoe, just a tap, but all us dogs know feet language. Be quiet or you'll get a solid one, it means. I shut up. Once I stop barking all I can do is think and I think fast. I think furious. I think desperate puppy thoughts until I know what I'll do the moment they let me out.

A puppy has just one weapon, and there really is no word for it but puppyness. Stuck in that bag, I muster all my puppyness. I call my tail wags and love licks up from deep way back, from the dogs going back to dogs unto the beginning of our association with these strange exasperating things called humans. I hear them stroking the steel on steel. I hear them tapping the boiling water pot. I hear them deciding I'll be enough, just barely. Then daylight. The bag loosens and a grandma draws me forth and just quick, because I'm smart, desperate, and connected with my ancestors, I look for the nearest girl child in the bunch around me. I spot her. I pick her out.

She's a visitor, sitting right there with a cousin, playing, not noting me at all. I give a friendly little whine, a yap, and then, as the grandma hauls me toward the table, a sharp loud bark of fear. That starts out of me. I can't help it. But good thing, because the girl hears it and responds.

"Grandma," she says, "what you going to do with the puppy?"

"Where'smyogleyzigzichaogleyzigzicha," mumbles Grandma, the way they do when trying to hide their actions.

"What?" That gets her little-girl curiosity up, a trait us dogs and children share in equal parts, what makes us love each other so.

"Don't you know, you dummy," shouts that boy cousin in boy knowledge, "Grandma's going to boil it up, make it into soup!"

"Aaay," my girl says, shy and laughing. "Grandma wouldn't do that." And she holds out her hands for me. Which is when I use my age-old Original Dog puppyness. I throw puppy love right at her in loopy yo-yos, puppy drool, joy, and big-pawed puppy clabber, ear perks, eye contact, most of all the potent weapon of all puppies, the head cock and puppy grin.

"Gimme him, gimme!"

"Noooo," says Grandma, holding me tight and pursing her lips in that terrible way of grandmas, when they cannot be swayed. But she's dealing with her own descendant in its purest form—pure girl. Puppy-loving girl.

"*Grandmagrandmagrandma!*" she shrieks.

"Eeeeh!"

"GIMMEDAPUPPY!GIMMEDAPUPPY!"

Now it's time for me to wiggle, all over, to give the high-quotient adorability wiggle all puppies know. This is life or death. I do it double time, triple time, full of puppy determination, desperate to live.

"Ooooh," says another grandma, sharp-eyed, "quick, trow him in the pot!"

"Noooh," says yet another, "she wants that puppy bad, her."

"Give her that little dog," says a grandpa now, his grandpa heart swelling up. "She wants that dog. So give her that little dog."

My girl's doll-playing fingers are brushing my fur. She's jumping for me. Spinning like a sweet maple seed. Straining up toward her grandma, who at this point can't hold on to me without looking almost supernaturally mean. And so it is, I feel those ancient dog-cooking fingers give me up before her disappointed voice does.

"Here."

And just like that I'm in the most heavenly of places. Soft, strong girl arms. I'm carried off to be petted and played with, fed scraps, dragged around in a baby carriage made of an old shoe box, dressed in the clothing of tiny brothers and sisters. Yes. I'll do anything. Anything. This is when my naming happens. As we go off I hear the grandpa calling from behind us in amusement, asking the name of the puppy. Me. And my girl calls back, without hesitation, the name I will bear from then on into my age, the name that has given so many of our breedless breed hope, the name that will live on in dogness down through the generations. You've heard it. You know it. Almost Soup.

Now, my brothers and sisters, shortly after I received my name I was transported up north to this reservation. Here on the ground where we now sprawl and scratch, I have lived out my years of strength, fertility, and purpose. As you see, I have survived into my tranquil old age. It is said of course by Ojibwas that those Indians who live on the plains eat dogs while they, the woods Indians, eat rabbits. However, it is my dog experience that this is not entirely true. I tell you now, relatives and friends, it is best to beware. Even in Ojibwa country, we are not out of danger.

There are, of course, the slick and deadly wheels of reservation cars. Poisons, occasionally, set out for our weaker cousins the mice and rats. Not to speak of the coyotes, the paw-snapping jaws of clever Ojibwa trapper steel. And we may happen into the snares set as well for our enemies. Lynx. Marten. Feral cats. Bears whom of course we worship. I learned early. Eat anything you can at any time. Fast. Bolt it down. Stay cute, but stay elusive. Don't let them think twice when they've got the hatchet out. I see cold steel, I'm gone. Believe it. And there are of course all sorts of illnesses we dread. Avoid the bite of the fox. It is madness. Avoid all bats. Avoid all black-and-white-striped moving objects. And slow things with spiny quills. Avoid all humans when they get into a feasting mood. Get near the tables fast, though, once the food is cooked. Stay close to their feet. Stay ready.

But don't steal from their plates.

Avoid medicine men. Snakes. Boys with BB guns. Anything rope-like or easily used to hang or tie. Avoid outhouse holes. Cats that live indoors. Do not sleep under cars. Or with horses. Do not eat anything attached to a skinny, burning string. Do not eat lard from the table. Do not go into the house at all unless no one is watching. Do not, unless you are absolutely certain you can blame it on a cat, eat any of their chickens. Do not eat pies. Do not eat decks of cards, plastic jugs, dry beans, dish sponges. If you must eat a shoe, eat both of the pair, every scrap, untraceable. Sit quietly when they talk of powwows. Slink into the woods when they pack the vans. You could get left behind in Bwaanakeeng. Dog soup, remember? Dog muffins. Dog hot-dish. Don't even think of hitching along.

Always, when in doubt, the rule is you are better off underneath the steps. Don't chase cars driven by young teenage boys. Don't chase cars driven by old ladies. Don't bark or growl at men cradling rifles. Don't get wet in winter, and don't let yourself dry out when the hot winds of August blow. We're not equipped to sweat. Keep your mouth open. Visit the lake. Pee often. Take messages from tree stumps and the corners of buildings. Don't forget to leave in return a polite and respectful hello. You never know when it will come in handy, your contact, your friend. You never know whom you will need to rely upon.

Which is how I come to my next story of survival.

Within the deep lakes of the Ojibwa there is supposed to live a kind of man-monster-cat thing that tips boats over in the cold of spring and plucks down into his arms the sexiest women. Keeping this cranky old thing happy is the job of local Indian humans and they're always throwing their tobacco in the water, talking to the waves. But when the monster takes a person in whatever way—usually by drowning—there is some deeper, older, hungrier urge that must be satisfied by a stronger item than tobacco. You guessed it. Lay low, animoshug. I tell you, when a man goes out drunk in his motorboat, hide. Say he's just good-timing, lapping beer, driving his boat in circles, and he hits his own wake coming at him. Pops out of the boat. Goes down.

Humans call that fate. We dogs call that stupidity. Whatever you name it, there's always a good chance they'll come looking for a dog. A white dog. One to tie with red ribbons. Brush nice. Truss in a rope. Feed a steak or two. Pray over. Pet soft. Not worth it. Stone around the neck. Then, splash. Dog offering!

My friends and relatives, we have walked down the prayer road clearing the way for humans since before time started. We have gone ahead of them to present their good points to the gatekeeper at that soft pasture where they eat all day and gamble the night away. Don't forget, though, in heaven we still just get the bones they toss. We have kept our humans company in darkest hours. Saved them from starvation—you know how. We have talked to their gods on their behalf and thrown ourselves in front of their wheels to save them from idiotic journeys, to the bootlegger's, say. We're glad to do these things. As an old race, we know our purpose. Original Dog walked alongside Wenabojo, their tricky creator. The dog is bound to the human. Raised alongside the human. With the human. Still, half the time we know better than the human.

We have lain next to our personal human shrouded in red calico. We have let our picked-clean ceremonial dog bones be reverently buried in bark houses. We have warned off bad spirits from their babies, and talked to the irritating ghosts of their suicide uncles and aunts. We have always given of ourselves. We have always thought of humans first. And yet, for me, when Fatty Simon went down I did not hesitate. I took to the woods. I had puppies, after all, to provide for. I had a life. Next time, there was a guardrail accident way up on the bridge and Agnes Anderson met her end that way. Again, not me. Not me tied like a five-cent bundle and tossed overboard. Nor when the lake took Alberta Meyer or the Speigelrein girls, not when old Kagewah fell through that spring sitting in his icehouse or even when our track star Morris Shawano disappeared and his dad's boat washed up to the north. Not me. Not Almost Soup. Bungeenaboop. In the Ojibwa language, that is my name and I refuse to give it up for human mistakes or human triumphs.

I refused, that is, until my girl weakened and got sick.

Cally was her name. The girl who saved my life. She loved me best of any other dog, put me up there with her human loves. As I told you, she saved my life, but also saved me from worse—you know. (And now I specifically address my brothers, the snip-snip. The big *C*. The little *n*. The words we all know and watch for in their plans and conversations.) My little Cally hid me whenever her Mama tried to drag me to the vet.

Thus, she saved my male doghood and allowed me full dogness. I have had, as a result of her courage, the honor of carrying our dogline down the generations. For this, alone, how could I ever thank her enough? And then she got sick, as I say.

One foul night in a blizzard far off in the bush, she got sick with a fever and a cough and it worsened, worsened, until the truth is, I sensed the presence of the black dog. We all know the great black dog. That is, death. He smells like iron cold. Sparks fly from his fur. He is the one who drags the creaking cart made of sticks. We have all heard the wheels groan as they turned, and hoped they kept on past our house. But on that cold late winter night, up north, he stopped. I heard his hound breath, felt the heat of his lungs of steam and fire.

9

Lazy Stitch

Almost Soup

Curled underneath the beading table with the unshoed feet of women, you hear things you'd never want to know. Or things you do. Maybe it's the needles, Poney Number Twelve, so straight and fine they slip right through the toughest hide. Maybe it is my own big ears that catch everything, and more. Maybe it's the colors of the seed beads that work up in stitches so intimate and small—collect, collect—until you have a pattern to the anguish.

We dogs know what the women are really doing when they are beading. They are sewing us all into a pattern, into life beneath their hands. We are the beads on the waxed string, pricked up by their sharp needles. We are the tiny pieces of the huge design that they are making—the soul of the world.

See here, Rozin says, holding out her work with a trembling hand.

We dogs know already what happened down in Gakahbekong and why she left for her mothers' house. Her twin mothers. Well, she doesn't know which one of them is actually her blood mother. They won't tell her. But she also was a twin, at first anyway, and so she is not confused that her mother comes as a set.

She left the city because her own child breathed poison and was spirited off to the other side of the world. Deanna passed through the western door. Her father didn't. He slept off his whiskey head and went out to the garage the next morning. The truck had shut down. Had to use the gas can he kept for the lawn mower. Mad at himself, he drove to town for aspirin or maybe the hair of the dog. Decided against that last remedy. Bought groceries. Loading the pickup, he dragged the coats off his little girl. At first, he thought she was sleeping.

Rozin. She swam in the grief, she cooked with it, she bagged it up and froze it. She made a stew, burned it out in the backyard, dug a hole and threw it in, sacked it for garbage, put it up on a shelf, brought it to the trees she loved, and set it free out in the leaves. She worshiped it, curled around it like a sweet dog, smoothed the hair of her remaining daughter underneath her hand, and decided to have nothing to do with men. Rozin left her husband and her lover both behind. Took her daughter Cally and came north to live with Zosie, Mary, and me, Almost Soup, once again.

Let me tell you about this flower, she rambles to her mothers now, this leaf, this heart-in-a-heart, this wild rose, this child of mine.

She knows everything about me.

What things, for instance?

Ridiculous things!

Rozin lowers her velvet and the old twins' eyes glide over at the swimming vines, the maple leaf in three blends of green beads, the powerful twist of the grape tendril, and her four roses of hearts that she's finishing in a burst of dangerous pinks. Rozin is shrinking into the wall of grief, becoming tiny and bird-boned. She has developed a drooping eye. You could think this eye was giving you the curse. Or you could think it was giving you the come-on.

So how, ridiculous?

Just listen!

My girl Cally, she and I get confused about each other. It happens with mothers and daughters, you know it does. Deanna. Why didn't she come inside, change her body with mine? Why didn't we switch minds? Why didn't she use my body for a while to rest so that she could understand this thing.

Eyah, n'dawnis.

They look at each other briefly, under their eyelashes. Rozin is talking fast, to either outrun the big stash of antidepressants she is on or beat the pain they won't solve. Either way, both Zosie and Mary nod her onward and listen.

She was only eleven years old! That's too young, Rozin says a million, two million times. Plus around that age we're so close with our daughters. Closer than when they are stuffed inside the same body. She'd look deep into my eyes, completely seeing her mama, but I would never get to the bottom of hers. She would hold me, and she was just the right height for holding, too, her grass-smelling hair.

Rozin jabs her finger with the needle, then jabs it on purpose, again.

There, she says, sometimes I have to stop these sad thoughts.

Next month it will be a year since that late March snow. One year. The temperature sinks bitterly that night in the moon of crusted snow. All day, Cally does exactly what the trees do in that fickle seesaw month of warm and cold snaps. Days, the sun shines so hot on the bark it fools the tree and brings the sap up, only to freeze. The sap expands, the veins crack, the trees pop and fall ill if they're young. That's what Cally does. I play along with it. She stomps massive clearings out on her snowshoes and throws her jacket off, her hat, for me to run with and toss. We see a mink flash by. She loses her mittens for me to find. Then she loses her indis, her bead-wrapped indis, where I can't retrieve it, ever. She tears into the house, face dark with joy, cheeks blazing, the raw cold and sweat of icy breezes swirling in her hair.

Rozin is confused with the sorrow over her one twin into lack of care for her other one. That's what her mothers see. She lets Cally run wild and shrugs when they tell her, saying, What good did all my worry do for Deanna? Just cut into her good-time fun, her pleasure in life. Now Cally, she can have all the fun she wants. No, Rozin isn't always careful with her only daughter. But then, Rozin was the only daughter, too, used to being taken care of by two mothers. Rozin paints her fingernails a golden satin pink while Cally burns her mouth on hot bread behind her back.

Cally . . . !

Ow, Grandma!

But Cally is laughing, fanning off the tip end of her tongue, taking the next piece of dough her grandma fries with more care. Instead of eating once it cools, however, my girl suddenly sets down the golden crust, unfinished. She coughs hard, not hard enough to stop herself, and then she is tired. She curls up by Zosie, who keeps a stack of old newspapers by her easy chair. I sneak under the edge of the couch cover fringe. They usually don't let me in the house—only when Cally sneaks me.

Zosie reads all of the summer news through long winter nights. She calls out to Mary occasionally, exclaiming over a visit from the Pope, another shooting, the practices of cults and movie stars. Now she shades Cally from lamplight as she curls into a knitted afghan. It is only later when my girl wakes, flushed in her first misery, that anyone except me even knows she is sick.

Her fever shoots up abruptly. Rozin takes the steel bowl and washcloth. She wrings the cloth reluctantly, sloppily, and bathes down the fever, wiping slow across her daughter's arms and throat. Faster, faster!

I think desperately, whining. She touches the girl's stomach and Cally weeps. Her face wrenches suddenly.

"Mama!"

Rozin bundles off the knitted blankets, brings fresh sheets and remakes the couch. All that night they are up, then down. I am constant. Under the couch, I keep faith and keep watch. Rozin falls asleep on the roll-away in the next room and Mary sleeps beside Cally's couch in the recliner, covered up with an old hunting jacket and a giveaway quilt. Every hour, Cally cries out and is sick with nothing in her stomach, her whole body straining, her face fiery with heat again.

There is almost six inches of new snow on the ground next morning, and Rozin wakes to a still and contained brightness in the tiny bitterly cold closet where she slept as a child. She curls for a moment into the sleeping bag, deeper, then rolls wearily over when Cally whimpers for help. She closes her eyes, aching for the warmth again, waiting for Zosie or Mary to respond. Cally continues to cry softly. Rozin rips the covers down with an almost angry gesture and hops out, stretching. Shit, she mumbles, walking into the next room. Her hand, though, touches down gently on her daughter's forehead and cheeks as she strokes. She refills the basin, then sponges her daughter's blazing gold forehead, throat. She lifts her head and puts the cloth against the back of her neck and again rubs her daughter's chest, again waits out the dry heaving.

An hour passes, and then she pours a little ginger ale into a cup and sits down, careful not to jostle Cally. She feeds her daughter teaspoon by teaspoon, waiting for each spoonful to settle. Cally's lips are dry. Rozin puts a bit of Vaseline on her finger, rubs their deep and punished color. Cally lies back in the pillows, impossibly still.

When Mary comes in the door, Rozin turns.

It's no good, Mary's look says. The phones were unreliable anyway, now cut off.

Then Cally can't keep down even those precious teaspoons of ginger ale and the whole miserable process begins again. She'll get dehydrated, Rozin says as her mother comes in from outdoors, from her lean-to where she's been searching through rolls and bags of bark for the best slippery elm, the strongest sage to boil to make a healing steam. Zosie goes back out and all morning they hear the regular fall of her ax as she builds up the woodpile. I go out to encourage and guard her. Slip back in, dart under the couch. Hardly eat. By the end of the afternoon, Mary's eyes narrow, her lips crease with worry. The smell of cooking upsets Cally. More snow falls and all day they take turns sleeping and eat cold food.

Cally is shrinking, thinning, hardening on her bones, coughing in explosive spasms that shake the springs just over my head. Weeping tiredly. Cranky. Then she loses the energy to fight and grows too meek. I lick the hand that hangs over the edge of the couch until Mary calls out, *Gego!* I curl up, retreat, call upon my ancestors and their old ones for help. That night, she seems even worse. She stares blankly at Rozin, who takes the sleeping bag and sleeps in the chair and sends Zosie to sleep. Rozin coaxes her daughter back to sense after that odd stare, and falling instantly into my own sleep, I dream of hissing cats.

Bad omen! Bad things! I wake at Cally's cry and Rozin jumps to her. Cally thrashes her arms and legs, but then silently and rhythmically. The regular movement of the seizure stiffens us to a calm horror and Rozin holds Cally as best she can until the climbing movements of her arms and legs cease. She sags, unknowing, her face at her mother's breast, eyes staring out of the whited mask of her features.

Cally.

Rozin's voice is deep, from a place in her body I have never heard. Cally. She calls her daughter back from a far-off tunnel path. Cally's mouth opens and she vomits blood into Rozin's hands, her shirt she holds beneath her daughter's mouth. She calls until her daughter stops looking through her mother and brings her troubled gaze to bear. She regards her mother from a distance, then, with eyes that soften in a grown woman's pity.

Rozin wipes her daughter's mouth, her forehead, her twig wrists, the calves, so fine, burning, dry. The soles of her feet. She wipes and wrings and wipes again until Cally stops looking at the ceiling. Rozin keeps on stroking with the cloth, finds herself humming. Slowly singing, she wipes up and down the pole arms. The forehead, her daughter's beating throat. She wipes until Cally says, I'm thirsty, I'm so thirsty, in a normal voice.

You have to wait. Just wait a little bit. Rozin's voice shakes.

Cally falls back. Her eyes shut. Her lips have darkened, cracked in fine, bloody lines, and her skin dries the wet cloth. Rozin keeps on wiping the fever away. I know she feels it underneath her hands, swirling, disappearing, but always coming back. After a while, I can see the fever itself, a viral red-yellow translucence creeping behind the blue of the wiping cloth. She puts the fire out, all night she puts the fire out, wiping until the sweet blue trembles in her daughter and she herself is light, lighter, rising to her feet to get the teaspoon again, shucking off the bloody shirt, fetching the ginger ale, the cup. She adds more water to the boiling kettle on the stove, more bark. The air is steaming, the windows a solid black with frost, a heart-rent blue, a dim gray, then white when Mary rises to take her place.

Rozin sleeps, but her nerves are shot through with adrenaline. She lasts one hour and then rises strong with fear. She washes her face—the water icy from the tap—brushes her teeth. Her eyes in the mirror are staring, young and round. She slicks her hair back into a tail and chews a nail impatiently.

Go to bed.

Mary sends her back, fierce, almost slapping at her. And so a day passes. Another evening. Another night in which Rozin and Cally do as before, the same routine, no change, except that Cally is weaker, Rozin stronger in her exhaustion.

You get too tired, you'll get sick too.

The twins send Rozin to bed with hard words, but their eyes are warm and still with a mixture of worry, sympathy, and something Rozin has not seen in their faces before. Drifting away she wonders at it, but then the dark well opens and she drops into an unconsciousness so profound she does not hear the four-wheel-drive winter ambulance groan and whine down the road that Zosie is killing her heart to shovel.

The ride down to IHS is complicated by new drifts and whiteouts. I jump in the back and hide just as they swerve off. No way that I'll get left behind, though there are only a couple of gunnysacks to crouch on for warmth. The dark comes on quickly as we drive along, silent. In the back Rozin holds our girl in the sleeping bag. Snowlight flicks through the branches as the wheels grind and tear and the ambulance swings patiently along. Rozin stares into her daughter's face and whispers. Cally's skin goes white as wax, her dark eyes bore into her mother's face, intent and strange. Her skin is rough as velvet when cool, then slides up to the skid of wax again when hot. They finally get there, carry her into the emergency room, into the hands of the nurses and doctor.

One look at her blood pressure and the doctor orders an I.V. Cally has surprising strength. I watch through the hospital window. Hear her yells and shouts. See her tug away, or try to, but Rozin holds her close in a fixed and tender grip saying calm words, calm though wrenched inside out at her daughter's feeble terror. They put a cot up right beside her in the hospital room and then, with Zosie downstairs on the phone, signing papers and arranging things, with Cally on the I.V. suddenly unhollowed, full of color, strengthening and falling into sleep, Rozin lies still, breathing calmly.

It is then, in the hospital room, halfway asleep, that Rozin feels me put her daughter's life inside of her again. Unknown to her, I have taken it with me to keep it safe. Waiting for her daughter to return, Rozin feels some confusion, a fall of silver, a branch loaded with snow, the snow crashing through her arms, and then Cally is back in her own bed and they are separate, drifting off under different cotton blankets, in sterilized sheets, into deeper and deeper twilight, entering new ravines.

Rozin is sewing the roses onto a shawl of black velvet, a border of madder pink and fuchsia flowers, twining stems, fancy leaves that never grew on any tree except in her mind. She has an odd thought—Cover the whole world with lazy stitch! Then Cally walks in the door and says, There's nothing lazy about it! Rozin rubs the corner of her one drooping eye, but she says nothing. It's a small thing, this mind reading that Cally does on her these days, and it's harmless except that sometimes her daughter gets big feelings that she's not ready for yet. The old, dead, angry love between her and Richard, unfinished sadness so big and devouring that she can't understand it herself. The worry at what he has become. The lonely wish to walk small between her mother, her aunt again, their arms curving over her like tree branches, making a smooth dim path for her to travel.

She takes agonizing stitches. Uses harrowing orange. They almost shoot fire in the dark room, these pinks. The word for beads in the old language is manidominenz, little spirit seed. Though I live the dog's life and take on human sins, I am connected in the beadwork. I live in the beadwork too. The flowers are growing, the powerful vines. The pattern of her daughter's wild soul is emerging. With each bead she plants in the swirl, Rozin adds one tiny grain.

10

Nibi

Klaus and Richard had medicine breath from the family-size bottle of Listerine they were drinking. They were sitting by the art museum, half asleep in the heated shank of the day. The air was stifling. Cars rushed by on the other side of the bench.

"Nice to get that breeze from the traffic!" said Richard. "That carbon monoxide. Ah." He took a deep breath, sat up, and struck his chest. Klaus, a red bandanna wrapped around his head and a T-shirt torn from collar to waist, lay curled, booze-thin, his legs folded neatly as a cat's, his arms a pillow. He opened his eyes and croaked.

"Nibi. Nibi."

"Oh shut up. I got no water, Klaus. Go to the drinking fountain."

"Where's it at?"

"Over there."

They both knew it was dry, always was. No fountains worked in this part of the city. They shared out the last of the Listerine. Richard screwed the black cap carefully onto the empty bottle. He set the bottle on the margin of grass beside the museum steps.

The bench felt good to Klaus, hard but broad enough to curl his knees on. He was so comfortable that he did not move, decided to endure his thirst. He shut his eyes.

A woman came out of the museum. She was carrying a huge orange cloth purse slung over her shoulder. It thumped against her as she walked, like a big soft pumpkin. Richard called out, "Hey, white lady!"

She frowned.

The woman wasn't all white. She was something else. Hard to tell what she was, exactly. Richard thought maybe a Korean or a Mexican or maybe, but probably not, she could be an Indian from somewhere else. She took some money from her purse and put it in his hand. Bills.

"Oh," said Richard, "that's very nice of you. I'd like you to meet my friend."

The woman walked away.

"Still," Richard called after her, "I thank you. I'll put down tobacco for you." She did not turn around. "That's a sacred gesture. We're still Indians."

"You got cigarettes?" Klaus peered at Richard and held out his fingers.

Richard gave him a cigarette. "That is my last cigarette," he said. Klaus held it lightly in the palm of his hand, in his fingers again. He did not smoke the cigarette.

"How much did that lady give?" he asked.

"There's four here," said Richard, counting the bills over slowly, twice.

Holding the cigarette, Klaus shut his eyes again and listened. There was music. A sweetheart song playing between his ears. He was still dancing from some long-ago night, as he always did in his dreams. Even now, though her image sagged like air was escaping, he pictured his wife and her twenty-six sisters and her daughters in shawls of floating hair. Over and over again they sprang into his dreams. Galloped at him. Brandished their hooves like polished nails. He batted them off. She was alone again. There for him again. But he couldn't stop his mind from turning his sweetheart to a Disney character. The Blue Fairy. Her light increased. Her smile spread slowly into jag-toothed mercy and then her voice flowed, the cool of a river. Once, very drunk, he had watched the movie *Pinocchio* eight or ten times in a row with successive nieces and nephews, their friends, their friends' cousins, then the cousins' cousins and friends. By the time the night came on and the children were draped in slumber on the floor and on pillows and heaps of blankets and clothes, he had fallen in love with the Blue Fairy.

"What should we do with this money?" said Richard.

"I'm sick."

Klaus stretched out his arm, too heavy, and then let it drop. Unconscious again. Two men came out of the art museum. Surprisingly—what day was this?—one of them handed Richard money too. Coins. Then a group of people emerged from the big doors and skirted the men as they passed talking loudly to each other about where to go for lunch. More people came, the two men went invisible. Some event sponsored by the museum was letting out. No more luck. The streams of people soon disappeared into their cars.

"That was exciting," said Richard.

"I'm sick," said Klaus. "Water."

"I wonder if they'd let me in to look at the paintings. Maybe we should make a donation."

"Don't do that!"

Klaus surged to life and propped himself against the steps, a big loose-jointed man doll. His lady love was still there in the back of his mind, standing in a ball of blue light.

"I'd like a drink of water," he said to her. She had a glass of water in her hand, too, Sweetheart Calico, but she poured it out in front of his eyes. The molecules dissolved all around him and did nothing for his thirst.

"Did she do that to you, too? Did she?" Klaus was disappointed, outraged.

"What?"

"Pour the water out right before your eyes!"

"No."

"What *did* she do then, Sweetheart?" Klaus asked, jealous. "Tell me every detail or I'll kill you right here."

"With what?"

"My bare hands," said Klaus lazily.

"Klaus," said Richard in a fatherly voice, "you're sick." Gently, he took the cigarette from between Klaus's fingers. He unpeeled the wrapping from the cigarette and began to sprinkle the tobacco on the clipped grass. Klaus and Richard were very quiet, watching the flakes of tobacco fall to earth. Above them, in the trees, a cicada began. A long drawn-out buzzing whine. The day was heating past bearable. When all of the tobacco was shaken onto the grass they got to their feet. Klaus steadied himself. His knees shook. As they slowly began to move down the street past the museum, on both sides of the sidewalk the sprinklers set into the sod of the lawn sputtered on and then sprayed out cones of mist. Klaus bent over, put his mouth on the little holes in the ground, the spigots, and tried to drink.

A museum guard in a dark uniform, a large woman bland and bored, walked down the steps and told them to leave.

"You're supposed to say," Richard admonished, "quit the premises. Better yet, vacate them."

The woman shrugged and walked back up the steps.

"Vacate," said Klaus, his face beaded with spray, "I'm still thirsty. It's hard to get much. That spray is thin."

"Well, let's go." They decided, taking themselves back down the street, to find a Wendy's hamburgers. Sneak in a side door to their bathrooms. If challenged, show their money.

"Where is this supposed Wendy's?" said Richard after they'd walked in the broiling sun over to the other side of Minneapolis.

"I'm thirsty," said Klaus.

They stood outside a grocery store next to a liquor store on Hennepin and they felt good, laughed, making the choice.

"Mad Dog or Evian?" Richard asked Klaus.

"I'm going in there," Klaus said, pointing up at the grocery sign. "I'm asking for a drink of water."

He was in and out the door in seconds and a security guard nodding with satisfaction yelled, "Good luck anyway, finding a fountain."

"He didn't want to do that," said Klaus. They walked into the liquor store. "He was just doing his job."

"So were the Nazis," said Richard. "I opt for a subtle white." He addressed the storekeeper. "Something with volume. I don't get too hung up on the bouquet."

"That's good," said the clerk.

"My circumstances won't permit it." Richard nodded. "I can tell the difference between a dollar ninety-nine and a two fifty-nine bottle of white port wine, though, you can't fool me. Don't try."

"I wouldn't."

The clerk scraped their money off the counter and bagged up three bottles, each in its own individual sack, and set them on the counter for the men to take.

"You wouldn't have a cup of water handy, would you?" asked Klaus.

"Not really," said the clerk.

"Did he mean not as in reality or really not," asked Richard as they went out the door.

"He meant they don't have a glass of real water," Klaus said, gazing back into the window with longing, "just those cardboard pictures on the walls."

"That's all you need," said the Blue Fairy, holding up the bottle before his eyes. Twice, with her glass hoof, she struck the hollow ground. "Let's mogate."

"To the big water. Mizi zipi."

"Howah."

They walked. Hotter. Hotter. A few times they took a drink from their bottles, but mainly they wanted to get there, so they walked. Shaking a little, hungry. Went around the back of a pizza place where the manager left unclaimed orders every once in a while. Past the Deja Vue Showgirls. SexWorld. Fancy café garbage Dumpster and outdoor bar. Nothing there. A woman exiting an antique store held out a dollar and the moment Richard touched the bill she dropped it like he'd run an electric wire up her arm. She darted away.

"It's that sex thing," said Richard, his look sage. "I have that effect on women."

"They run like hell."

Klaus laughed too hard, furious, thinking of how his antelope girl could take off and sprint.

They reached the broad lawns and paths beside the river, went down the embankment and edged along the shore until they found a clump of bushes, familiar shade.

"We were here a while ago. I remember this place," said Richard. "We should put down some tobacco."

"Or smoke it."

"We just got two cigarettes left."

"Let's smoke it like an offering then."

"It don't mix with wine, not for religious purposes."

"That's true," said Richard. He slowly decided, and then he spoke. "This afternoon, let's just regard our tobacco as a habit-forming drug."

Klaus swayed to his knees and then painfully, slowly, he inched down the bank of the river, leaned over the edge to where the water began. At that place, he lowered his face like a horse. He put his face into the water, sucked the river into himself, drank it and drank it.

"That's Prairie Island nuclear water," Richard yelled.

Klaus kept drinking.

"He can't hear me," Richard said to himself. "Besides, that plant is down the stream farther."

Richard lit a cigarette, took a drink of wine.

"Some beaver might have pissed up near Itasca."

Klaus kept drinking and drinking.

"For sure," said Richard, worried, "they dump the beef-house scraps in it up at Little Falls."

Klaus didn't stop.

"Wowee," said Richard, taking a drink of the wine, swishing it around on his tongue, "full-bodied as my sour old lady."

"How about you?" Richard yelled to the river. "Klaus?"

Klaus was still face in the water, drinking, drinking up the river like a giant.

"What do you think he sees," said Richard, helpless without an audience, wishing he could open Klaus's wine already. "What do you think he's looking at? What do you think he sees?"

After another drink, Richard answered himself.

"To the bottom."

And he was right and she was down there. Klaus was watching her float toward him—his special woman—the Blue Fairy, merlady—a trembling beauty alive with Jell-O light, surrounded by a radiance of filtered sun and nuclear dust and splintered fish scales. The water was medicinal, bubbling, hot turquoise. She stopped for a moment, flying backward in the great muscle of the current pushing south. It tugged at her hair. She had to go, Klaus knew. Longing for her scorched him through and through. He stretched toward her with all of his soul, but she only looked back at him over her shoulder with her hungry black eyes. Gave a flick of her white-flag tail.

PART THREE

NISWEY

SOUNDING FEATHER, GREAT GRANDMA of first Shawano, dyed her quills blue and green in a mixture of her own piss boiled with shavings of copper. No dye came out the same way twice. According to her contribution, always different. The final color resulted from what she ate, drank, what she did for sex, and what she said to her mother or her child the day before. She never knew if she'd end up with blue dye, green, or a dull combination. What frightened her was this: One morning, after she had lost her struggles, done evil in the night, resented and sought revenge of her sisters, slapped her husband and screamed at her child, the quill worker peed desultorily and finished her usual dye. Dipping the white quills into the mixture, she found that the blue she made that day was unusually innocent, lovely, deep, and clear.

11

Gakahbekong

Cally

My mother sewed my birth cord, with dry sage and sweet grass, into a turtle holder of soft white buckskin. She beaded that little turtle using precious old cobalts and yellows and Cheyenne pinks and greens in a careful design. I remember every detail of it, me, because the turtle hung near my crib, then off my belt, and was my very first play toy. I was supposed to have it on me all my life, bury it with me on reservation land, but one day I came in from playing and my indis was gone. I thought nothing of it, at first and for many years, but slowly over time the absence . . . it will tell. I began to wander from home, first in my thoughts, then my feet took after, so at last at the age of eighteen, I walked the road that led from the front of our place to the wider spaces and then the country beyond that, where that one road widened into two lanes, then four, then six, past the farms and service islands, into the dead wall of the suburbs and still past that, finally, into the city's bloody heart.

My name is Cally Roy. Ozhawashkwamashkodeykway is what the spirits call me. All my life so far I've wondered about the meaning of my spirit name but nobody's told it, seen it, got ahold of my history flying past. Mama has asked, she has offered tobacco, even blankets, but my grandmas Mrs. Zosie Roy and Mary Shawano only nod at her, vague and shrewd-eyed, holding their tongues as they let their eyes wander. In a panic, once she knew I was setting out, not staying home, Mama tried to call up my grandmas and ask if I could live at their apartment in the city. But once they get down to the city, it turns out they never stop moving. They are out, and out again. Impossible to track down. It's true, they are extremely busy women.

So my mom sends me to Frank.

Frank Shawano. Famous Indian bakery chef. My Mama's eternal darling, the man she loves too much to live with.

I'm weary and dirty and sore when I get to Frank's bakery shop, but right away, walking in and the bell dinging with a cheerful alertness, I smell those good bakery smells of yeasty bread and airy sugar. Behind the counter, lemony light falls on Frank. He is big, strong, pale brown like a loaf of light rye left to rise underneath a towel. His voice is muffled and weak, like it is squeezed out of the clogged end of a pastry tube. He greets me with gentle pleasure and shakes his hair out of the thin dark ponytail that he binds up in a net.

"Just as I'm closing." His smile is very quiet. He cleans his hands on a towel and beckons me into the back of the bakery shop, between swinging steel doors. I remember him as a funny man, teasing and playing hand games and rolling his eyes at us, making his pink sugar-cookie dogs bark and elephants trumpet. But now he is serious, and frowns slightly as I follow him up the back stairs and into the big top-floor apartment with the creaky floors, the groaning pipes, odd windows that view the yard of junk and floating trees. My little back room, no bigger than a closet, overlooks this space. Gazing down, through the pretty fronds of oval leaves, I can see an old brown car seat below, a spool table, spring lawn chairs, a string of Christmas lights.

I'm so beat, though, I just want to crawl into my corner and sleep.

"Not too small, this place?" He sounds anxious.

I shake my head. The room seems safe, the mattress on the floor, the blankets, the shelves for my things, and the somehow familiar view below.

"Call your mom?" Frank gives orders in the form of a question. He acts all purposeful, as though he is going back downstairs to close up the store, but as I dial the number on the kitchen wall phone he lingers. He can't drag himself away from the magnetic field of my mother's voice, muffled, far off, but on the other end of the receiver. He stands in the doorway with that same towel he brought from downstairs, folding and refolding it in his hands.

"Mama," I say, and her voice on the phone suddenly hurts. I want to curl next to her and be a small girl again. My body feels too big, electric, like a Frankenstein body enclosing a tiny child's soul.

We laugh at some corny joke and Frank darts a glance at me, then stares at his feet and frowns. Reading between my Mama's pauses on the phone, I know she is hoping I'll miss the real land, and her, come back and resume my brilliant future at the tribal college. In spite of how I want to curl up in my city corner, I picture everything back home. On the wall of my room up north, there hangs a bundle of sage and Grandma Roy's singing drum. On the opposite wall, I taped up a poster of dogs, photos of Jimi Hendrix and the Indigo Girls, this boyfriend I had once and don't have anymore, bears, and Indigenous, my favorite band, another of a rainbow and buffalo trudging underneath. Ever since I was little, I slept with a worn bear and a new brown dog with wiry blondish hair and a red felt tongue. And my real dog, too, curled at my feet sometimes, if Mama didn't catch us. I never liked dolls. I made good scores in math. I get to missing my room and my dog and I lose track of Mama's voice. Tuning in, I hear a wistful bantering as she asks about Frank.

"He's fine. He's okay. You want to talk to him?"

I know the answer. She hardly talks to him directly, ever since Deanna. She doesn't want to talk to him now, but must keep her distance.

"Just say hi," I urge her. "The world won't crash."

But I know she doesn't believe that any more than anybody else does. They are the most famous separated lovers I ever knew. People talk about them. Speculate. Everybody wonders what would happen if they ever got together. Mama is sure, anyway, that she knows. Their love is too powerful, she says, to contain in one place. Their love would explode walls. Fry windows. Jell the concrete. She thinks, though she will not ever say it, that their love killed my sister. She is afraid their love will come down on someone else. So she stays on the rez, Frank has the city. Since their love future died with my sister, Frank has become a driven man. He works too hard, has become professionally jealous, secretive about his recipes, perhaps a little strange.

I remember him differently, whenever he came around. Basically, a pushover. Sugar-cookie baker. Cancer survivor. Lover of little kids. I used to sit on him like a sofa until after Deanna died. Even when he got sick, took radiation treatments, and said that he needed my mother's presence just to live, she would not come back to him.

My branch of the Ojibwa sticks to its anokee. That word, which means work, is in our days of the week. Monday is First Work Day, Tuesday is Second Work Day, and so on to Ishkwaa Anokii Wug. No day for lazy. Even our Saturday is Clean the Floor Day. I start right in and learn the cash register, the prices, how to handle the pastries with a plastic glove or wax-paper tissue. The first morning, I'm already selling doughnuts. Also maple long johns, hot pies, raised braids, and crullers. Things go fine except that I get vibed from the wife of Klaus.

I am behind the display case with a spray bottle of lemon glass-cleaner when I get this tickly, hairy, sifty feeling I am being watched. The store is empty, that dead hour just after lunchtime. The air is quiet though the growl of motors on the street barges and recedes. A few passersby glance in, neutral, full, no interest in the display of breads or cakes or even the scent of fried dough that Frank has purposely vented where it will attract the casual customer. I hear the scritch of nails on paint, twirl. Nobody. I turn back to my work and then there is the tap, tap, tap of heels. I drop my polishing rag and spring to the door leading back to the ovens. I'm supposed to mind the till, not leave the counter, but the tiny noises and the staticky feeling at the nape of my neck bother me. Nobody is there, and I am about to turn back to arranging cookies when a light touch at my shoulder spins me into her gaze.

Sweetheart Calico. Auntie Klaus. She hasn't got a name so we call her by her husband's name. Klaus. Or by the fabric that once tied her to his wrist. He brought her back from a powwow out west while he still had a job with a big company and was, on weekends and so forth, a successful trader. That was years ago. Right from the first, they say, she seemed uncomfortable. No one knows just exactly what happened because those two disappeared for a while, cut themselves off from everybody, left. Once they came back, Frank says, his brother wasn't the same. Upshot is Klaus walks the streets drinking from a bagged bottle. Lives in the shelter now and sleeps in the city parks. Meantime, Frank cares for his wife.

She never speaks. I've heard she's beautiful, and it is true. Her lean face, clear and smooth and pale milk-caramel, sweet as a hen's egg, her tea-brown eyes, her hair a powerful wing sweeping down her slim back. She has slender, jutting hips, long legs, on her feet black stiletto heels like shiny fork prongs. Perfect honed features. I smile at her and open my mouth to talk. A mistake. For then she smiles back at me.

When she opens her mouth, her eyes go black. Her grin is jagged, teeth broken and sharp as nails. Her smile is fixed, frightful. Her gaze thrills upon me. The scariest thing of all is this: I can sense she is glad I'm here. Excited. She wants me near and as I stand quiet before her I feel it all—her hating need and strangeness and eager sly wishing washes toward me like an oily black wave. She wants me in her house, the apartment upstairs, in her part of the world, Gakahbekong.

She wants to steal me. I think this without any rhyme or reason. Then the wave recedes. She is gone as suddenly as she appeared.

My hands are clumsy as I rub the display glass, smearing it. I am not the same afterward, nor will I ever be until I understand the design. I don't know how to take this, don't know what to make of it, have never known and do not now want to know a person like Sweetheart Calico. For she alters the shape of things around her and she changes the shape of things to come. She upsets me, then enlightens me with her truthless stare. She scatters my wits.

Sweetheart Calico lives upstairs in her own room not much different than mine. She hums in her sleep, I notice, loves the smell of burning sage. Our apartment household consists of her, Frank, me, and Frank's younger sister, Cecille. But the four of us never get together and are never in the same place because we all keep different hours. Frank is up all night baking and sleeps through the morning. I am up in the morning and sleep in the night. Cecille is at her kung fu studio all day and then out at the movies. She is rarely anywhere she can be reached, which is also true of Klaus's wife, though I suppose you could say she is out of reach in another way, since she doesn't talk.

If she is around, Sweetheart is sitting in the corner, down in the yard, poking through things in the basement, doing the house chores somehow not quite right—sweeping with her broom between drags on her cigarette, but then forgetting to pick up the piles of dust. Washing dishes but not rinsing them so for a week everything we eat tastes of soap. Dusting knickknacks onto the floor. Leaving them there. Washing mirrors with toilet paper so the little papery bits are stuck all over. She takes hours putting makeup on and hours taking it off. She lotions her face. Sits in the tub. Often, just before she leaves, she tries to get me to go with her. Tries to pull me down the stairs and out the door. I don't go, though her face is desperate. When she does get out, she walks and walks, sometimes for days, going places nobody knows. Returning with a silent, baffled, pitiful look on her face, she sleeps for a week.

She likes to sit in the kitchen, listening to the radio and watching the telephone to see if it will ring. Every night she is there when I call my mother. Every night I report on every member of the household.

"Frank's okay."

"Good." I can tell Mama wants to ask more. I don't volunteer anything unless she pays the price, though, of actually saying his name. Most often, she won't.

"Cecille, I never see her."

"And Klaus?"

"Him either."

Meantime, his wife sits in the kitchen corner smiling her shark-tooth smile and smoking a Marlboro. She is watching me talk on the phone, blinking her hexing eyes slowly and openly staring. Fascinated with my every word.

"What about her?" my Mama asks, meaning Auntie Klaus of course.

"Yes," I say.

"She's there again?"

"Geget," I say, then I think maybe with her thin, sensitive ears Sweetheart Calico takes in and understands Anishinabe. I don't want to get her attention, make her grin. That spooks me. I turn away after a quick, weak smile and feel immediately, right in the small of my back, the calm prickle of her gaze.

Often, while I am on the phone and can't get away, Auntie Klaus veers close and gives me a hug. It is a strange, boney, upsetting, long stranglehold that twists me in the phone cord so I can't speak. She is gone before I can untangle myself. All that is left upon me is the scent of her perfume and I find, even once I hang the phone up, that I can't get rid of the smell. I can't get it off me. I can't stop thinking of her and I see things. I see her in my deepest thoughts. I dream. Her perfume smells like grass and wind. Makes me remember running in the summer with my hair flopping on my shoulders. Her scent is like sun on my back, like cool rain, like dust rising off a waterless, still, nowhere-leading road.

"I could use a little support," I tell my mother on the phone one night, "with her. You know. She scares me when she looks at me."

"You call Grandma?"

"I call her every day. She's never home."

Mama makes a dissatisfied sound. She's all irritated with my two grandmas, Mary and Zosie.

"They're bopping around like celebrities," she grumps. "Don't have any time for their own grandkid."

A funeral here, bingo there, workshop up north or on an exciting Canadian reserve. From traditional to merely ordinary, they are constantly on the move. My grandmothers are also somewhat mysterious by choice. Their past history as murder suspects haunts them and they like to shroud their whereabouts. Love to confuse others, even their own daughter and granddaughter. For the past year they have enjoyed sending us postcards from various states, reservations, even cities.

They're hard ladies to visit, that's for sure.

I decide to find out more about them by asking all who enter the store whether they knew of the Roy sisters, Zosie and Mary. I ask politely. I ask nicely. I ask in a friendly way. I ask a lot of people, not just relatives or Indians, and the thing I am surprised at is this: How many people know them or have seen them. How many people talk to them all the time.

I hear they live down the street, exactly where though, what address, none can remember. I hear they live in an apartment, an old folks' high-rise, with their daughter. Those old ladies? Sure! They're healers, beadworkers, tanners of hides. They make cedar boxes. Or they work as language consultants in the school system. Maybe one's a housekeeper for a priest. The other dances. I hear she won the Senior Ladies Traditional twelve years in a row. Bums, they roam the streets.

Windigos, they ate a husband. Oh, too bad, one or the other died and was buried the month before. Tough luck, I missed her. But then, once I worry she's dead, the next day it is in the paper how Mrs. Zosie Roy or Mary Shawano just won a big jackpot at bingo. It is amazing how much information there is, and how little of it useful.

One night, I get yet another number from my mom and I call the grandmas.

Shock of shocks, there is an answer.

"Boozhoo," Zosie or Mary, her voice hard as a nut.

"It's me, Cally."

"Oh."

"Indah be izah inah?"

"If you want."

Not exactly a raving welcome. I get that uneasy sense I always get. You see, because they are twins, they share the grandmahood—my mother's mothers refuse to admit who is the actual mother. In truth it should hardly matter, they're so alike. But it does to me. Like now, when she is in a rotten mood, I wonder if maybe this grandma on the telephone isn't the real one after all.

Yet, at my naming, both Grandma Zosie and Grandma Mary blessed me. They raised their female golden eagle fans and swept me with the smoke of sweet grass. I still remember the holy scent and hear their creaky, sly voices. Grandma Mary, then Zosie, made a long talk in our old language, then my Mama put on a feast of cakes with maple sugar frosting and plates of sandwiches and fried walleye. I think of that feast as I hang up, uncertain.

Mrs. Zosie Roy. Mary Shawano. All they have seen, all the names they've named. Just a few people at one time are born to name. They have to dream certain dreams, hear them in the wind, get the instructions just so. I do know that my grandmas' dreams were big-time powerful. They got a lot of names you never heard, as well as some brought to them as spirit gifts. New names. Old ones. Zosie got my sister's name. Mary got names told to her by little frog woman. Names off the sun and weather. From the mouths of animals. Thin air. That day we were named, I ate until I stuffed myself and then I watched my sister walk in the hold of her new name given by the spirits.

It is a name I do not speak. That name couldn't save her. That name, it died with her. My sister, I miss her so bad. She went before me, broke ground for me, tested my mother's body. Then she made a path for me to the next world, left her footsteps for my shoes.

What we do with our names is one thing. Where we get them is another. I am a Roy, a Whiteheart Beads, a Shawano by way of the Roy and Shawano proximity—all in all, we make a huge old family lumped together like a can of those mixed party nuts: The big-time professors and ferocious aunties and tribal politicians are the cashews. Then there are the peanuts, the kids, me included. The Public Intoxicateds, PIs, the street cousins and uncles, bitter walnuts. I've got a cousin in sheet metal and a few in public health. I've got an artist uncle and a sort-of aunt who is studying to be a radio personality and is a martial arts athlete.

Not long and I get a jolt of her. Baby Cecille. She's like a caffeine surge. She runs her kung fu studio right next to the bakery shop. Through this, and peroxide, she has made herself a bicep blond Indian with tiny hips and sculptured legs that she shows off by wearing the shortest shorts. She also has the glitteriest, most watching eyes. Green glints reveal her Irish, way back in the Shawano line. She's a proud one, and, as opposed to Auntie Klaus, she likes to talk.

Some bloods they go together like water—the French Ojibwas: You mix those up and it is all one person. Like me. Others are a little less predictable. You make a person from a German and an Indian, for instance, and you're creating a two-souled warrior always fighting with themself. I'm nondescript, I think. Average-looking girl, is what I'm saying—olive skin, brown hair, rounded here and rounded there. Swedish and Norwegian Indians abound in this region, too, and now, Hmong-Ojibwas, those last so beautiful you want to follow them around and see if they are real. Take an Indian who shows her Irish, like Cecille, however, and you're playing with hot dynamite.

I think it's the salt.

Cecille, she sat down for lunch with me. First thing, she gets the salt shaker. She salts before she tastes. I have read that's a habit can lose you a job in an interview lunch. This salting before tasting is supposed to indicate some kind of think-ahead deficiency. Some lack. Me, I think different. To my mind, the pre-salting indicates this notion that the world is automatically too bland for Cecille. Something has to be done, in big and little ways, to liven things up and bring out all the hidden flavors. Something has to be done to normal everyday life, time spent, to heighten and color the hours, to sprinkle interest.

As salt is to food, so lying is to experience.

Or not lying, that sounds too bald. How about sprucing up, spicing, embellishing reality? That's better. Now at first as I got to know Cecille I didn't understand about this. I thought everything that happened *happened* just the way it really occurred. But even after lunch, which was simple—health food for Cecille, nuts and carrots and a swipe of peanut butter—she sits back and tells me stories of her students, their progress, then lectures me on all of the amino acids she's imbibed. On the legendary qualities of the naked almond and the undisclosed secret of ginkgo.

"My memory," she tells me, "used to be a blip. Now I recall every single thing that happens hour by hour, minute by minute. Things I've read, even license plates. My memory is getting close to photographic." She doses herself with more grainy pressed oval pills and swallows watercooler water by the gallon to clean her liver.

"I'm all set," she informs me, "to live a hundred years. I want to be around to see my grandchildren."

She has no kids as yet. I stare at her, a little blank-eyed, surprised she isn't over that. Or does she have a child by someone else? She answers my thought.

"We Shawanos," she says, "as opposed to you Roy women, don't start menopause until well into our fifties. And then, since we're running around with a two-year-old upon our hip, we just don't notice. We don't have time for that hot-flash shit. We bear late."

"And take no prisoners," I say. She gives me a little curious look.

"So how come you're here, anyway?" she says. "I mean, not that I'm criticizing you, but shouldn't you be in school or something?"

"Here's how it is," I start.

I am glad to be asked. Pleased that my drama of identity is something we can talk about. All my reasons. I list them quickly, before she can change the subject away from me.

"I was never in the city, since a little girl. Very sheltered. Not yet recovered from losing my sister. And my name. I think I want a new one, or at least I want to find my grandmas to ask them a few things about the one I've got. Plus this. I don't know where my dad is."

"Whiteheart Beads?"

"Who else?"

She eyes me significantly.

"I know where he is," she says.

I do not press her. I say nothing, because the truth is, I really don't want to know where my dad is or to see him. I am mainly concerned with making sure I have enough reasons for doing what I want to do, which is simply to stay here, in the city, work awhile, see what happens.

"Don't you have an ambition?" She asks this suddenly, with a kung fu swiftness that I don't anticipate. It is like she reads my thoughts, again, and sees how shallow they are.

"Well, yeah." I sit up straight.

"What is it?" she asks.

I open my mouth to tell her, but I can't put it into words. There is this big thing stored up in me, but I don't know what it is. Some smooth, round, important piece of data. Information. I keep tapping the sphere but I don't know what's inside. The globe is huge, yellow, sometimes changeable of shape and substance. A weather balloon, sometimes it bobs to the surface of my day and I must bat it aside, this thing, this compelled ache, this ambition. I shrug at Cecille now, helpless to describe its bounding weight.

The bakery has huge steel witch ovens and a concrete floor slippery with grease. There is a dough-pounding table of blocky wood covered with sparkle linoleum. The windows, high in the walls and coated with years of dustings of flour, look to me like something from a fable or a movie with their tiny blocks of glass. A tulip, gold stem and leaves, bursts fierce red in the pane. It is an old bakery, much loved and tunneled to by rats, floors creaky with shadows and all the doors set crooked or stuck. There is this built-in deep-fry pit, too, which can be zapped up to bubbling or let glaze over. It takes up one entire corner of the kitchen. There is a wonderful scent that rises when the grease is fresh. Frank slips in the little slabs of dough and they bob there, bubbling, reminding me of back home at powwows and sweating ladies at the fry-bread stands laughing and pushing those gold rounds at you, hot and welcome.

I work alongside Frank when I can, basking in the unfamiliar man aura. He is absorbed, melting and beating at some transparent substance in his treasured copper pan. I ask questions. I can't help but ask questions. I ask questions even though it takes him so long to answer that I've thought of about twenty more before I manage to pierce his distraction.

"What's that pan made of?" I ask, knowing, just a question to warm him up. But he takes a long time even to answer this.

"This pan is made of spirit metal," he says at last.

"What's that?" I put forward immediately, so he won't lose his train of thought.

"Miskwa wabic," he mumbles, absent in his work. "They say the thunder people sent down this red stuff, put it in the ground."

"Why's it your favorite pot?"

"Conducts the heat real good."

"What about those bowls?"

"Smooth the batter out."

The answers are getting closer, quicker.

"What are you making?" I ask, even though I could maybe look into Frank's sweat- and butter-stained recipe notebook, a tattered spiral-bound, and find out for myself. He won't answer for a long while, though, and this makes me naturally curious. So I peek over his shoulder at the notebook, see this word I have never seen before, although I have heard of it. Blitzkuchen. Written on top of the lined paper in tired ink.

Blitzkuchen! All of a sudden, he gets talkative. He's trying to reconstruct the recipe. Trying to win the state fair's highest honor. The cake is a fabulous thing, he says. The cake is holy. Extraordinary with immense powers of what sort nobody knows. He calls it the cake of peace. The cake of loving sincerity. For years, he tells me, he has searched and tested for the exact recipe. In fact, the hunt for this recipe could be called his life quest. Always, between other concoctions, even inventions like his popular rhubarb sludge bars, when he has a little moment to himself, Frank Shawano makes a trial cake. Attempts a variation on the length of time he beats the batter. Amount of ground hazelnuts. Type of sugars and butters. Whatever.

"Of exquisite importance," he says to me, waving a darkly wrapped bar of chocolate now, his wide-boned, pleasant face remote and concentrated. "Cocoa content seventy-seven percent. Strong and dark." He writes this in his notebook, scrawls it, and sighs over the batter he is now whipping in the bowl.

"Perhaps," I say, "it is all in the stirring."

He frowns, irritated now, and doesn't answer for the longest time.

"Frank," I say, wanting to break the spell between us and change the subject, "why don't you do the nose trick?"

He looks at me, startled. "Oh, you remember that?"

"Sure I do."

Frank could push his nose all the way to one side and tape it there. Looked ridiculous. He could also pop his joints, vibrate his ears, and roll back his eyelids. He was like this big high school clown, Frank was. He used to be ironic and jolly, always with a sly humor and a broad goofiness we kids loved, until he had the radiation treatments. From what I understand, the rays killed the tumor and also zapped his funny bone. He kept his taste, touch, sense of smell, and so on, but he lost an Indian's seventh sense. He lost his sense of humor. Now he is the only Indian alive without one.

It is a terrible burden.

Humor or the suggestion of it reminds him he doesn't know how to laugh. Jokes make him nervous. Puzzle and panic him. Put him in a sweat of anxious lather. Like right now, just thinking of a stupid old funny trick that made him look like a big dork, he gets upset. He thrusts his smooth hands deep in the flour barrel. Looks like he'll cry until a teary dough forms around his fingers. Maybe, I think, watching him knead and sugar and tenderize, this is how he works through his loss. Slowly, with grand determination, yeasting and sweetening, he will form the gist of his angst into a personal triumph. Simple things—cake, bread, pie. Also complicated European torten. These are Frank's ways of making sense of the world. When confused and when challenged, he bakes as though the order he imposes on his raw ingredients will straighten out his thoughts.

"Let's go visit my grandmas," I say to Cecille the next day. If anyone can find them, it is her. "I've got a lead on their address. Let's search."

Mama has told me they are staying with a lady who lives over a grocery/health-food type of store. Cecille agrees. A health-food place is just her cup of tea. As a martial arts enthusiast Cecille eats and drinks nothing that is not healthy. Except for an occasional root beer. Just the word *beer*, she says, somehow helps her to imagine she is still self-destructive, which she misses. Yes, Cecille pursues her physical and spiritual discipline at all times. She has a deep belief we are what we eat and she is trying to change her brother's serious demeanor, she says, through feeding him careful amounts of only wheat-free and also soy-based products. This is on the theory that his lack of humor is an allergy. My suggestion to her, feed him foods that look funny, smell funny, does not take.

We start out to the grocery/health place over which my namer supposedly lives, me almost jogging to keep up with Cecille's short but energetic stride.

"What's the rush?" I keep saying.

"Geez you're slow," she answers.

We reach the little supermarket in the Crossing Mall deep in the city, go up the back stairs, knock on the markless door. Who answers, instead of my Grandma, however, is this young woman, frail and velvety dark–eyed, veiled, from I think Ethiopia. She opens the door and puts out her tiny, thin hands in a graceful gesture.

"Does Mrs. Zosie Roy live here?" I ask.

"Fun Coy?" she says, hopeful.

"Sounds like she's saying 'funky.' What's she want?" says Cecille.

"Fun Coy," the woman says again, dialing with her fingers, holding up an imaginary receiver to her lips.

"Oh, she thinks we're the phone company."

Cecille tells her we are not US West. By then we can tell that Mrs. Roy does not live with this lady. We leave. That is it. That is all. We walk downstairs into the market, pick up some natural root beer and tofu wieners, which we plan to smother in bean chili and eat with a nutritious salad of corn and raisins.

Back home in the upstairs apartment, we create our dinner, put it all together, and then serious Frank comes up the back stairs and sets the egg timer. He is always timing—this, that—because of course there always is something in the oven to rescue or to check. Anyhow, that day, Frank is working again on his life project. This cake is from an old German recipe given by an actual prisoner of war to Frank's father. The cake of all cakes. The blitzkuchen. Early in his life he tasted it—light as air with a taste of peach. A subterranean chocolate. Citrus. Crumbled tears. Sweet lemon. A smooch of almond.

"It explodes on your palate," he says, eyes fixed and grave.

"Oh, gimme a break," says Cecille, who has heard this before. "Stick with our daily bread."

Frank considers. An aura of furious effort. Concentrated baker's conversion of heat, light, energy.

"I make the staff of life," says Frank Shawano in a dignified and measured voice. "That is my calling. But I will never stop attempting the blitzkuchen."

Cecille raises up her eyebrows, shrugs.

"Lighten up" is all she says, but her voice is sad. I guess she wishes she had the big brother she once knew, the sweet funny guy, back in her life.

Frank wipes his face, wet with the strain of his delicate decisions, and he sits down at the table. He stares at the pot of tofu wieners and then at the bowl of corn and raisin salad, back and forth, with reflective detachment. He is deciding which way to go first, how to settle things into his stomach. He starts with a piece of his own bakery rye. "Got to put down a good base," he explains. He then proceeds, as he always does, to eat with careful aim and calm deliberation everything in sight.

Cecille keeps trying to get a rise out of her brother. Just as the cake is his quest, his laughter is the challenge of her life. She wants him to crack up so bad, or at least smile. I suppose maybe this, too, has made her into a liar. At any rate, here's how she tells about our day: Frank, oh Frank! This mysterious thing has happened. She does not know what to make of it. I'm all intrigued. Cecille lets us in on the occurrence: A woman in foreign dress answered Mrs. Roy's door and asked Cecille, because she looked so prosperous apparently, if she would pay her phone bill for her.

"Pay it!" Cecille hoots. "Just like that! I don't know what to think about these unusual people in veils who just choose you because you happen to have a certain assurance, or confidence, whatever I've got, and they ask you to take on their responsibilities! So I said to her, 'Why would I pay your phone bill?' And she said to me, 'Because you are a rich American.' So I said to her, 'Haven't you heard, honey? We are hurting here in this country. Look around. Rich assholes in the suburbs. Us here, we got no cable, no AC.' And this woman she said, kind of like, I guess, the equivalent of 'wow' in her language and she walked off into the mist."

"Mist?" Frank was eyeing her, giving little nods. Of course, he's been inside, either napping or managing the ovens all day, so Cecille, she can make up (and does, I soon learn) all kinds of outside weather. Frank never knew it had been for instance a slightly overcast day, medium warm. There had been a pea-soup fog out there, apparently.

"Collision of a low- and high-pressure temperature system," says Cecille, flipping her blond hair, her face intense, "which means a huge amount of condensation formed."

She doesn't even look at me to shush me or warn me not to give away the true fact it was a normal day weatherwise and encounterwise. No. Cecille doesn't need to do that because Cecille's reality is solid. Doesn't matter that it is different from mine or anyone's. Hers is it. This shakes me a little. That night, I lie awake. I wonder. I even have the notion I should switch on the late-night weather in case I was looking the other way when that fog blew in and covered the Ethiopian woman. I have to tell myself what I experienced was true. I have to tell myself I know what is what.

As the days heat up, we rise earlier and earlier. You can balloon up fast on day-old muffins, so sometimes I go running with Cecille. This jogging suit she wears, made out of the same silk as a parachute, bright yellow, flares up and down the street and over to the river, her route. With her hair in a ponytail and neat black ribbon, she is like this fixated kung fu bee. Shadowboxing. Leaping. Posing with her hands cocked and her eyes steady. Man-eating tiger eyes. Irish-Anishinabe-girl-Wing-Chun-Jackie-Chan-flying-monkey demeanor. While she works off more of her breakfast in her studio, I handle the customers and clean the glass counter and display case of their eternal fingerprints.

Sometimes, when I rise even earlier in those blue morning hours,

Frank teaches me everything he knows about the attractions of flours to yeasts to butters. He explains the temperatures that make them brown and rise. I learn to skim with serious efficiency the bits of blackened dough from the Jacuzzi-sized deep fryer full of boiling fat and to run the whip cycle on the mixer that froths up lard and sugar. My favorite part is to add the food coloring in drops. Instant red, blue, lavender. Killer frosting, whipped high.

All day, people stagger in from the kung fu studio next door, exhausted from Cecille's workouts, craving butterfat icing and reflex-slowing caramel-fudge fritters. They have to touch the cases where these things are displayed on doilies. They press close to the delectables, breathe, smudge, cough the air full of predatory microorganisms. I can see their instant relief, too, after they have paid. Opening the crinkly white bag, exposing sweet deep-fried dough, biting into the spot on the powdered bismark that holds the squirt of cherry jelly, they sometimes give out a small involuntary moan of intense pleasure.

While they chew, their eyes rolling, I usually come forward with my question. "Do you know where Mrs. Zosie Roy or Mary Shawano are living these days?" The pastry usually pauses before the mouth and there is, often, a tiny bolt of information given. Just a line. They have a craft shop. They live over in the housing development. Teach at an alternative college. Counsel alcoholics. Do drugs themselves. Run ceremonies. Coach the little league. Have between them six Ph.D.s. What have you. I nod and take in the new bit. I add it to the barrel of confusion.

One day, along about late morning, however, the confusion thickens when one of my grandmas finally enters the shop.

I know it is Grandma Zosie because she is still wearing a pair of pink-beaded earrings that I gave her. The two have grown into their differences, however, and I could probably recognize her anyway by the implacable set of her mouth, not to mention her lipstick, which Mary does not use. I get to take Zosie in all by herself, now, no twin to compare with. She is small as ever and her face reminds me of one of those squashed-in little dogs. Soft round flat cheeks, heavy chin, a grim wide mouth. Her nose is pug round and brown as a knot of tobacco and her eyes dark and yielding with kind of liquid mournfulness. Her big gaze sweeps over the cakes and cookies. The contents of the lighted case seem to her a tragic puzzle. She sighs over all the choices. She slowly opens her purse. And here's where I know I am in trouble, not one word yet exchanged. Her little plastic snap purse is held together with a rubber band.

Those rubber-banded snap purses. Watch out. You see an old lady slowly draw one forth and you know you are going to pay for her lunch and pay beyond that in ways more than money or time. An old lady. A snap purse with a broken snap. A rubber band. I remind you. No way you can spiritually afford to charge an old lady with a broken, old, green-plastic snap purse who has, in her pride, saved and used to close it a blue rubber band off a bunch of broccoli she bought to aid her slow digestion. No way you can charge her a dime. Even if she points at the biggest, puffiest, creamiest, most expensive piece of cake in the case you can't charge her.

"Please," I say, sliding the piece of cake at her over the counter, already on a six-inch paper plate, with a plastic fork and napkin beside. "It's on the house." She rears back as though suspicious.

"Cally," she says like she just noticed, but I see already her snap purse has vanished.

"I've been looking all over for you." I come around the counter to sit down with her, intent on not letting her out of my sight.

"Megwitch, my girl," she growls. "What kind of cake is this?"

I tell her, pulling out a chair, tidying the corner I'm going to try and keep her in. "This is Frank's attempt at the world-renowned blitzkuchen."

She takes an immediate bite.

"Needs something."

"What?" I say, thinking I can clue in Frank.

Her face goes intent with thought, trying to discover what spice or ingredient the cake is missing. I watch her sit back, solid as a gray lake rock, chewing in meditation. In the window, looking out as she slowly licks the schlag from her plastic fork, she gives a secret little smile. A familiar expression from up north. I'm the one suspicious of her now. She's toying with me, this old bulldog lady.

She knows, but she won't tell.

"So Grandma, I've been looking all over for you," I start again.

"Oh?" She opens her eyes in what may even be real surprise. She loves me, at least I think she does. "Good thing I came in here then. What did you need?"

She asks me this, right out, what I want of her. Just like that. And just like that, faced with the question, I come up short. My mouth opens. I search and scan. I have so many things I want to say—What does my name mean? Where is my sister? What about my father? And Mama, will she ever stop avoiding Frank and make him her destiny? And what about this frightful wife of Klaus's? What does she want? And you, Grandma, you and Mary—I look into her too-young brown eyes and get lost in all that I don't know.

Instead of asking her any one of this tangled ball of questions, I get bashful. I have this streak of frustrating shyness that comes on big now. I don't know where to start all of the things I need to say, and my Grandma daunts me with her ease of command. Anyway, she seems not to mind that I don't tell her what I need. She plucks from the load of our family life a problem close at hand and gets right into it, right there.

"Well, you might want to know why I'm here," she says. "I saw your dad on the street with my dad's cousin's boy Klaus, Frank's brother, and it's getting real bad."

She makes significant eye contact, tips an imaginary bottle delicately to her lips.

"Does your Mama know?" she wonders.

Of course we know, in a way, but that is only a general way. What I mean is that we heard things up north but never saw Richard for ourselves. So we don't know in fact how he is except through other people. And I don't care, the truth is, don't want to open up that piece of my heart I locked shut after Deanna. All his fault, my heart says, all his fault and his alone. So many times, I can feel my twin with me. She talks in her little-girl voice, in my own voice, in the whisper of leaves.

"I never, and I mean ever, want to see his face again," I say with a firm note in my voice that surprises me.

"Then you better leave here," my Grandma says calmly. "You better go upstairs."

For just as she takes another bite of her cake, my father enters. With Klaus. The two of them trip off the little bell on the door.

Richard Whiteheart. I can't say I recognize my father at first, for he is saggy-skinned and drooping like a week-old helium balloon, and he is sick, with a bruise the green of old cooked liver on his cheek, and puffy eyelids. Around his head a frayed handkerchief, knotted. A Georgetown Hoyas sweatshirt from the Salvation Army with its sleeves chopped off and the bulldog faded. Shorts sagging underneath a watermelon-tight paunch. Shorts held up with rope. Flapping tennies and no socks. He stands before the counter barely holding himself upright and then he turns, and directly, as though he knows, he fixes me with such a stare, like looking down into the bottom of a dry well. His mouth opens. A powerful wave of sour horror hits me as he croaks three times like a raven, "Cawg . . . Cawg . . . Cawg . . . ," then stops, gulps dry, and looks even harder at me and croaks in a terrible whisper.

"Deanna . . . "

Wheeling backward, whirling his arms like a suddenly light scarecrow tossed by a wind in the air, he stagger-skips backward to the door, and just as I lean toward him in a desperation of conflicted feeling he is out, and then into the street. From the window, we three watch his runaway figure round the corner and vanish.

"That was quick." Grandma returns to her cake, presses up the remaining crumbs with the tines of her fork.

"Aawww . . . " Klaus is still standing in the middle of the store. He has my dad's same wracked voice, bone-dry and awful. I can't move, just stand there, fixed, watching as Klaus tries to speak, tapping his throat. He's in a worse state than Richard, even, and as he sways back and forth the noises he makes are pitiful.

As though Frank's ears are tuned from the back ovens to his brother's voice frequency, he's suddenly there, his arms big and pillowing, lowering Klaus before he can pitch down, dragging him with an arm over his own shoulder back into the bakery. Once behind the swinging steel doors, he rolls him gently out on a stainless-steel bread table. Turns down the lights. Frank takes an apron or two off the wall hooks and drapes them across his brother's arms and chest and bare legs.

"Now," says Frank to me, his big face steady, "you come on out to the front and take care of the customers. Your uncle Klaus needs to sleep."

I look back. Grandma, she is gone.

For an hour or so, Frank works out front with me, doing nothing more than checking the ovens in the bakery, the specific one in which he's got the next blitzkuchen. From time to time, he makes sure that his brother is still peacefully passed out. We sweep and shine the cases from top to bottom, restock the register tape and make sure all the money is counted, all the bills straight and faceup. Frank, in an unusual move, mops down the entry floor and even goes outside and sweeps off the spotless sidewalk. I watch him standing there gazing out at street life, massive from behind, casting a shadow around his feet like a little black pool. A dog pauses, just for a moment, out of the searing noon sun. The day, a hot and sticky ninety, is most likely the reason Klaus became desperate enough to throw himself into the entry of the bakery shop.

"They don't come here much," says Frank when he steps back in. "It shames them."

"What happened, I mean to Klaus?"

I know enough about my dad's nosedive.

"We don't know it all yet," Frank tells me softly. "Just like he was here," Frank steadies his hand flat in the air, "maybe a few drinks, nothing over the edge. Then more drinks and less time between. They move out together. We don't see them. It is like three, four years and they come back. She don't talk. Well, she never did. But Klaus, he is the way you see."

Frank shakes his head, and it is just as we both glance toward the big lightly hung bakery door that there's a noise from behind. Rustling, groans. Frank starts forward but the bakery door barges open and Klaus has thrown it wide. He is staring at us like a confused scraggly dog who doesn't know how it got into this body. Or understand why his clothes are covered with shit and vomit or what to do with the feet that can't steady the rest of him. His hands reach out, shaking, his face twists like a rag.

"Nibi," he cries, and staggers forward.

Sweetheart Calico comes down the stairs. She stands behind Klaus as he staggers forward, and in her eyes there is something I can't name at first. Not kindness, not love. I can only call it now a savage mercy. She grabs his arm. Turns him. In her hand there is a plastic cup of water that she offers and he, stumbling and reeling, tries to accept. His hand won't cooperate. He swipes toward the cup and misses. Holds his elbow with the other arm and concentrates. Stumbles. It takes Frank sitting him down on the floor and crouching next to him, holding the cup to his lips, to slowly get that water into Klaus, sip by delirious sip.

And all the time she is sitting across from him, looking at him, her eyes fixed in his eyes, their minds locked in some form of knowing. They are talking between them, I know now. They rise in unison. She somehow imparts his grace to him and although Frank is on the telephone now calling for a medic, someone, trying to get his brother for the hundredth time into detox, those two are floating out the door with their arms around each other. Hand in hand, their eyes in each other's eyes. Between them, the pilot light of alcohol, dead blue and steady.

Gakahbekong. That's the name our old ones call the city, what it means from way back when it started as a trading village. Although driveways and houses, concrete parking garages and business stores cover the city's scape, that same land is hunched underneath. There are times, like now, I get this sense of the temporary. It could all blow off. And yet the sheer land would be left underneath. Sand, rock, the Indian black seashell-bearing earth.

12

Windigo Dog

The dog was standing on his chest again, looking down into his face and grinning the same curious, confiding dog grin that started Klaus drinking. The dog was a scuffed-up white with spooky yellow-brown eyes and a big pink dragging tongue. The damn thing had splayed wolf paws, ears alert and swivel-based like a deer's, and no pity whatsoever for Klaus.

"Boozhoo, Klaus, you are the most screwed-up, sad, fucked-in-the-face, toxic, skwaybee, irredeemable drunk I've talked to yet today," said the dog Klaus called windigo dog.

"Get off me," said Klaus.

Weary. Tired. Klaus had thought windigos were strictly human until this dog came to visit him on a rainy afternoon not long after his ass got rightly and properly canned. Sweetheart Calico had, of course, left him, too. Come back. Then left again. Sent back this dog in her place. Windigo. Bad spirit of hunger and not just normal hunger but out-of-control hunger. Hunger of impossible devouring. Utter animal hunger that did not care whether you were sober or brave or had your hard-won GED certificate let alone degree. No matter. Just food. Klaus was just food to the windigo. And the windigo laughed.

"Shit-faced as per usual." The dog yawned. Its black gums gleamed and its ears pointed straight at Klaus. "I suppose we should have one of our little sessions?"

"No!" Klaus firmly said. "No!" Louder. "Nooooo . . . "

But windigo dog was dragging his fat blazing purple killer tongue all over Klaus's face, feet, hands, everywhere. With each tongue lick Klaus shrieked and gagged with laughter until he was crying in hysterical hiccups, at which point the dog leaned down into Klaus's face and breathed month-old fishhead dog breath on Klaus.

When he was utterly immobilized, then, he leaned down and told Klaus his latest dirty dog joke.

"So Klaus, not too long ago I overhear these three dogs. A Ho Chunk dog. A Sioux dog. Ojibwa dog, too. They're sitting in the veterinarian's office waiting room talking about why they're here. The Ho Chunk Winnebago dog says, 'Well, the other day they were eating that good stew they make, just lapping it up right in front of me. That night they put the cover on the stew pot but they forgot to put the pot away. So I sneaked into the kitchen and I took the top of that pot in my teeth, set it down careful, and ate all the rest of that stew. Then I got in the garbage and ate the bones and the guts of everything that went into that stew. Then I wanted to sleep but oh, by that time I had the worst stomachache. I just had to go. I barked, but the Winnebagos, you know they sleep good. They never even stirred in their sleep, so, well, I just went ka-ka all over the house. Now, I guess, they're so mad they're going to put me to sleep. What about you?'

"'Me,' said the Sioux dog, 'I have a similar story. You ever heard of the stew the Dakotas make with guts? It's mighty good, and my owner had a big plate of that plus all the makings for Indian tacos in his pickup one day. He was driving home and I was proudly sitting in the cab of the truck when he stopped. He get out, left me sitting there with all that good stuff and I just couldn't help it. I wolfed it all down. Every bite. Man, was it ever good! But then I waited and waited and my owner, he was having a good time, and he didn't come back. I tried to hold it for a long time but finally, well, I just had to go. I went all over that cab of his pickup. Boy, when he came back, was he ever mad! First he was going to eat me but then he decided that was too good a fate for me. He brought me here. I'm going to be put to sleep too. And you, what about you?'

"'Well me,' said the Ojibwa dog, 'I was sitting on the couch one day just dozing off. I was half asleep and my owner, she likes to vacuum her house in the nude, she was doing her usual housework. She was working on the carpet right in front of me and usually, even though I'm not fixed, I've got a fair amount of self-control. But then she bent over right in front of me and I just lost it. I went right for her.'

"'Sexually?' asked the others.

"'Yeah,' the Ojibwa dog admitted.

"'Gee,' said the other dogs, shaking their heads, 'that's too bad. So she's putting you to sleep too.'

"'Gaween,' said the Ojibwa dog, modestly. 'You know us Chippewa dogs, we got the love medicine. Me, I'm getting a shampoo and my nails clipped.'"

"You're a very sick dog," said Klaus.

"You're the blooming picture of health yourself," said the windigo dog. "I gotta motivate out of here."

"Listen." Klaus tried to look pitiful. "Go get her, will you? Bring her back to me."

"Get who?"

"You know," said Klaus, very shy, "please. My sweetheart."

"Good-bye," said the dog.

"Don't go now," said Klaus. "Just as we were starting to have a nice little talk."

"You tell me then," the dog said, yawning, rolling over to have his belly scratched. "You tell me a story."

"What kind of story?"

"Love story. War story. Food story. Any story."

Klaus rolled over, lay on his other side, staring into the bushes, into the unlocked leaves, into deep penetrable green.

"Okay then," he said. "I always get asked this question: 'Klaus. Klaus. What kind of name is that for an Indian?' I heard how this story went from uncles, from my mother, from the old ones and my mother, who was there. So here, psycho pooch. Here's your story. Here's the story of my naming."

13

The Blitzkuchen

Klaus Shawano

When the ogitchida came home from the land of the frog people he was strange, but that is often how warriors are when they return. 1945. End of the war. So many spirits out, wandering. And, too, the ogitchida, that is my father Shawano, had lost his cousin who in the warrior's blood relation was more like another self and could not be adequately revenged.

"*Owah,*" my father cried suddenly. They were sitting at his uncle's house. "I tried. I made his mark on every German soldier that I killed!"

"Was it a deep mark?" hissed old wrinkled-up and half-unstrung Asinigwesance, whose opinion was that the proper way to deal with this thing was for the USA to make all the Germans into slaves. Ship the whole country full of people here and teach them to be humble. That's how they would have done it in the old days. He couldn't get over how he had heard our government sent them money, help, Red Cross boxes of food and soap.

My father was a slim and handsome boy when he left, but his look when he returned was reeling and deathly. His face was puffed up and his eyes, they were like pits in his face. He had a thousand-year-old stare.

"He took a stomach wound," said Shawano. "I had to stuff my cousin's guts and loops back into his body, and all the time he kept his eyes on me. He couldn't look down. When I had them back in, his teeth were clicking together and he got these words out. 'You sure you got them back in the right order?' I said I did my best. 'Because I don't wanna be pissing out my ears,' he said. His voice was real serious and I answered, 'I checked. Your pisser made it. No damage, cousin.' He seemed real happy with that statement. The ground shook around us. Close one landed. I lost my hold and they all poured out of him again."

Shawano was exhausted and they got my Mama, Regina, to come in where the men were and put him to sleep. She was big with her child, that is, myself. Calming. To her, my dad would always listen. Before he slept, though, he gave Asinigwesance a funny look and repeated himself, "Old man, I did what you told me. I sent as many as I could with him after that to be his slaves in the land of spirits. It didn't help."

Old Asin looked at him long, deeply, watching.

"Maybe," said Asinigwesance at last, "you need to do the next thing."

"Which is what?"

Asinigwesance hunched into his gnarled body and then tapped a leathery bone finger on the pocket of his shirt just over his heart.

"Replace your cousin with a slave brother."

Shawano mulled this one, took it in slow.

"Where do I get one, a German?" he wondered, at last.

"Oh, they're all over the place here," Asinigwesance said, sweeping at the air side to side with the flat of his hand. "All over here like frogs."

Why we call them Omakakayininiwug I don't really know, unless it was because they popped out of nowhere. In the beginning, there were whole village tribes of them, we heard, shipped over here from Omakakayakeeng to tear up our land. They took it over. They killed it. Most of the land is now half dead. Plowed up. Still, we had no ill feeling versus any one individual. Even the Germans who made the war.

And lost it, too. As they tell it, there was a whole bunch of prisoners shipped over in the beginning who wanted to stay in this country now. They moved up north and worked the timber, two on a cross-end saw. Ditched timber roads. Learned only swear English. Walked along piercing the earth with pointed iron bars, tamping in seedlings with their shoes. It was only a short while before Shawano would get word of them. Waiting for D.D. status, they were living inside the fence of the state work farm. Yes, they slaved away, they worked, but none of them belonged to anyone personally. Someone should have told that to Shawano. Before anyone could give him the information, though, he listened to Asin. Overcome with the proximity of Germans, the old warrior encouraged my dad to fetch him one. A moonless night, then, Shawano clipped a hole in the wire fence, sneaked into the work camp.

The men were summoned the next morning to his house.

"Of course, I stole the German at night," said Shawano, explaining. "I crept right up to the barracks without detection."

"Without detection." Asinigwesance gloated. He was excited by this ancient working out of the old-way vengeance, pleased young Shawano had taken his advice. He nodded all around at the other men, grinning. I remember the old man's teeth were little black stubs—all except for the gold one. That tooth glinted with a slightly mad sheen.

"I dropped the gunnysack over the Kraut's head when he came outside to take a leak," Shawano went on. "Bound his arms behind him. Goose-stepped him. Got him right back through the fence and from there, here."

Silent, they looked at the figure sitting bound in the corner.

Barefooted. Wearing a baggy shirt and pants of no particular color. And the man, his head covered by the gunnysack, was quiet with a peculiar stillness that was not exactly fear. Nor was it sleep. He was awake in there. The men could feel him straining to see through the loose weave over his face.

My uncle, Pugweyan, got spooked by the way the guy composed himself, and suddenly he couldn't stand it one more minute. He went over and ripped away the gunnysack hood. Maybe some expected to see a crazy eagle—how they stare mad into the air from their warrior hearts of ice—but they did not see an eagle. Instead, blinking out at us from spike tufts of hair, a chubby boy face, round-cheeked, warm and sparkling brown eyes. The men all reared back at the unexpected sense of warmth and goodwill from the German's pleasant smile.

"*Owah!*" Expectation was something more impressive than a porcupine man! His hands were chubby, his skin almost as brown as ours. Around his circle eyes his stubby hair poked out like a quill headdress. His smell—that came off him too now—was a raw and fearful odor like the ripe armpit stink of porcupine. He moved quite slow, like that creature, his deep eyes shining with tears, and he took us all in one by one and then cast his eyes down, bashful, as though he would rather be under the porch or inside his own burrow.

"Put the bag on him again," said Asin hurriedly.

"No," said Shawano, hurt and surprised at the meekness of his catch.

"*Grüssen!*" the prisoner bowed. His voice was pie sweet and calm as toast. "*Was ist los? Wo sind wir?*"

Nobody answered his words even though he next made known by signs—an imaginary scoop to his mouth, a washing motion on his rounded stomach—his meaning.

"*Haben Sie hunger?*" he asked hopefully. "*Ich bin sehr gut Küchenchef.*"

"Mashkimood, mashkimood." Asin's attitude was close to panic. He wanted to put the bag over the boy's head. Because he had once been known as a careful and judicious old man, the others had to wonder if there was something in the situation they just hadn't figured yet. The kitchen, a window shedding frail light on an old wooden table, the stove in the background of the room, the prisoner blinking.

"'Skimood!" Asin cried again, and Shawano picked up the gunnysack uncertainly, ready to lower it back onto the porcupine man's head.

"Hit him! Hit him!" Asin now spoke in a low and threatful tone. At his command, everyone fell silent, considering. Yet it was apparent, also, that the old man was behaving in an extreme and uncharacteristic fashion.

"Why should we do that?" asked Pugweyan.

"It is the only way to satisfy the ghosts," Asin answered.

"Haben Sie alles hunger, bitte? Wenn Sie hunger haben, ich werde für sie ein Kuchen machen. Versuch mal, bitte." The prisoner asked his question, made his offer, modestly and pleasantly, though he seemed now in his wary poise to have understood the gravity of Asin's behavior. He seemed, in fact, to know that his life hung in the balance although Asin had spoken his cruel command in the old language. Not only that, but he suddenly, with a burst of enormous energy, tried again to make good on his offer using peppy eating motions and rubbing his middle with more vigor.

One among the men, of the bear clan, those always so eager for food, finally nodded. "Why not?" said Bootch. "Let him prepare his offering. We will test it and see if his sweet cake can save his life."

He said this jokingly, but Asin's gleam and nod told that he took the baking test seriously and looked forward to the German's failure.

The porcupine man drew a tiny diagram or symbol for each thing he needed. Little oval eggs, flour in a flour sack, nuts of a rumpled shape, sugar, and so on. By now, even though the men had no money extra, they had to go along and so they all dug deep for whatever food money their we'ewug trusted—into their hands, socks, the liners of their shoes, and the rabbit fur inside their moccasins. They sent my brother Frank to the traders' for these things and he returned with his lower lip stuck out and fire in his eyes. He was just at that young age where he hated to be bossed and yet loved to be taken care of by his relatives.

The stove. The German seemed to have a problem with that. So did my mother, who refused to take on my father's name or to marry him and felt in bearing his sons and giving us her bear dodem, since Shawano's windigo family had lost his, she'd done enough. And it was true. She had picked these red berries for us, though, odaemin, the heart berry, from the clearings. So fresh and dewy and tender the red melted in your mouth. She gave her makuk full of them to the prisoner, and was surprised by the emotional way he accepted the offering. He lifted the container in his hand, inhaled the fragrance of the berries. His dark round eyes filled again and this time spilled over with tears.

"*Erdbeeren*," he said, softly, with mistaken and genuine sincerity. "I fuck you thank you."

The men stood there in the kitchen before the stove and looked down at their feet, at the floor, anywhere, not knowing what to say. Regina reached out, and they got in that moment a sense of her grace, another side of her. She shook the German's hand, or paw, which we saw with a certain fear had fur on the back.

"Gaween gego," she said, meaning it was nothing special.

Her kindness was a match to Asin's low fury and he flared up, insisted that Klaus had just delivered a most clever insult veiled in ignorance, fixed Klaus with a crushing stare, bared his black teeth and then just a hint of a snarl, so that the men had to step away from the clash and out the door, leaving the original Klaus, who waved the watchers away from the smoking woodstove abruptly, anyhow, to begin his efforts.

From inside the kitchen, then, where Frank had stubbornly placed himself and from where Regina, heavy as the stove herself, refused to move, they got as much of the story as they could, or maybe as I was ever supposed to know.

First, the prisoner pounded almonds to a fine paste between two lake rocks. Took the eggs, just the yellows in a little tin cup. There was, in my mother's house, a long piece of wire which he cleverly twisted into a beater of some sort. He began to work things over, the ingredients, grinding with the bottom of the iron skillet pods and beans and spices into the nuts and then adding the sugar grain by grain.

When he was finished, he took the thick syrupy batter and poured it as though it contained, as it did for him, the very secret of life. He made dark pools in four round baking pans. He bore them ceremonially and with extreme care toward the oven, which yawned, perfectly stoked beneath with coals glowing in the firebox. Bending with maternal care, he placed the pan within the dark aperture. Closed with a toweled hand the oven door. For a moment all of the men, who had slowly returned, drawn by the composed fury of his efforts, regarded the words set in raised letters upon the oven door. The Range Eternal. Then, as a body, they backed slowly away and sat down, lighting their pipes, to smoke and wait.

They paid respect to the east. In their thoughts, in their prayers. They respected the manito who guards the south. They regarded with humble pleading the direction of our dead, the west. North was last. And now you may ask, in all this time, where was Shawano, my dad, himself?

He sat with them and he sat alone. He sat in a deep embarrassment of thought. He sat wondering, he sat appalled, he sat in memory. He sat just like the rest, waiting for the next thing to happen.

My mother did not wait, of course. She was a woman. What woman sits waiting for something to cook in the oven? Disgusted by the male mystery and presence in her kitchen, she bustled ostentatiously. In. She bustled out. Made a lot of noise coming, going. Banged her washing board and banged pots. Banged anything she could, including the heads of her children and the chairs of the men, who jumped. Once, but just once, she banged the stove. At which point Klaus leaped high and with a scream that still shakes in our hearing, grabbed Regina by the apron strings and swung her toward the door. She flew as though shot from a bow. With as quick and lithe a bounce as some limber wildcat, Klaus poised, light on the balls of his feet, and motioned one and all to hush.

Again the men sat, now staring and caught in the grip of what the prisoner sensed happening behind the raised Range Eternal letters and the blue enamel of the oven door.

Light in the window turned subtly more golden. Klaus set pans of water into the oven like offerings. A breeze sprang up. Welcome. Leaves tapped. Nobody said a thing. Their inner souls leaned toward the stove, their outer selves didn't even smoke. Asin's eyes grew bloody. His hands trembled and the air whistled between his teeth. They sat until finally Klaus rose and, like a groom pacing tranced toward his bride, approached the oven. At the lip of the door he closed his eyes, cocked his head to the side as though listening, and then slowly and pliantly bent, hands wrapped in two thick rags. Carefully but with firm control he pulled the handle on the door until it opened and then, just for a moment, the waiting men lost their bearings as the scent of the toasted nuts and honey and vanilla and sugar and subtly united oils and flours escaped the oven box and trembled in the air.

More than delicious, the fragrance that floated. Impossible. Perhaps an Anishinabe vision word comes close and perhaps there is no way to describe the premonition they all experienced then, as he tenderly drew the pan along the rack until it rested secure between his thick, furry, rag-protected paws.

More sitting while the brown cake cooled. Eyes of Asin sunk, blackening. He made everyone uneasy now with his wild breathing and in the silence of space in which the creation cooled, the watchers remembered things they'd rather have forgotten: how Asinigwesance had suffered from time to time with nameless angers, which now had assumed a name and form in the person of the porcupine man. Klaus.

The original Klaus. My namesake.

Air poured in the screen door, cooling and healing. Dusk air. Pure air. Moved onto Shawano. Pugweyan took his fan, the wing of an eagle, and with immense care he swept the air toward Asin, whose face now worked in and out like a poisoned mud puppy's, and who said, hissing, fixing us with eyes crossed from behind, a strict power in his gaze:

"Let us deliver him to the west. We are Ojibwa men—the name

has a warrior's meaning. We roast our enemies until they pucker! Once, we were feared. Our men brought sorrow. What have we here? Chimookoman? Women? Our enemy is in our hands and we do not make him suffer to console the spirits of our brothers. We let him cook our food. It is this . . . Klaus," he scoured the name off his tongue, "whom we should burn to death!"

In the space of quiet that followed on his words, then, each man realized and understood Asinigwesance was lost.

They were talking to the old man's bitter ghost.

"Ohhh, ishte, my grandfather," Pugweyan said, drawing the wing of the eagle through the air in a soothing and powerful fashion. "Good thing you've told us this." Looking at the rest of us meaningfully, he said to Asinigwesance in a calm tone, "We respect your wishes, grandfather. However"—and now Pugweyan held the wing of the eagle stiffly pointed toward the cake–"would we be honorable men if we did not keep our promise even to our enemy? Before we roast the prisoner, let us try his offering."

And Klaus, whose intuition of their meaning just barely kept him horrified, then took from his pile of ingredients a tiny packet of white sweet powder and, with a gravity equal to Pugweyan's, coated the top of the cake with the magical dust and then motioned to the men to cup their hands, each one of them, Asin, too, as he cut the cake into a piece for everyone, including Regina and my Shawano brother, Frank, who jostled into the circle. When they all had the cake in hand, they looked at it hungrily and waited for the elder to taste. Asin, however, was too slow and my brother too tempted. Frank bit into the cake. Before he chewed, he gave a startled and extraordinary squeak and his eyes went wide. It was too much for the rest of them. They all bit. Or nibbled. Tasted. And every one emitted, according to my mother's memory, some particular and undiluted sound. There was not a one who'd ever tasted the taste of this thing or come into the rare vicinity of such a quietly extreme sensation on the tongue.

We are people of simple food straight from the earthen earth and from the lakes and from the woods. Manomin. Weyass. Baloney. A little maple sugar now and then. Suddenly this: a powerful sweetness that opened the ear to sound. Embrace of roasted nut-meats and a tickling sensation of grief. A berry tartness. Joy. Klaus had inserted jam in thin-spread layers. And pockets of spices that have no origin in our language and no experience on our part or in the Zhaginash tongue and so, too, there was no explanation for what happened next.

Together, they sat, swallowed the last crumbs, pressed up the powdery sweetness with their fingers. When they had licked every grain into themselves, they sat numb with pleasant feelings and then, over the group, there stole a sweet poignance. Some saw in the lowering light the shadows of loved ones who went before us on the road, whose spirits they had fed as well as they could, food of the dead. Curious, they doubled back. Others heard the sharp violin string played in the woods, the song of the white-throated sparrow. Regina spoke to me, knew my name, and I believe I heard her voice. Some saw their mother's hands plunge in and out of flour and some tasted on their faces the hot sun and breathed warm thick berry summer odor and the low sigh of the moving dancing white grass that grows all along the road to the other world.

They breathed together. They thought like one person. They had for a long unbending moment the same heartbeat, same blood in their veins, the same taste in their mouth. How, when they were all one being, kill the German? How, in sharing this sweet intensity of life, deny its substance in even their enemies? And when there is an end of things, and when I all so sudden fade into the random scheme and design, I believe I will taste the true and the same taste, mercy on the tongue. And I will laugh the same way they all did, at once, in surprise and at the same sweet joke, even old Asin.

So that is how the German was adopted into the Shawano clan, how Frank got fixed on duplicating that sweet hour, and how I got my name.

14

The Gravitron

Cally

They are giving out free figures of gods of the underworld along with Happy Meals at McDonald's. Driving up to the window, I get Hades, a sinister blue guy with skinny arms, and Mama gets two plastic halves of the three-headed dog Cerberus who makes me wonder immediately whether, if Hades went into a pet parlor to get the dog clipped for the summer, he'd have to pay triple.

"Cerberus has one body. That's definitive."

"Put together, the heads equal something."

"You don't groom the heads, really," she points out.

"Anyway, in reality, we've got enough to worry about," I tell her.

She laughs shortly and, although she is studying in night school to be a lawyer now, she agrees with me.

In the city, you watch the swaying of the branches of the trees. I have that rattling old window. My outlook on the world. And the trees are that kind of black locust and tree-of-heaven tree that grows everywhere, tough, with small, oval pointer-finger leaves that flip over in a breeze. Sometimes I watch the dull underside roil, and bathe my brain in long streams of four-o'clock gold, streaming from the west. Sometimes a branch tosses high, like a horse against the bit and I think of it out there, streaming against the wind, and the very thought of that same wind ruffling my leaves and heading north along no highway to ruffle the leaves of my mother's house pulls at me with a longing I cannot make sensible.

Some days, I feel home's pull more than others. At least she's here now. It's still August, but already leaves are turning on the driest trees. Bright, then blackening. A low wind rides, trembling in the stiff grass, unwinding and slowing my steps. The gravity tugs harder. Lead instinct. Grave soul. And then I break into a short run, startled. What if? What if, just as sure as we are pulled toward earth and destined to go down into it at last, we are also at the same rate pulled toward heaven?

No wonder we are stretched top to bottom from both ends of our being. No wonder the soul can't decide where to wedge itself. Of course, there are those who aren't troubled by these things, for instance my mother. As I said, she has decided to get her law degree. She moved down here to live with Grandma Zosie and Grandma Mary, go to night school. During the day, she works as a checker in a big discount food warehouse. From this, I guess she has learned to question nothing. She knows that prices change constantly and yet are precisely fixed. Every evening, I run the city lake while she walks the curved shore in startling peace. We meet at the bridge. There, her profile held simple against the sky, it seems to me that my mother is held equally by sky and earth, home and city. Some days with her I feel the perfect suspension, the balance. Other days I know how small a thing it takes to throw us off.

For instance, Frank.

There he is one sudden eight P.M. when I go to pick up my mother from work. Frank is standing at the checkout, big and quiet, looking faintly Dakota with braids, glasses, a crooked smile above the six cantaloupes he carries in a red plastic basket.

Cantaloupes that my mother refuses to check.

"Go put those back." Her sleek face stretches bleak, annoyed and alive with irritation at the man she loves. "I'll wait. Those aren't ripe. You've got to smell them for the test."

He startles us both then, with his direct line. His love pitch, although at first he is so bold we don't process it.

"I need you."

"Cally here can help you. She knows how to pick a melon."

"I mean, I *need you*."

"Step aside, sir," my mother advises the lover she hasn't seen or really spoken to for years. "Next customer!"

Almost with admiration, for certain with respect, he backs away from the cash register. Light on his feet, he turns. Walks down the aisle bearing the cantaloupes. Mama is glaring and snapping her eyes in barcode messages as she drags cat food and cheeses across her scanner. Canned beans. Bottles. Bulk items. Part-time work, but she likes the change from studying. The store, her store, is an employee-owned co-op arrangement. OWNER, says the badge on her work shirt. Rozina Roy, in print. She took her own name back. Right below that she has written Waubanikway, Dawn Woman, with a black pen that leaks corner tears. She writes her name because she uses her Indian name on everything she can, insistent that the chimookomanug get used to her language as she'd had to theirs.

I walk back to find Frank inhaling the air over the cantaloupes.

He looks at me with his head tucked down and raises his eyebrows. His eyes are brilliant, opaque. He thumps the melon. "That's how I was taught. It's wrong, I guess. And I do like them ripe." He puts his face to the stem scar of the cantaloupe. All of a sudden, he grins into the nowhere of the aisle, a nice smile, modest but full of meaning.

Walking with Mama across the parking lot, I decide I am a generational anomaly. Some type of odd woman out. In the historical days, my mom would have worn down her teeth chewing hides by now. The sun would have fried and refried her skin to sheaves of wrinkles. She would be considered ancient, an elder, past all hope or desire, contented with advising the young and passionate. But now, a melon to weigh in each hand, her disposable contact lenses in place and her hair cut, set, brushed, sprayed, she is antimatter. Ageless. Serene and bitterly competent. Though she lived through the steam of her youth, her husband, Frank too, she has no seeming interest left.

"He still loves you," I say on the way home, driving.

She swats at the window in irritation, but she is too sharp and disillusioned to play coy.

"I know it. Coming through the line after, with those melons up over his chest, no less, he asked me out."

I can't help it. Strange hope and loss bite my heart. In my mind I want my mother to be happy. In my heart, I want her all mine.

"Just like that? Already?"

She lifts up her hands, exasperated and resigned. "He's lost his funny bone for sure, too."

"What did he say?"

"His biological clock was ticking. I told him mine needed new batteries. 'I'd like to charge it,' he replies. Then as I am about to get a good one off in answer to that, of course he hands me his credit card to wipe through the machine."

"Acts all innocent, I suppose. 'I'd like to charge it.' Lame."

"Pah! He's been around once or twice since me."

"No shit."

"I told you not to say that kind of thing around your mother."

"I'm twenty."

"All the better reason."

"Twenty is the age of reason," I say, resigned. "That's my problem. Too much reason."

"Too many reasons. Excuses." My mother prods at me. "Why don't you go out with somebody?"

"According to Frank, men like them ripe," I say, and then we both start laughing and we can't stop, the two of us, laughing our heads off in the car on the way home, where he'll call her and call her until finally she says between the two of us she's tired of fighting the magnetic pull and okay she'll do it. The state fair is on. She'll go.

End of August. It is night, the cheese curd stands frying curdled milk, the Australian batter-fried potatoes, the chili con carne bars at war, the dip cones, and the beer gardens. Eating something long, snakey, and blue, we watch the show horses practice outside the arena in a sawdust ring. So delicate. So fine. Hooves like sewing machine needles, they do fancy stitchwork up and down the sides of the metal fence. They pass so close we can feel the breath off their velvet noses and smell the warmth of their glossed hides, braided manes, sense the determination of their stiff little riders.

Mama is uncomfortable, even standoffish with Frank Shawano. Or it could be that she is locked up in the past. She figures that she is done with, finished, all over with love and those complications. No more. A relief. I understand her and that makes sense. But here is Frank, so kind, his hands plucking cotton candy off a paper cone to hand first to her, then me. And so unassuming. He looks at the prize rabbits of every shape and size, and the bread sculptures and the Elvis faces made of beans and seeds, and he makes no jokes whatsoever about the size of the prize boar's sexual equipment. Nor does he look as though he feels entirely outclassed in that matter, like some men, staring back over their shoulders at the pig in envy and fascination. Frank would be good for her, I think, walking behind the two of them. I don't want to be too obvious, however. I stay evasive, stand aside, simply follow as they make their way zigzagging to the sizzling zipper lights of the midway. We walk past the howling bungee jump, over the Chinese bridge, on and on until right before us the Gravitron rears.

Twenty is the fulcrum, the sawhorse beneath the seesaw of young and responsible. Twenty is the balance. What my mother means by excuses is that I keep saying I'm twenty as though that should excuse me from having to make the decisions of either a child or a grown-up. I've never been in the center of life and people. As I stand in the drama of light and music and fair noise between Frank and my mother, I realize that the center is not as invisible a place as I've wished. I watch the people as they move up like happy zombies to the entrance of the ride, a big crowd. Just over their heads, I see the exit and entrance of a new bunch of people slightly nervous and chattering as bored attendants strap them in. The operator of the ride looks way too young—brush strokes of a soft yellow beard, hair in a braid, earring. Vacant. He disappears for a minute under the equipment and then jumps to his music monitor control panel and begins rattling some strange Wolfman Jack spiel into the microphone.

The Gravitron starts slowly with the purr of a giant motor and a lurch of gears. The deep bass throbs to life, heavy rock beat, a flame of guitars. Strapped in standing, hands at their sides, the riders are hugged by welded bars to the inside of a gigantic pie plate that starts turning now, turning against the night. Green lights in refracting bands. Rippling blue. Pink. A maddened cake stand that swivels on its base! Tipping side to side, it spins faster, faster, gravity a hand flattening the faces of the screamers to one green dimension. . . .

"Looks like fun," says my mother.

I must be hearing things. She says it again. Her tone is so dry I think she's kidding, but she's actually not. This is how on the next run I find myself watching alone, astounded at Frank and my mother. They walk up the ride stairway and climb into the cages that close over them like alien claws. Again the Gravitron comes to life, now, Frank and my mother clinging to the bars and straps, blurring into one unit as the ride commences. Since I've seen it before, I turn away for a moment. Turning back the other way around, I casually catch the eye of the operator, or not his eye so much as the strange fixed grin that he is shooting right through me from the little cage he inhabits next to the gears and motors.

He stares at me and I stare back at him until I realize he's not seeing me. Staring through me as though he's disordered, his whole body fixed and frozen, he's a shirt-store dummy.

High, I think in total understanding. I am seeing the pure drug, the human chemical configuration.

"Hey you!" I wave my hands at him, yell. He whips his head away from me then, and with a screech of Wolfman laughter only crazier and nastier, he accelerates the ride. Faster. Higher. Cranked up and down with fire shooting from their eyes, the riders scream. The operator starts to blow froth bubbles. Rabies! An overdose! And he's garbled, makes no sense. There's only this overarching manic howl that penetrates the Hendrix "Purple Haze" lick and funk. I am certain he's hit the far edge. I start forward. Others, concerned, do the same. We surround his lighted booth and start to knock, and then we find that his door's wedged shut. We previously sane ones claw and beat and yammer like those horror-show blue-faced undead. He's spouting chilling warbles and declaiming as he revs the inner body of the Gravitron.

What follows from above is frightful, the riders understanding now that something, something, something has gone most horrifically wrong and the ride, a killer to begin with, now juiced up to unbearable, is whipping them mercilessly through time and space. They're roaring. Puking. Blurred. They're like those tigers turned to butter. They're all one face of horror smeared across the inner circle of the Gravitron. They'll die. Brain damage, inner organs turned to mush. I'm so terrified I grab a railing and begin, with another desperate and grounded loved one, to wrench the bar from the walkway. We'll use it to batter in the Plexiglas window, flail against the door, somehow jam the mechanism. But no, someone is there before us. With a tire iron she is beating and beating in the window until it smashes. People jump to the marked controls and now, at last, the ride is slowing. Each rider, coming into focus, is the very picture of sick and dazzled terror except for one.

My mother. She steps out of her cage, doesn't falter, not a single misstep. She helps a wobbly, limp, gray-green faced, sweating Frank off and leads him to a place in the grass where he sits in grateful wonder with his eyes still spinning. She strokes his hand. She holds his shoulder, puts her arm around him, and holds him lovingly, the way I cannot ever remember her holding my father. The way she acts is so different, so natural, so real, so warm and naked that I suddenly have this picture of what has just happened to her.

My mother has been scaled. All the scales of convention and ironic distance have been scuffed off her. All the boney armor she affects against the world. She has been stripped by centrifugal force and jumbled up inside. The wrench of gravity has undone all her strings.

He calls, that night. I hear them long on the phone. She leaves, comes back, goes to sleep. The next day he calls again. She's jumping up and pacing back and forth. Strewn with a blasted weight of emotion. I can sense waves of feeling, banners with cutting edges, huge sensations ranging from her, all set loose. Dressed, but awkwardly, her collar turned inside, she bats away my hands when I try to fix it. Goes to a corner of the room. And it is here from watching her back and shoulders tremble that I understand it is too big for her, too much. It is pulling at her with inexorable weight. She's falling into it. Gravity. She can't contain her feelings anymore. And as for me, I am emptied out, hungry, and chilled. It is terrible to see your mother in love.

We have these earthly bodies. We don't know what they want. Half the time, we pretend they are under our mental thumb, but that is the illusion of the healthy and the protected. Of sedate lovers. Not my mother. For the body has emotions it conceives and carries through without concern for anyone or anything else. Love is one of those, I guess. Going back to something very old knit into the brain as we were growing. Hopeless. Scorching. Ordinary. He feels it too or she would certainly go crazy. Already in the other room, the phone is ringing and my mother as she walks toward the receiver with her hand outstretched seems to shrink and fall into the steady pull.

15

Tears

Klaus Shawano

Richard was crying again. We were tired of him when he did it, never knowing if he'd stop. My clothes were dirty, so I borrowed and put on my counselor's pants, left our recovery lodge, and walked six blocks over to the priest's residence, a green wooden frame house with a porch. Waited on the porch. Father came to the door and I said to him, "Richard is crying again." Father looked at me like, Hey, I was all involved in doing something else and now I got to do this. Still, he made a swing motion with his head and arms, accepting it, and got his old brown jacket off the hook. He turned the key in his door lock, walked beside me back down the street.

"How long has he been going for this time?"

"Two days."

Sometimes drugs, the prescription kinds I mean, don't do anything for a person. There are griefs beyond their dosage limit. Richard's hand in what happened to his little girl was that kind of untouchable sorrow where you can't even drink it off, no matter how long and hard you try. I know. I have those sorrows too. Now, going sober, Richard was flashing on the loss once more and every time he did that he would start telling the wrong tragedy, get all caught up in some other scenario of death and loss, blame it on a woman, get into the crying thing again. And the five of us trying to maintain ourselves sober in the house would want a drink just to shut out the sound of his man-sobbing, which turned late at night to alien barking, words in a dog language. Sometimes when he thrashed it sounded as though a whole herd of dogs were in the room, it sounded like, moaning and discussing what it was like to be a dog and in the state of life inside the skin of a dog.

We all slept with pillows on our heads.

I'd come to get Father this afternoon, though, because Richard was turning himself inside out. A faulty water system. You could hear the painful burst of air in his lungs, their blue crackle like dry cleaner bags. His ribs creaked. The pressure popped in his neck joints. He had gotten to that kind of crying, and his anguish was taking up the entire house. And he wouldn't come down from his room, which of course was central. Couldn't eat. Mouthfuls would catch in his throat, gagging him. Sip on a cup of milk—that was all he could take.

"Father, do you mind, I can't get him to come down, going upstairs?"

Now that he was into it, committed, Father went.

In his room with the door not barred or anything, Richard was weeping in quiet. I was not fooled when walking in all was silent. I knew for an hour he might lie there on his bed pumping tears from his eyes like a defective sprinkler and the tears slowly soaking the bed from down the sides of his face, the back of his shirt wet and the nape of his hair and his shoulders, all wet from tears. He sat up when Father entered. His face was leaking. It was like a bucket had been dumped over him. I stood behind the priest. A couple of times just the entrance of Father had helped get the tears Richard shed underneath control.

"Father," said Richard, very earnest and real for a moment. "It isn't that I mind my kids dead now. That, I have accepted. It is that they had the time to be afraid."

This was an old one—unable to say what really happened, Richard took on other half-heard stories and made them his long enough to cry himself to sleep. The worse the better. Of course, Father was never sure which of all the stories was true. This one, I think, was the apartment fire where all of his children—sometimes four, five, never just one—went up in smoke.

"You don't know that, Richard," said Father.

"I'm afraid I do," said Richard, his face twisting red. "Yes, I'm afraid I do."

Father was silent. Hands cupping his knees. He is a big pale man built rough with a round, flat, pan face, tired skin, and a golfer's slow body. Thick and loose-jointed, he settled himself on Richard's chair, a folding chair held together with creaky bolts. I could tell that Father was trying to think of what to say next, which I was hoping to catch. I mean, here's a professional. But he couldn't think of anything to say that good either, not for a while. Richard lay back on the damp bed once more and tears came out of his whole face like sweat.

"You loved them very much," Father stated at last.

In answer, a huge gravelly roar poured out of Richard, like out of some kind of zoo animal. He turned over in the bed. Then he put his forehead on the wall, holding it there, a gesture for the effect, I couldn't help see. Something crinkled in me. Irritated by forty-eight hours of continual crying, I went along with this story, the way he always wanted, except I didn't let Richard Whiteheart Beads off the fucking hook.

"You loved your kids so much you went on a drunk and let their mother party down. She was on the first floor with the landlord. At least," I said, "she made the rent, sold the truck."

There, I'd mentioned a real thing, his truck. Oh shit, I thought. I was surprised at my slip, but I was tired. Richard's air bubble sobs had kept me awake. At first, he didn't appear to have heard the slip, anyway, going on with his delusion of woe and blame. He nodded eagerly and took up the story.

"If only she had stopped at one month. Not tried to make the entire lease! Apparently, Father, she did such a good job on the landlord that he passed out with the age-old cigarette in his hand while she, not being a bad person in many ways, my wife Rozin, clean anyhow, took advantage of his hot, working shower down the hall. Barely squeezed herself out the bathroom window. Once his curtains went, it was like a wick to the floor above. And then some gas pipe blew."

"I don't think they had time to wake up," I said to Richard now, trying to make up for my weary slip about the truck but also realizing what I said was giving Father the wrong idea. Sure enough.

"There was an explosion, remember?" Father was getting into this, emotional now, voice shaking. "You said there was."

"I wanted to believe that. I imagined that," Richard cried from behind a pillow, "but the fact I have a problem with today is this understanding I got later that they were found under their beds. They had to crawl there, right? Scared. Huddled together."

"Richard," Father said, "kids sleep under their beds all the time."

"No they don't," said Richard. "They go under the bed to hide, that's all. I was a kid once."

"So was I," the priest said. "I liked to sleep underneath the bed. My brothers and I brought our pillows down there."

"No pillows," said Richard, argumentative. "They found no pillows. Which proves they went there out of fear."

"Not really," said Father. "You said before that the pillows burned up. Evaporated. Heat like that. Richard, it was instantaneous. They never even woke."

"Never had a chance," said Richard, as if this was a cue. "Oh God, oh God, never had a chance."

Oh shut your face, I thought. You were Deanna's chance.

He was feeling sorry for himself. He was an asshole then and he was an asshole now, the only difference was now that he was a recovery asshole people listened to him and I really was starting to wonder exactly why, because as human beings go, Richard would never contribute much even cold sober. If anything, he'd rise to the level of a social mollusk.

It made me think of the food chain and wonder why this guy deserved to be at the top of it? Theoretically, he could devour whatever grazed, pecked, crawled, rooted over earth, or swam in the sea. And what had he ever done to earn such status?

"A cheeseburger Happy Meal," I said, as though ordering from out of a car window in the much better days of someone else's youth. "Do you deserve the three-ounce patty? I'm not saying yes and not saying no. However." Then I added, "You probably haven't seen one since Deanna died."

Richard stared at me with a mysterious look on his face. That I should mention his daughter in such a down-to-earth and factual way. Taboo material, his Deanna, naturally. But I was at the end of my patience to be merciful, which was why I got Father. I have an industrial cleaning job I have to be awake for, two alarm clocks, plus trying to get my own failures into some new order is itself the job, the real one. Just staying in my life is hard. When I came here, entered in alongside my buddy, Richard, I didn't own shit. We used garbage bags for clothing and comfort and shelter. Anyhow, I used to say, it was designer garbage bags. Quality. No tissuey plastic for me! My suave black tuxedo by Hefty. I brought all my stuff in my Indian suitcase. Hefty. I camped out. Hefty. Ten-ply. Tough. Garbage belongs in these things—i.e., me. That's what I thought at the time.

"God don't make trash, Richard," I said, more to myself. "Maybe you can sleep." Meaning: maybe you'll give *me* a chance to sleep. "Having talked to Father, you may feel more at peace or something."

But my face was saying all I really felt about Richard, I guess, because one look at me and his eyes went cold and tiny, a bitter coffee-dreg brown. His slapped-red cheeks froze, pulled in and out.

Impatience. Betrayal. I was afraid big sobs were building up again, monsoon sobs, but when he spoke his voice was chilled and nasty.

"You threw yours away," he said, now talking to me. "Letting her suck whiskey. You fucking kidnapped that woman, didn't you?"

"She wanted to go." I got it out though my voice was real faint.

My face went flat, stunned, slapped.

"Yeah." His voice contemptuous. "You bet. You stole her and then you beat her up and got her drunk. Her daughters are still out there, somewhere. They'll get you, Klaus, they know you're a sucking jackal. You destroyed your woman, Klaus. I saw how pretty she was when you brought her and what a lousy old wino you turned her into now."

He knew all from our meetings, each detail.

"You're a dead man. You're dead in the water!" I screamed.

But Richard was laughing and laughing at me now. All my excuses do and will forever fail. Father's hand was on my back. I shrugged it off. Nothing in that statement, even the jackal part, was more vicious than what I say to myself. Still, it was as though a dog sleeping on the floor went for my ankle. Numb, then oh god. Like that. And suddenly you felt its teeth hit bone.

"Father"—I nodded sideways at Richard—"he's all yours. I can't take any more. I better not."

Outside, there is a little bench down the street in a dogshit triangle of lawn. Some strangled dark red ambrosia-colored snapdragons are planted there by who knows who? *Better go there,* says a voice. I guess it's my dog, Windigo. *Get out. Don't look back. Don't go back until that fuckhead Richard stops crying.* Now, right now, attend to yourself and focus on the next fifteen minutes of your life. For I was never able to do it a day at a time, not me. An hour. Two hours. Half a day at a time. Or not.

And I think of her. Now and again they'll ask me, the others, what was so fucking great about her? What did she do, in bed for instance, or what did she cook? Was it something she did with her hands, her face, some way she had perhaps. A love way. A food. Not one thing in particular, I say. She never cooked anything from a recipe. Potatoes, mac and cheese, that kind of stuff. It wasn't that. They'll ask did she have my children. No, I'll say. No kids. Was she related to you? Was she from your own clan?

Sometimes I think she was. Yes.

In my worst down and outs, I get comfort from the thought she was just a fragment of my imagination, my pretty antelope woman. But I know she is actual in every way. What scares me worst is this: The simple knowledge that my Sweetheart Calico is another person than me. Lives in another body, walks in a different skin. Thinks different thoughts I can't know about. Wants a freedom I can't give.

She dragged me in, I say greedily, can't she handle it now?

Yet I know with bleak shame I'm excusing my trapper's appetite. I'm tangled in a net of holes. I don't know how to stop wanting her in me, with me, part of me, existing in my food and water and the booze I drank. I don't know how to stop the circle of my thoughts.

In the old days, they used to paint the red stripe of the drum down the middle of their faces. Right now, sitting on the carved bench in the hopeful little ugly park I close my eyes. I imagine the painted stripe. I try to divide myself up equally—two parts. *Send half of yourself to each direction.* West, east. Let her go with the western half, free. But the part of me that goes to the west reaches out and clings to my love like a baby, following her into sky-hung space.

16

Kamikaze Wedding

"There is a species of trouble women long for and sigh after and regret once they get it, like a too expensive dress that cannot be returned. That trouble is marriage," said Cecille. Studying to be a radio commentator, she constantly practiced her low, smooth, custardy voice. "It is not automatic. There is no singular improvement. Status. Contentment. Sex anytime you want it, even. All men are not even *into* sex. Those white satin pumps my darling new sister-in-law paid a mint for, those may be shoes of red-hot iron that fuse to her feet! I've tried to tell her! But I could not budge the wand set to that age when we feel we are destined to reproduce."

"As it happens," said Cally, with an attempt at like pomposity, "my mother has already reproduced—me. And I would venture to say that she is made of different stuff and has chosen the right husband for the right reasons in life."

"So you say. So they all say." Cecille Shawano had a tight, square grin and her long incisors glistened when she laughed. "We'll see." She was making fry bread. Delicately, as she removed one golden round with tongs she slipped another pad of dough off her gleaming spatula into the pond of sizzling oil.

Behind the closed doors of the bakery, the kitchen of the wedding was a calm madness of women. Each emanated personal intensity, moved in an aura of decision and risk, behaved as though the completion of her smothered noodles, fry bread, buttered vegetable or rice ring or mayo-mustard potato salad was a matter of just bearable weight. Failure was not considered, though occasionally someone did fail, put down a spoon, set a fist to her jaw. Here the implacable nerve of each Shawano or Roy woman stood the test, showed the bloods—French, German, Ojibwa, surely a little Cree—in all composite zeal. Steaming in despair, the author of the dish would dump the foul batter ruined by an unperceived bad egg, ruthlessly wash down the sink a separated gravy that could not be whisked back together, then go on grimly refashioning and remeasuring, until the reconstructed offering was set into the stuffed refrigerator under foil or plastic.

Though finicky cooks, these were professional women, high-achieving women, as were (and they cooked, too) the Roy and Shawano men.

Outside, in the small backyard, beneath the wedding reception tarp, the men were more relaxed, however. Their duties at this point were not so crucial. The day was generous for autumn, clear and with a fugitive warmth. Brothers and cousins, work and fishing buddies, they casually set up chairs and tables for the feast to be held later. The Roy and Shawano men were pronouncers, fishing philosophers, joke tellers, and also waste control engineers, bakers, lawyers, teachers like the women. Rozin's new brother-in-law, Puffy Shawano, was a tribal judge. The groom, Frank, was working on the wedding cake. Klaus was trying to stay away from the beer cooler. Failing, he tried to sip, only sip the beer his hand had mysteriously grappled. Gulped. Put the beer down, picked it up again. And again and again while occasionally pausing to fold canvas bags or stuff nylon tent straps away or strip off the cellophane tape from a pack and tap out a cigarette.

"In this world, there is always the element of risk." Puffy straddled a white chair to watch Klaus resist the can, which sat, glowing, dripping gold sweat in the grass.

"We're all predators." A cousin of the groom, Darrell. "That's why something like this is meaningful. These two, they're decent. He's a man, my cousin. He does as a man does. Mr. Frank Shawano. He's no whiner."

"Neither was Whiteheart Beads. However, he was a tribal politician."

"He's come down in the world."

"How much further down can you get?"

"A reporter," said Puffy. His foot went out. He tapped the beer can over. Klaus gave him a look. "In real life, Richard's a wino, I guess."

"In other words," said Klaus, trying to ignore the spilling beer, the dizzying scent of hops and foam, "he's come up in the world."

"Rozin's going to be a lawyer!" said one of the bride's cousins.

"Not yet. There's still a chance she'll revert to her human origins."

"She'll pass the boards no sweat. She's gonna be a good lawyer."

"A prosecutor."

"No, a D.A. That was her hope. Or is she still waffling?"

"No more. No more, my friend. Sympathy for the devil's a thing of the past."

"That's because the devil's got his hooks in us all."

"They're all the same—the cop, the criminal, the defense, the prosecutor—they all share a fundamental belief in the malleability of truth," said Puffy.

"The truth is that there are many truths," said Klaus. His brain was shaking at the proximity of more iced cans and bottles. He thought he might take a walk to clear his head. He plunged his hand into the freezing tub, and this time, although his fingers longingly grazed Schlitz, he grabbed a soda.

Frowning at the sky, nodding at the perfect cloudlessness, the men signaled an organic goodwill agreement among themselves and shifted the subject.

"They'll do okay."

"That's plain."

"Who wouldn't?"

The men paused to watch the bride, in cutoffs and a tight purple T-shirt, catapult herself across the yard on some errand or other vital to her future. Rozin. Even now, back inside the kitchen, the women were doing a cousinly compare and contrast. This one she was going to marry, Frank, they'd finished holding their breaths over. He was seemingly normal. There was passion, which all agreed she needed. But so far no self-destructive weirdness involved. Not yet, that they had seen. A relief.

They were thinking of that other disaster—Richard Whiteheart Beads.

"He was slim, but he was big obsessed."

"And the man could dress."

"Dapper."

"That's it. He was dapper."

Yet the word to them seemed sinister. Richard Whiteheart Beads, in his youth a tribal chairman hopeful, now turned skid row. Just the night before, he had called up Cally, to ask why he was not invited to the wedding.

"He wanted to be the best man!" She grinned crookedly, hiding her shame over her own father, crossed her eyes. "Flako!"

The call had troubled her. Richard knew all of the details of the wedding ceremony, to be held at a nearby state park, and of the reception afterward, back at the house. Spooky, but typical. In and out of recovery, still connected, he always had the inside dope. When he had asked why he wasn't invited, there was a note of aggrieved strain in his voice. Cally tried to stutter a polite excuse, but he had slammed down the phone abruptly, midsentence.

Frank's solidity was thus improved by contrast, and the family boasted unreservedly about the relationship between the bride and groom. Apparently, so the men believed, the groom was subject to the most stubborn love of all, based upon the most primal attraction. Only he, of course, knew and yet even Frank did not know all of it. And the women, though they knew it was a legendary deep love, did not know all of it either.

Frank had told Rozin somewhat piously that he loved her for her practicality and strength of mind. In truth, he was wild for her because she smelled to him of the raw silk of his mother's dress in childhood and of the dreamy terror of a hot summer thunderstorm. She smelled like the radishes his mother ate in secret as she read historical novels in the hay barn. She tasted of browned onions. Of silty ice. Of civet sweetness. Tart raspberry sweat and yeasty bread. She had, in other words, captured his soul on a subliminal level beyond the reach of mortal rescue.

That love could be seen, all agreed, in his eyes when he looked at her as she passed, swift and radiant in her professional bearing, or slumped tantalizingly against a chair, a marionette with the strings cut, in sudden exhaustion.

As for her love, it was based on a similar message received when her world was young—Frank's easy bearing, the powerful sloped shoulders and elongated bearish muscles of a strong swimmer, and his thoughtful mouth were familiar in the deepest way. His voice, ringing above other people's heads like a railroad conductor's, direct with a chef's assumptions, thrilled Rozin with pride. When his peremptory gestures occasionally irritated her, she told him. Their honesty with each other was a wonder to them both.

The problem, on that day of days, was from the past. From history. Richard Whiteheart Beads. History is grief and no passion is complete without its jealous backdrop.

Rozin's two oldest cousins were Vatican twins, not much more than a year apart. Ruby and Jackie. They had shed their jealousy of Rozin long ago along with most of the long dark hair their mother fiercely set and combed and protected from their much longed-for pixie cuts. Now, along with Cally and Cecille, they were the short-haired organizers and handlers of the event, while their luxuriant-haired mother and aunts presided over the greater issues of food and dress and took on the tasks of dispatching men to do their bidding. There was a lot of bidding, and there were a lot of men. Falling somewhere between the levels of authority was the sister of Frank Shawano, Cecille.

Ruby and Jackie were square brunettes. Cecille, small, preternaturally and pridefully slender, with stiff, newly colored red-streaked yellow hair and very pink lips, was a contrast. She was a frightening egoist who absorbed every conversational tidbit instantaneously with an experience of her own. She never reacted, she eclipsed. She did not appreciate, she upended, overthrew, and dominated everyone around her by the simple and obdurant means of aggressive non-listening—though sometimes in a freakish way she did listen, but only for some connection to a story that would allow her to start in on a complicated and self-referential tale.

The habits of Cecille's nature gradually drove off all friends, but she possessed a sad and cunning power within her own family. She had not yet reproduced, which gave her a certain power. Each detail of her life seemed crucial to her and therefore important to impart. During a crisis, she had the ability to drive other people nearly out of their minds.

At this moment, as the wedding party prepared to travel to the place of the wedding ceremony at a lovely site cliffside, just where Frank had proposed, the women were making certain that every detail for the feast was taken care of in perfect order. The tension rose to a magnetic hum. Cally was in a nervous state over how the spectacular wedding cake that Frank was making was to be cut and served to each of the guests. She had just realized that wedding cake plates made of silver paper would be an absolute necessity. Six months ago, she'd purchased them. Just that morning, she had misplaced them.

"Would you please, would you please . . . oh." Her voice rose from deep in her throat. She stood with hands to her head, trying to think. "I can't find the paper dishes for the wedding cake. Oh no. They have to be here. In some sort of sack, a plastic sack, I think!"

"I lost some dishes once. Or *thought* I did." Cecille immediately diverted the crisis to herself. She touched Cally's shoulder as if in sympathy. "Listen . . ." And was ignored.

"Did anybody . . ." Cally's voice rose sharply as she whirled, rattled frantically underneath a sink.

"They turned up at a neighbor's yard sale," continued Cecille. "Can you imagine it?" She glared intensely into the middle distance as Cally directed a young cousin now helping her search.

"No. They're not underneath the sink. Those are buns! Put them down. They're for tomorrow's—"

"The funny thing was this, Cally, are you listening? Jackie, the funny thing was this—" But Cecille could not manage to gain her ear.

"If we don't find the plates for the wedding cake soon, I'm going to have to send someone out to buy some." Her voice rang out, tense and wary.

"Send Chook."

"He's been out, I mean, we sent him out *twice*."

"So what, Janice and him never showed up with the turkey cold cuts they were supposed to. He just brought the moose."

"Yeah, the tough moose."

"And now he's sitting back there, smoking."

"His truck's blocked."

"Then get Puffy! Get Klaus! Get somebody!"

Whirling to the refrigerator intent on her task, Cally nearly bumped into Cecille, who saw her story losing ground, unshaped, unnoticed, and fiercely resumed her narrative.

"Well, the thing is, I couldn't stand it. I didn't know whether the plates were mine. I just didn't have a mark on them, you know, labeled! I'm hardly that compulsive. But I did remember I had chipped one and reglued the chip. Now, listen Cally, Jackie, how many people would do that?" She gestured to them all in retrieving energy.

Cally put her hands on Cecille's shoulders to move her out of the way, as though she was a store dummy.

"Excuse me."

"Not many." Cecille answered herself in a stouthearted voice. "Not many!"

"Let me find my purse!" Jackie jumped in the opposite direction. "The cake plates have to be here right when we return!"

"And what do you know. There it was, the little chip I repaired. So the next question then was this." There was a considerable, though unremarked, dramatic pause as she drew in a deep, deep breath to continue. "Do I confront her or do I just buy back my dishes?"

"We've got to, we've just got to find them . . ." Cally whirled in a circle, eyeing each cupboard. "They're in there somewhere, I know."

"Can you imagine being faced with such a question!" Cecille nearly shouted, panicked to recall her interrupted story.

"Jesus. I suppose they're outrageously expensive, too, but here. Fifty dollars. Shit! Tell him to rush."

"That's *done*, anyway. *Oh god.*"

"Cally, Cally, you said a brown sack?"

"No? But yes! Folded over on the top! That's it!"

"Tell Chook not to go! We have the cake dishes!"

"He's gone."

"Oh . . . oh for the . . . "

Cecille's voice was gathering, strengthened as though from a power beyond herself.

"So anyway, Cally, Jackie, you guys. Listen! I had to ask myself what kind of person I was. It really came down to that. Was I the type to bring this up, risk unpleasantness and so on. You know. With my neighbor whom, I might add, watches my house and has the key to my house? And no telling whether she could make or would think of making a copy before she gave me back the key, you understand. So I would never know and would then have to think of changing the locks, or—"

"Well, if we ever do another wedding," Jackie cried. "Oh, I'm hysterical!"

Cecille leaned forward and low and intense. ". . . or, Jackie, was I the sort of person who would simply buy back my own dishes?"

"This is so much fun." Jackie hugged the other women. "We should go into business. I'm choking!"

"Stop, stop it. I'm going to split a gut." They laughed maniacally and stared directly at Cecille, but did not hear what she was saying.

"What kind of person was I? Am I? What do you think? What do you think I did? Jackie? Ruby?"

"I haven't the faintest idea!" Jackie actually shrieked, but Cecille was too immersed in her tale to take offense. There was no stopping her.

"Well, I'll tell you, I'm the kind of person who does both! I bought them back. Five dollars. Then I said to her while I was paying, 'These look exactly like a set of dishes I once had.' And she gave me this strange—no, I'll call it this *assessing* look in return, and she said to me, her exact words, 'These are your dishes.'

"I was just floored. That she would admit this! Anyway, I said to her, 'These *are* my dishes?' And she said, 'Yes'. And naturally I questioned her. 'How did you get them? The whole set?' I felt like the ground was giving way, you know, like maybe she was over to my house day after day taking one dish at a time, and I'd never noticed. Things were happening too fast. And then she said to me, 'Cecille, I bought these dishes from you at your yard sale. Two years ago. I paid you ten dollars for the set, but Kerry tripped and broke two plates, so now it's incomplete.'

"I counted. Two plates less. She was right. I tell you, I was listening. I was listening hard to something beyond what she said. I was sunk in confusion. Because to this day I do not remember, I swear to this, I do not remember having ever sold those dishes."

Cecille's voice now fell and she panted, breathing deeply, looking all around her for confirmation, and for a moment the other women returned her beaten stare, blankly, for none of them had followed her story to where she now stood. She was alone with it. Luckily, the phone rang. Cecille grabbed it like a lifeline. Listened, her mouth opening and opening, wider. No one was watching her, but she mouthed the name Richard to their backs and profiles. Cecille hung up the phone.

"Richard"—she inserted a dramatic pause between the two words—"threatened—"

"Oh wait. Chook's back. He forgot something." The others were still embarked on the drama of the cake plates.

"Tell him not to go out in the first place!" Jackie cried.

"I am! I will!" Cally turned her back on Cecille, anxious.

Cecille shouted to them, loud and desperate, stopping them a second only.

"Listen! He's going to show up! Don't you get it! Richard."

Jackie finally faced her and in the annoyance of wedding planners, the exasperation of one hounded to her limit, said what she thought.

"That stupid plate story didn't wash so you just made up another one. Richard show up. I doubt that, I really do."

"He did . . ." Cecille was momentarily nonplussed. "He just called. He was on the phone."

"All right all right all right."

Jackie patted her shoulder, patronizing. Cecille shrugged her off, shocked, indignant, and then all of a sudden hurt. But her range of emotions was ignored.

"Don't blame me when he does show up," she said in a small voice. No one heard her, or acknowledged her, anyway, except Cally, who was thinking of the veiled Ethiopian woman and the unreality of Cecille's view of conversations.

"I hope he doesn't," Cally said, tense, then a need struck her, and she bolted. "Wait! Let's make sure we have everything we need before we stop Chook. Do we need something from the store?"

"Rice!"

"We have rice, wild rice, look . . . "

"For throwing."

"Oh come on. We're not going to throw that old white rice."

"It's a custom."

"Why?"

"Well, I don't know exactly," said Cecille in irritation, "where it came from. But I'd venture to say it's fairly meaningful, if you examined it and all. I would be surprised if there weren't some tradition involved, going way back into the medieval Christian times."

"They didn't have white rice then."

"Rice is thousands of years old!"

"But it's cultivated in the Far East."

"True. So how did it get to be a custom, do you think?"

"Hey you."

"Chook."

"It's too late. Now he's parked his truck and he isn't going to go anywhere again. He won't want to risk going out in his truck. It's too late!"

"Besides, rice kills birds. Haven't you heard that? They peck it up, sip water, and explode!"

They wedged themselves into their cars, drove off, and soon arrived at the decorated area cliffside where Frank had made known his intentions. A wild vista hung below the stone outcrop—river, woods, islands, a sparkling haze of warm fall sky. Beneath a domed awning, white chairs were set. The sister and cousins composed themselves, barely mentioned or even recalled the disturbing phone call. Yet Richard Whiteheart Beads did show up. Just as the wedding couple walked up the aisle to gather around the Reverend, a woman dressed in gleaming hand-sewn robes of steel gray and magenta, he appeared at the very back of the crowd.

Richard Whiteheart Beads was wearing a tuxedo tailored to his stronger, pre-alcohol body, and carrying a huge cone of roses. The flowers were pink-yellow, velvety, and scented the air around him so that their sweetness preceded him into the gathered crowd whose attention—absorbed by the bride's off-shoulder gown and the draped state-park plaque that served as the altar—passed over him lightly. The entire wedding party assembled and the Reverend calmly organized her thoughts to welcome all to the service.

Chairs spread before the sun-smitten lip of the altar in a gentle fan and everyone smiled at the Reverend's first words.

"Today!" she exclaimed softly, with feeling. "We are here to appreciate, to witness, to support the love shared by Rozina and Frank. Let us now share their joy!"

An electic bunch of people had gathered—for the mixed-blood families had intermarried not only with neighboring tribes of Winnebago and Lakota origin, but with at least one sub-Saharan African and an exchange student from Brazil. But in spite of their worldliness all were surprised when the haggard man with the cone of flowers burst into raven-hoarse, false laughter. Heads turned, craned, and a dismayed sibilance of hushing sounds came from the protective mothers and aunts. Still, the strange guest's withering laughter accelerated. Would not be hushed. And then to their horror, from the back of the crowd, Richard Whiteheart Beads advanced.

"Excuse me, excuse me!" he cried to either side. "I should be the one joining these two in unholy matrimony. After all, the bride was mine first and you know what I'm saying"—his voice cracked—"in the biblical sense!"

Cecille breathed, I told you, and Cally gasped, Stop him, and stretched out her arms as though to do so with fingers bent, but Whiteheart Beads was at the altar now. There, the groom grabbed him instantly by the throat, cutting off the laughter, half throttling and choking him. But Richard Whiteheart Beads was possessed of a manic energy. He batted the groom fiercely with the thorny roses and then there was a swirl of white net obscuring all as the bride rammed forward to try to thrust the two men apart. In the confusion Richard freed himself. He popped out of the net of foam and flailing arms, scrambled toward the stone barricade above the scenic overlook, and lightly gained the top—beneath which, of course, the cliff shot down in a sheer vertical drop. There, he teetered.

The Reverend, accustomed to all sorts of wedding surprises and to counseling suicides, could be seen assembling her training and mustering her intuitions—it took but a moment—and then in a gesture of serene power enhanced by the authority of her swirling vestments and robe, she raised her arms. She told the others to retreat, and they were glad to. She and Richard were left in a circle of silence, he on the wall, she just below. It was then that she asked him in a normal tone of voice, though her stomach was folded in two, where he had acquired such beautiful flowers.

"I know you're thinking of jumping over that cliff," she continued calmly, "but you don't have to right this minute. Believe me, they'll all wait."

The wind came up a little and the two, Richard poised on the stone wall and she situated in her breeze-stirred clothes, just below him, regarded the crowd of wedding-goers who pushed back their swirling hair and gaped and huddled, comforting one another, Rozin red-faced and weeping, the groom restrained by his brothers from charging forward to push Richard over the edge himself.

"Mr. Whiteheart Beads," said the Reverend with great courtesy, "will you allow me to make an announcement so that I can ask you a question in private?"

"I guess." He was breathing heavily, desperate and suspicious. The sun swirled. White puffs of clouds. A clear blue limpid sky.

The Reverend made a cup of her hands, called out through it. "The ceremony will be slightly postponed. Feel free to mingle. And have a glass of champagne if you wish!"

There was a general rush toward the alcohol.

"Now," she said, turning to him, "we have a few moments to ourselves. About those roses." Aware that he was losing his audience,

Richard edged backwards and the Reverend's heart disconnected from the rest of her body. She felt it thud unpleasantly and she grabbed his ankle with both hands.

"Wait a minute." Her voice was motherly, annoyed. He struggled, attempting to pull away. His cone of paper broke and petals spilled about them. Her voice remained steady and she gripped his foot tight as the lid on a canning jar. "You haven't told me where you got those beautiful roses and they are my favorite flower. Richard?"

It was then that Whiteheart Beads looked into her face, so exceeding pleasant, the features all dauntless maternal curves, and realized that she would not let go of his foot.

"I bought them at the supermarket," he whispered.

Sadly, as though betrayed, he shook his head. "Let me go." His face was crumpled in anxious grief and he smelled of the skin-through saturation of days of alcohol, as though he was sweating old vodka. Yet there was real sorrow in his voice. "This is real, Reverend, real. And God is no help. I am in a dark place."

"I have been there, too," she said, her voice sad with assurance. "I have been where you are."

He didn't reply. Mistakenly, she felt compelled to say more.

"Terrible as this may seem to you . . . ," she carefully began. The comfort she offered enraged him.

With all his strength he then lunged away over the lip of stone. For a moment he hung beyond in air, straight as a statue, and then he crashed headfirst directly onto the other side of the wall. For although yanked against the rough stone and nearly over, the Reverend had not let go and still held Richard two-handed by the ankle, a deadweight, unconscious. And the wife of Klaus, whose eyes had never left Richard, was there suddenly too. In a flash of physicality she lunged to the wall and snagged Richard's other leg. Otherwise, desperate as she was, the Reverend could never have held him. Arms straining, alongside Sweetheart Calico, overlooking the brink, she yelled for help. As the men came running, she saw an odd thing: The other savior was smiling. Her lips peeled back from her dreadful teeth, she was smiling dreamily into the sheer air and watching the petals of the roses drift calmly down in pink quiescence, hundreds of feet.

For the first time in her life, the Reverend had a glass of champagne before the wedding ceremony, two glasses in fact while the blue-uniformed emergency ambulance technicians collected Richard, peering into his pupils with a tiny flashlight, strapping him with businesslike dispatch onto a gurney. They tucked him into light, warm blankets, rolled the gurney into their vehicle. After they latched the doors shut, they nodded to all, politely, and left. When the sirens finally receded, the wedding party, shaken but excited in their relief, slightly intoxicated by the bubbles and warm autumn sun, reassembled and then there commenced, in all of its touching glory, the witnessed uniting of two complex middle-aged hearts.

The tiny particulate unyellowed leaves of the locust trees flickered and swam in the moving air. Trembling, stammering, golden and clear, the four o'clock light fell across the yard in a yolky radiance. Inside the apartment and the downstairs kitchen the shadows threw upon the interior of the window shades a supple language, changeable and rushing. The cooks whirled, carrying covered bowls, spoons, dishes out the door. Cars pulled up constantly with people arriving for the dinner and wedding cake.

The meats of the day were all game acquired by the brothers and uncles and prepared according to their own special methods. The moose was unearthed from a cooking pit in the backyard. Fish, dunked in fluffy beer batter, fried, dripped a delicate grease in a bedding of paper towels. Deer sausages sizzled in light gold fat. The refrigerator was carefully emptied. Ambrosia appeared. Wild rice and onion. More wild rice with shredded ham. Macaroni. Cecille's self-advertised carved watermelon boat filled with exotic fruits strewn with plump grapes and toasted coconut. Six types of potato salad. Fry bread in a cardboard box. Still to come, pies of winter saved and fresh picked fruits. Marshmallow Krispy Bars, studded with colored chocolate bits. Fudge.

Of course Frank's cake. Towering. Glistening. The blitzkuchen. Curls of white chocolate. Raspberries. Stiffly whipped cream.

And still no plates.

"Here's my damn purse! How much do they cost per dozen? Those little plates? How many dozen do we need?"

"Six dozen in a hundred and two hundred to be safe so a dozen dozen!"

The guests moved in and out of one another's circles, families of Ojibwa elders with children and grandchildren of varying tones from palest laughing blond to swirls of ocher and obsidian, all poking, eating, tasting, organizing. In one corner, the older ladies had gathered, comfortably served by teens threatened into momentary good manners. The ladies accepted heaped plates and commented on each dish, voicing all approval in English and criticism in Ojibwa to spare the feelings of the younger cooks.

"This moose is tough!"

"Dahgo chimookoman makazin!"

"Magizha gaytay mooz."

"The old are the tenderest, though. Really they are!"

"Magizha oshkay."

"Or they cut the meat against the grain."

"Probably that."

"Chook said he thought there was something funny about those steaks when I unwrapped them."

"I guess Puffy gave the meat away because he didn't like it."

"He poached it!"

"Owah!"

"No he didn't. The moose stepped across the line."

"He says."

"His weh'ehn's the game warden."

Cecille understood enough Ojibwa to know that they were talking about meat and hunting, though she didn't understand that the grandmas thought the meat was tough as a whiteman's shoe, probably from an old skinny bull, poached midwinter, stored until it burned from cold, given by Puffy to Chook because he wanted to make room in his freezer. She smiled at them all and drew up a chair to sit. She got along better with the older ladies because they had no patience with her and shut her up with their own running commentary. They all, therefore, thought that she was a tractable and good-mannered young woman and smiled their collective approval at her, clucked and hissed, indignant, when she explained how nobody had listened to her right after Richard called.

"I warned them. I warned them."

The grandmas looked at her in radiant sympathy, but between them they spoke otherwise. She had so many men they wondered, wasn't her *place* all worn out? So many of them these days just had one or two, but somehow they kept themselves like young girls all their lives.

"Aerobics in *that place*," said an aunt of the bride in Ojibwa, and all of the woman laughed.

Cecille, earnest and tossing her red-streaked mane, asked if they knew about the elder's program of water exercises they could do to keep their strength up and build their eroding muscle fibers and keep themselves safe from osteoporosis.

"It is sponsored by the YWCA." She commended it to them brightly.

"Maybe her head wore out too," said an old cousin of the groom's father.

"Let her be," argued a grandma from the other side of the family. "She just wants us to live long."

"Sometimes I think I been here too long already."

"You're a nice girl," decided another, patting Cecille's hand.

"First I dug the pit," Chook explained, modestly. "I put volcanic rocks in the bottom, then the screens, two layers of screens, then all the buffalo and the moose meat wrapped up in tin foil. Then dirt over that. Then sod. Then more stones. Then wood over that, yet."

"What about old tires? You use any old tires?"

"Shut up, Puffy, this is good. Chook is the chief chef."

"Aaaay. Your pickup. Puffy. Eight-ply tires?"

"I don't know how many plies I have."

"How much air you put in those tires?"

"I don't remember. You trying to distract me?"

"Maybe. Forty-five when you're empty on those six-ply."

"I don't remember how many plies, though."

"That old husband was a few plies short."

"You said it."

"Holeee . . . "

"What?"

"There he is!"

And sure enough, walking with careful little steps, his head wrapped in a white helmet of gauze, Richard Whiteheart Beads, newly escaped from the hospital emergency room, approached the eating crowd from halfway down the leafy architecture of the alleyway. His tuxedo hadn't suffered in the tussle, although the rose in his buttonhole had dropped two blood red petals that clung to his lapel. The dressing that protected his head was enormous and seemed to bob on his shoulders. The men stood up in one solid group, approached him, walking down the back alley with set faces, a phalanx of heavy torsos. They stopped. Implacably, they folded their arms. Richard stopped too, there in the alley before them, and slid his hand slowly into the breast of his suit jacket.

"Wait." Puffy reached out and set his broad hand on Richard's hand.

"You got a gun in there?"

"No!" Richard exhibited grave shock. "No! I have a letter."

"Give it here then, I'll deliver it," said Chook. "You get lost."

"I loved her," said Richard in a ragged voice.

The men drew closer. An arm went around his shoulder, turning him away, back down the street.

"We all got to suffer," said an uncle quietly. "That's love."

"Now you go carefully. Take care."

The men stood quietly together, watching Whiteheart Bead's slow and bitter progress down the street. He disappeared into a side alley.

"You think that's the last of him?"

"He's got it real bad." Chook rolled his sleeves back down. "Could pop out of the wedding cake."

"I've seen other guys like that," Puffy said. "He thinks he's special, but he's nothing special."

"Go slice your moose."

"They're asking for another batch of fish."

"Maybe I should go after him, make sure he gets home all right," said Chook.

"Maybe you shouldn't."

"He's got his pride."

"Or something."

Two of the men stood watching the place where Richard had disappeared.

The Reverend turned from the conversation at hand just as Chook solemnly approached the bride, bearing a stiff white envelope. His earnestness drew her interest, and then the fact of the letter, too, which Rozin ripped open with an air of contempt and read holding the edges as though the paper was coated with a dangerous virus.

She stared at the words for a good piece of time, enough to alarm the others near her—Chook, who was about to retrieve the letter and was already sorry he gave it to her, and her cousins, anxious now to get on with the cutting of the cake. They stood expectantly near the photographer and the cake itself gesturing at Rozin to put down the letter, approach with Frank, and do the honors.

Rozin turned decisively from the gathering, crumpled the letter in one clenched fist, and then, lifting the edge of her dress and kicking off her delicate poke-heeled satin pumps, began to walk straight down the street, away from the gathering, faster, accelerating, until she was tilted forward in barefooted speed. Elbows out, she strode in deliberate intent and fury, hell-bent. One, and then another, and at last a huge group of the wedding party directly fanned out walking curious and worried in her wake.

When she broke into a trot and then a full-out run, many of the others dropped behind. Others ran, too. If the groom hadn't got such a belated start he might have caught her before she reached the corner supermarket, where she popped into the door and whipped in a froth down the frozen meats section at the end of which, of course, Richard Whiteheart stood as though considering the array of breaded fish cutlets lighted before his face.

"You!" She stopped, took in a breath. Holding the letter, she looked from it to Richard. "What do you mean you poisoned the cake? What do you mean? What is this?"

She shook the paper at him.

Richard stepped forward under his lopsided headdress in the hum of freezers, voice smooth as ice.

"I'm sorry, Rozin, but I had to pretend that I did something really serious, being you probably wouldn't want to talk to me."

"But, so, the cake's not . . . "

"Poisoned? Not that I know. I mean it could be, not by me of course, but not that I *know*! I'm so sorry. I didn't make that clear immediately." Richard's manner was light, reassuring, professional. "That was just a ploy to get you here, of course." His habitual slow, winning, sympathetic smile of practiced charm bloomed, grotesque underneath his gauze turban. "Don't tell me you could possibly have married Frank Shawano without the two of us having a private chat."

"Yes," Rozin stepped firmly backward. "I did. I could. Manager!"

Richard leaned closer, put out his arms stiff as a doll, talked double speed.

"I made love to you as though you were the most special thing on the face of the earth. An angel. I kissed your cunt and you spread your wings like an angel and you held my face between your thighs and told me you loved me and never would leave me and then you let me enter you as much as I wanted and for as long as I wanted and now"—he groped for the tag end of the sentence and story, found it, his voice rising—"you tell me you got married to another man and you meant to do it and you wanted him the same way you wanted me?"

Richard stepped toward Rozin nodding his head back and forth in a parody of avuncular chiding. He crooked his arms as though to embrace her but just behind him Klaus had crept, bearing in his two bottle-trained but now four-month-sober hands a solidly frozen twenty-pound turkey. This, he brought down on Richard Whiteheart Beads's head. Richard buckled to the floor. For a long moment, Rozin and Klaus stared down, waiting to see the effect of the blow. Richard blinked at them, stayed conscious. He rose, wobbled as he walked, only slightly disoriented, through the Employees Only double doors at the rear of the supermarket and then out to sit thoughtfully in the parking lot. Klaus replaced the turkey in the freezer, dusted his hands. As he helped the bride out the front supermarket doors, he murmured slow and helpful words that made no sense even to him.

Out back, Richard rested on a heavy box of waxed cardboard. It did not collapse, but when it began to sag he got up and staggered down a series of alleyways until he found a deserted backyard with a little bench underneath a grape arbor. There, he lay down. His brain throbbed immensely now through the hospital's painkiller and yet the skull itself felt thin and fragile as an egg. He tried to imagine his next move, cast away scenario after scenario until he saw, flickering and tensile, images fast-forward from an old Japanese war movie.

Where, he wondered, would he get a samurai sword? Bayonet? Machete? Or would a chef's knife do? Hara-kiri. He would kneel in the hotel lobby of their honeymoon destination. No, better, in the very hallway just outside their bridal suite. Kneel on a white tablecloth, take out the chef's knife, knock on their door and when they came to answer . . . but then again he'd never liked the word *hara-kiri* and heard that it was considered vulgar anyway by the Japanese whereas kamikaze, meaning "divine wind," was much more fitting for a man whose Whiteheart Beads ancestors had known how to change the weather. Yes, he saw himself crash over their romantic balcony through the sliding glass into their room. The needle nose split their bed in two. Flames spurted from inside the metal skin. Explosion.

Where to get a small plane?

"The perfect murder weapon," said Puffy to Klaus, marveling. "You beat a guy senseless with a frozen turkey, unthaw, roast it, eat. Presto. No trace except the wishbone."

"This is getting too weird even for me," said Cecille, who was drinking a beer with her cousins now, and who, with her disregarded phone call, had finally gained back every shred of lost status and respect by giving the police an interview. She was, however, visibly shaken by the truth of Richard's pain.

"They're not sure how he managed to get out of the emergency. But the doors are hardly locked, right?"

"He was gone when they got there."

"Jesus."

There was a tense feeling in the group, the paranoia of people confronting an almost supernatural, odd power, something unseen and spooky. Clever. Whiteheart Beads had disappeared, traceless, after the supermarket exploit. Hysterically weeping, Rozin had surrendered to the police the letter, which was a detailed, even convincing explanation of how he, Richard, had managed to replace the contents of one of Frank's favorite spices with tasteless, traceless, instantly deadly poison for which no antidote existed. The police sergeant uncrumpled and dusted the paper for fingerprints and dropped it in a Ziploc bag. For the second time that day, a group of sober professional people in uniforms took their leave of the wedding party.

Who were left in a great murmuring clump, staring at the blitzkuchen. The cake, surrounded by fresh flowers and curlicues of white and dark chocolate, reared high in graduated tiers of pristine frosting. The wedding guests' attention did not rest on the cake but scaled its height, returned, scaled again the sweeping precision of the icing and symmetry of each round. The low-voiced conversations stopped and silence held. Quietly, the party crowd regarded the magazine-cover perfection of the cake that, there was no denying, now seemed sinister.

Frank grasped the mood and acted on instinct.

"Let's cut the cake!"

There was a shuffle, weak smiles, shrugs and halfhearted inquiries around among the women, who, questioning one another, determined that there were still no plates.

"Hold out your hands then!" Frank brandished the shining knife and then, with Rozin's hand grasped firmly in his hand, cut a wedge firmly into the lowest layer. He then proceeded with the practiced alacrity of his trade to slice up the entire cake and lay out the pieces before the increasingly restless crowd of guests, all of whom he then, gesturing grandly, with an expansiveness unlike himself, urged to pick up a piece in their hand. He did, smiling now at Rozin. Holding the fragrant wedge aloft, first, he then lowered it like a sacrament and took a huge bite. At his reaction to the taste, the crowd stopped dead. His face, his expression, registered a stark, huge feeling. Amazement covered him. He opened his mouth wide and bit again. Even before he broke off a corner of his piece and placed it in Rozin's mouth he was already shouting.

The crowd began to taste the cake, exclaiming as they did, nervously, in trepidation, but unable to resist the next bite after the first, the next and next delicate yet dense bite of blitzkuchen. And so it was, so the secret was discovered. The final and the missing ingredient—fear. And they all ate together, and they all saw their loved ones moving in the present, around them, children running in the grass. The old people sacrificed a corner of the cake, with tobacco, for the spirits. The ones who had gone on before, the dead, even they came back for a little taste.

Frank slung his arm too carelessly around Rozin's trembling shoulders. "So you thought I was the kind of baker who would leave his cake batter long enough for some idiot to slip in poison?"

Rozin stiffened, stepped out of his circling embrace. "Not everything reflects on *your cake*," she said, her jaw set evenly on each word. "Not everything is about *your cake*." She turned. Her full skirt puffed up behind her as she ran up the steps into the house. She continued up the next flight of creaking steps and down the hall to the end and hurled herself into the bathroom, locked the lock, dried her tears, stripped off her bridal gown. Just for a few minutes, she told herself, to breathe. This was too much for anyone! Gradually, her breathing calmed. She sat at the edge of the tub, wiped the makeup off her face, and then stared out the little upstairs window into leafy gold light.

The theme of the hotel room was flowers, lilies mainly, a quiet vining wallpaper and tan throats and pink stamens patterning the quilted comforter. Some huge stylized imitation O'Keeffe petals and whorled knoblike spikenards, prints framed in golden metal. Innocuous lamp shades in rough eggshell. Blond wood. A television cabinet and underneath a little refrigerator stocked with drinks. In a celebratory bucket, champagne. Delirious with exhaustion, Rozin popped the cork into a hotel towel and poured a full water glass. Frigid smoke swirled from the thick green stub of the bottle's neck and she drank. She drank. Pins fell from her sprayed-up hair. Frank undid the bodice of her wedding dress and then began to lick the undersides and the nipples of her breasts and the tender inner skin of her arms.

"What's that?"

"Nothing."

"Room service probably."

The knock sounded again.

"Who's there?"

"Room service."

"See?"

"Somebody sent us something."

"I guess."

"Wanna get it?"

"No."

Again the knock sounded.

"Go away."

Another knock, harder.

"The fuck?" Frank exploded, jumped from the bed dragging a sheet around his waist and threw the door wide. Framed in the doorway stood Richard Whiteheart Beads. His head was bandaged more tightly now and he stood straight and neat as a boy playing soldier. He was holding a gun.

When he raised it with a flourish and pressed the barrel to his brow, Rozin took a long stride out of the bedclothes and went to the door naked, for his brown eyes had gone sheer black and drew her, their gazes locked in threatful knowing. She sprang toward him and it seemed clear to her that if she could only reach him and hold him physically in time he would not do this. As she came close still holding on to his eyes, she saw from the corner of her vision his first finger press the trigger. Just as she knocked his elbow, there was a loud noise. She lunged forward, following him back against the opposite wall of the white hallway. As she tackled him, her full weight across his body, the memory of his body upon hers covered her mind, the two of them moving together sexually, lightly as dancers, flooded into her and she thought of his delight in her ease and his wonder at the pleasures of his body and it was as though the whole unread substance of his love poured into her, bloody and pure. She lay holding him against her naked and uncaring as people filled the hallway.

It was unclear at first whether he was grazed by the bullet or going to die, and as Rozin cradled him looking into his eyes she felt the old hopeless mixture of tenderness, hatred, exhaustion. After the now familiar medics and police came and fetched him, Frank sat on the bed with his head in his hands and refused to speak or look up at anyone. So it was her cousins first that brought Rozin into the shower and put her in the water and let the water run down until the blood was off her. The water racheted down in stinging streams. All that time she couldn't stop thinking.

She remembered the times Richard took care of her. For those first days after Deanna, he would do anything. Still, she could not forgive him. It was not in her. He combed her hair, braided it, painted her fingernails and kneaded lotion into her feet. He tried his best to comfort her, and it was true, there was no one else who loved Deanna as he did. He drove her crazy. His desperate love, going back, all the way back to when they first married. The times he came on her, spilling on her, and pressed all of his semen into her skin and said that she was pregnant with him now. He had kissed her over and over with profound and desperate emotion, his tongue a wet flame. She had begun to plot right then, that first year, how in the world she would get away from him. And she saw now that all her plot threads had raveled into one seam. One thick black seam stitched of unforgiveness. His blood poured off her like a red shawl. Redness seemed to have soaked into her. It was a long, long time before the water finally ran clear.

PART FOUR

NEEWIN

THE RED BEADS WERE HARD to get and expensive, because their clear cranberry depth was attained only by the addition, to the liquid glass, of twenty-four-carat gold. Because she had to have them in the center of her design, the second twin gambled, lost, grew desperate, bet everything. At last, even the blankets of her children.

She won enough, just barely, for the beads. And then the snow fell. Gazing into the molten hearts of the ruby-red whiteheart beads, the children shivered, drew closer, chewed on the hem of her deerhide skirt. First one, and then the other, plucked up the beads from behind her hand. Even knowing they were not food, it was the look of them, bright as summer berries, that tempted their hunger. When her fingers finally closed on air, she turned, saw her youngest quickly swallow the last bead. The mother looked at her children, eyes dazed, fingers swollen, brain itching. All she could think of was finishing her work. She reached for the knife.

Frightened, the children ran.

She had to follow them, searching out their panicked trail, calling for them in the dark places and the bright places, the indigo, the white, the unfinished details and larger meaning of her design.

17

Food of the Dead

A cool fall night in the city on a dead-end street. Cottonwood leaves tapping and traffic a dim snarl to the west. The night after her wedding, Rozin is sleeping in her mothers' apartment, alone. She sleeps with her back to an open window. Later, she thinks of that window. Maybe that's how her daughter's spirit entered, climbing on leggy vines? Or the fan in the next room, sifting fire through its sleeves. The light socket with the bulb out. Thoughts. She wakes to the telephone's persistent ring. Downstairs, in the yellow wash of light over the kitchen sink, she raises the phone to her mother Zosie's voice.

"I'm calling from the hospital, Rozin. He never came to, Richard. He never made it. Frank's here. He wants to talk to you."

"No."

Rozin lowers the receiver back into its cradle. She passes her hand across her face, crumples a fist to her mouth, and wonders what she will feel next. Nothing comes. Just nothing, though her blood roars and her skull suddenly feels tight. A helmet. Her brain overstuffed with too many thoughts. She is just about to lift the phone again and call somebody, anybody, when Deanna's voice floats down from the top of the staircase.

"Mama . . . "

Rozin steps back out into the hallway, stands at the bottom holding the worn curl of the bannister.

"Mama?" Deanna asks. "Are you coming too?"

Rozin freezes. An excuse, a little laugh shoots up inside her and then her throat shuts. If she lets her daughter keep talking, Deanna will never stop. She'll go on talking. She'll talk to her mother morning and night and at last they'll put Rozin away. Still, she wants to hear so badly. Just a few words. Just get close to her, she thinks absurdly, don't talk to her but just get *near* her. Where is she now? She has to find her. Has to! The air at the top of the stairs is thick as black cotton and she can't see where Deanna went. Her knees give. Is she hiding in the closet? The covered bench?

"Don't go," she whispers. An unknowing thrill clamps her middle, shoots over her shoulders, and then spreads down like an ice cape. Still, silence. The dread passes over and a lighter feeling sails in. Her heart bobs and the longing is a stitch in her side. She gasps painfully.

"Come back," she calls out, hopeful and afraid. But there is no answer. Wax leaves clatter against the side of the house. She crouches on the bottom step, motionless.

The earth tips its farthest shoulder to the sun and the dark goes solid. Cold air seizes in bands along the mopboards. She sits there, waiting for Deanna to tell her what she came for, what she wants, what she can do. Incrementally, the dark motes thin to gray. The air stirs with the cold soupiness of dawn. She doesn't shift her weight. She doesn't lean or twist to move again, not until the starlings begin to argue in the tattered cedars.

When it is full morning, Rozin rises and slips her arms into an old shirt. One of Richard's that she kept, a black and white checkered shirt that reaches almost down to her knees. For he was a tall man, and she is more her mother's size. She removes the heavy iron pot from its cupboard place and brings it over to the bowl of the kitchen sink. She pulls the snap-in cord from the phone jack so that she can do what she has to do without disturbance. Into the pot, she pours an inch or so of wild rice. A fine sweet dust rises off the rice like smoke, smelling of the lake bottom, weedy and fresh. Next, she runs water into the pot, swirls her hand among the ticking grains. Black-green, brown-green, dotted with paler speckles and very fine. Uncultivated. Not the fake stuff. Knocked into the bottom of Zosie's beat-up aluminum canoe last fall. A few small hulls, sharp and papery, ride the surface. Poured off, the water carries away green clay, powdery silt. Another water. Five waters altogether, until the last comes clean and she sets the pot aside. Onions now. She holds a kitchen match tight between her teeth so the juice won't make her eyes water, then she crosshatches the onion from the root end, slicing the tiny cubes into a pile she keeps neatly triangled with the flat of the knife.

Broth will slowly cook the onions into the rice. Before she sets the top onto the pot she adds a tiny pinch of white pepper, but more than that Deanna never liked—simple foods, no spices. Odd she never got her dad's complex food tastes, neither of them did. Basic foods. Potatoes, cheese. Rozin remembers the stubborn genius of Richard's ways and sees him, now, before her suddenly. Brown hair and brown eyes with a curved smile and hollow cheeks. Shuts her eyes against the picture. He is a magnet, Richard Whiteheart Beads, with a prickly and unappeasable energy some people resent and others worship. Around him, she was like that herself, never doing things the easy way, always finding the method of most resistance. Even now, she prefers to cook food she'll have to guide and watch over for the next four hours. A soft vanilla pudding from scratch. Stewed turkey. Milky corn still on the cob. She slices off boiled kernels, butters them, pours them back into a plastic bowl. It is good, though, the care she takes with everything, for by the afternoon she will be tired enough, she hopes, to sleep.

On the table, at the western end because that is the death direction, she sets two places carefully. Spirit plates, with tobacco. A paper napkin folded once. Knife, fork, and spoon all on one side. She fills the plates with the wild rice in a heap beside the turkey, the milky, buttery corn, a bit of fruit salad containing strawberries, and, beside them, a large bowl of vanilla pudding.

Eat it, eat it all up, now, she thinks vehemently, heartsick, setting another smaller plate for her daughter at the head of the stairs, then go to sleep.

Startled at how forcefully she's spoken, even though not aloud, only in her thoughts, Rozin walks upstairs and slumps on the edge of her bed. She rolls over, curls on her side, and without even consciously closing her eyes, she falls into a dream. Long, disrupted, complicated, tense, she lives out a day with her daughters' father.

Once again, they are at the old BIA administration headquarters, walking the creaking floors to the very back of the building. Everything goes wrong. Around him, she is clumsy. He cuffs at her or explodes. She is trying to get the tape to stick properly. Her shoelaces spring apart. Her hair messes up in twisted knots. They go home. Fear grips her stomach when she realizes she has lost the ring he gave her, then the watch, then everything. His sandwich toast burns. Ants march across the doorstep and she can't sweep them back. Her beading loosens and then falls apart in his hands. His Christmas present. He does not want her present, the loomed watchband, she can tell that. Where would he put it? How explain the beads clittering off the ends of the watch, falling to the floor? The potatoes she serves him are cold and also she's missed an eye or two that turn up in a spoon of his, unmashed. Staring at her. Not enough butter. Too much.

Now, she lies suspended between her dream and the next morning. Easing into her old pink flannel robe, she remembers about the food, goes to the kitchen, on the way picking up the plate set on the stairs. She removes the plate from the table as well, dumps the food all together into a covered bowl, and then meticulously constructs a new plate of food and sets it piping hot on the table. Steps away from it.

"Eat," she whispers, frowning the way she did when Deanna picked at her food. She longs for her and at the same time feels in herself a knotted thing form, a twisted configuration of heavy, bold, recalcitrant tubes, yarns, and wires like a terrible science project, some uncontrollable failure for which she will be graded F.

Hatred for Richard. Longing. This tangle of blame and killing anger and wilted love.

That night a stranger appears to her in her sleep. She can see all of his features. His long face, straight nose, flared nostrils, and eyebrows like two thin wings. His eyes deep and remote. A mournful thin-lipped hardened mouth. He does not speak, but as he stands there he slowly unzips his body. It opens like a fearful suit. Inside, he is smooth as a cave of river ice. She can see, faintly, from within his rib cavity, faint glows of phosphorescence. Death has hollowed and scoured him out inside so that there is room, she understands when he beckons, for her to enter.

That morning she plugs her phone back in, calls in sick to her job, and then stays underneath the covers, afraid of what she has been offered. A windigo has visited. She is afraid but also hopeful. Her daughter might talk to her again. She ignores the ringing of the telephone that she knows is Frank calling, begging her to let him in the door. Rozin has already decided she can't possibly go live with him, not until she meets the windigo full on. Not until she feeds these spirits so they will stop circling her, hungry. Zosie has gone up north, to get Mary. Maybe they'll doctor her. Rozin can't even get out of the bed. She will have to stay with her daughter, right here. She sleeps all day, all night. When morning comes, again, she removes the plates and brings the food out into the backyard, where the squirrels will eat it, and the city raccoons and the ravens with their glossy arrogance.

Four days pass, the food she's made is used up, and the squirrels and the ravens come regularly to the stump in the backyard. Five days. Six. On the seventh day, there is a knock on the door.

Her body feels light and slow, drifting, a balloon. Whoever it is goes away. Probably Frank. There is a box of Cheerios. Rozin starts eating them one by one, but they dry in her mouth like sawdust and gag her. Stick in her throat. She can't swallow, as though a lump has grown there suddenly. She eats nothing. And then the walls shake and thimbles of red fire float in the air. She begins to weep and tears pour out of her.

Deanna is safe in her arms.

A woman's body is the gate to this life. A man's body is the gate to the next life. She is crying for the stranger to stand before her once again, to open himself. She knows who he is, now, this windigo. He is the original Shawano from way back in time, the windigo man whom the Shawano brothers took into their family in the old days, long ago. Here's how she heard it. They were hunting together way up north, those brothers and their families. Visited by this ice spirit of awful hunger, they let him in the door. They should not have. He was all frost inside, all ravenous snow. Still, she wants him to come to her again. This time she will enter. Cleave to the glossy ice. Pull his cold sky-colored skin around her like a grave.

Although she hasn't eaten in all this time, she feels stronger, normal in fact, on day eight. Just water. All her body needs. Warmish water. Not cold. Her body has apparently decided it does not need food. Her stomach pinches, radiating pains shoot through her chest, but she is calm inside and sleeps and sleeps. Her bed is soft, wide, deliciously warm, and safe. Two more days pass for Rozin, and by then she is a forest. She is growing small trees. Saplings shoot through her arms and breasts eager for light. Her skin is a protective mesh to shelter small seedlings and over her already big pines tower.

Every night, she walks down the wooded path of herself and waits for the stranger. She is sitting in a chair by a shallow river, at the end of the path in her dream, when she feels his touch on her shoulder, the nerveless threat of his presence. She turns, but it is Frank. He takes her into his arms and she is crushed against the man smell of his body, starch, oil, grass, heat, sweat. Against her cheek the tiny buttons of his shirt press. He is standing and she is sitting so she has thrown her arms around his waist and her face is mashed against his tough torso.

Suddenly he slides down, limp and heavy in her arms, a suit of leather, and she remembers she is caught up in a dream. Brown leather. Warm. A pale brown the color of his skin. She straps him on like body armor. Wears him like shields and breastplates. He has given her the gift of his big, warm, strong body to hide in from now on as she walks forward in the world.

Richard Whiteheart Beads had crazily but understandably wanted to bury the whole yellow truck. Rozin chose to bury her daughter in the old tradition underneath a grave house, built low and long with a small shelf at one end where food and tobacco could be placed for her to use. Sometimes Rozin goes up to the reservation on weekends, leaves a coin or two, copper, for some still believe that the water man exacts his price at the red stone gates. If so, she thinks, Deanna will have enough to pay her way time and time over. She can bribe the collector and pass in and out, keep wandering and exploring the woods the way she liked to do with Cally. Ride the pasture gate built in the fence between earth and heaven. Pick berries. Eat from a table loaded with cookies.

Still, she takes food to her grave.

A bag of airline peanuts. A bowl of oatmeal. She leaves a pack of playing cards. An apple. What she has in her purse.

One night, sitting at her desk, she hears Frank come in. She doesn't answer when he calls and his footsteps rise on the stair treads. Suddenly, he is at her shoulder and she tells him to leave. He says no, he won't leave her. He'll be there, annoyingly returned and unwilling to depart, even though she sleeps with the lights on and talks to her daughter's ghost.

"I'm seeing things," she tells him.

She has this life, this ghost to deal with. She warns him that she's feeling hateful, that she is going up north and chopping up Richard's grave house, that if he doesn't leave her alone she will set fire to his bones. She tells him that Richard is part of her now and she knows it. His suit of anguish has become her own skin. His too-far-seeing eyes her own eyes. And the way he despises her, too, that has become her until even the small praise she gives herself rings false. She tells Frank that she sometimes thinks of herself as an unwitting host and of Richard's personality as something like kudzu or zebra mussels or wild cucumber, a weed that advances daily or a sea lamprey, so that if she wants to purge herself of him she must poison the waters. Death might work. Only she has this thought: He will be standing at the western gate. And when she gets there, having shot herself or swallowed sufficient pills, it will only be to land in Richard's arms.

"I'm not leaving," says Frank.

It is a cool afternoon. Frank tells her that she needs to drink the chamomile tea he has made for her and take a nap. He tucks her in. Sun is blasting through the window, a scalding new yellow leaf-hung light. The cries of children are like birds, far off, and as she is drifting into sleep, unexpectedly, a radiance of goodness, a strange pleasurable intensity sifts into her body and floats her just an inch above herself.

Looking down, she sees how close it is, this line between alive and dead, two countries that don't know each other. Floating above, she stares into her own face. At first she is troubled by her sad skin, the straggling hair, the pallor and ashes of her lips, the slight softening of age. Then she realizes Richard is knit so far into her that she is the only person alive who can keep him alive and keep him safe. She wonders if he understood what she tried to communicate to him in the largeness of the moment she lunged for him in the hotel hallway. It was a simple expression of amazement that all they'd felt and said, all of the huge blockbuster fights and the little stabs of ordinary difficulty, the transparent cut-glass beading of their days, the intricate way they were woven together into Cally and Deanna, all the poignant effort should come down at last to one moment.

"It isn't that simple," she says now, past anger, thinking of Deanna's voice, of the gate of the windigo's body, of Frank in the kitchen scrambling eggs and toasting bread and pouring cold juice into a pottery cup.

18

NORTHWEST TRADER BLUE

CALLY

My grandmothers prefer the burnt heart of the turkey to the white breast meat and will accept cranberry sauce made from fresh berries only. Mincemeat pie gives Zosie the runs. Pumpkin stops Mary's bowels. Wild rice must be prepared with no salt, and garlic gives both an instant cramp. Otherwise, they are to me the perfect Christmas guests. They bring out the worst in everyone, all their wicked old stories. Then sometimes, surprisingly, they elicit graciousness and hope.

Misty snow, plump clouds, occasional breaks of sun. Ice on the sidewalks slick and treacherous under the white dusting. I am just approaching from a long emergency run to a convenience mart, when I see Cecille back the Shawano delivery truck with expert care into its space across the street. Inside the truck, both grandmas are sitting high and proud on grass blue vinyl, their stunning Miss Indian America profiles on display in the watery dark of the window. The truck is white, shelves built inside a hard-shell camper. The snow is neat, a new fall outlining the shoveled walk and steps. I breathe blue air stepping down to the curb below Frank and Mama's apartment.

"Take this. Here!"

Zosie opens the door. She holds a casserole pan in her lap, a meat-fragrant oblong warming her knees through her red and white trader's-blanket coat. I take the food carefully from her, remarking on her looks as always, for she'll notice if I do not compliment and ask me later if she's slipping anywhere, if her lipstick or eyeliner is crooked, mascara smudged, hair spurting a cowlick in back. Now, reassured, she is free to concentrate her attention on the endless sparring love with Mary.

These two are exhausting together. They don't even get out of the truck—they're too busy reminding me of their complex digestive needs.

"Mary takes no salt. I eat the whites of eggs only, yolks will kill me. Plus Mary's got that sugar in her blood. She craves it, though. Try not to tempt her," Zosie whispers, "don't leave the cookie plate alone in the kitchen. She'll make a pig of herself behind your back and then she'll lapse into a coma. Me, you know I'll eat whatever."

"No you won't," I tell her. "You're picky as your whole family put together. Mama already put celery in the stuffing. You'll have to divide it out."

"She made the stuffing already? That's ours to make."

"You're late," says my mother, coming down the steps. "But it was such a relief to have the whole apartment to ourselves for once!"

She raises her eyebrows until I acknowledge the unknown significance of her statement. One, she is annoyed as usual with Cecille, who stays with them every so often, and me, here too. I did the shopping while Cecille fetched the grandmas. We left the two alone. She and Frank either made love in the quiet apartment or they finally finished doing their quarterly taxes or she studied for and passed the law boards. You never know which it is with Mama anymore—love or the bottom line. She's become distractingly like Cecille, who talks run-on about her own illicit pleasures and you think she is clinically comparing the lovemaking skills of men of different ethnic groups and faiths, and then suddenly you realize she actually means bookkeeping skills and is on to the growth of her favorite penny stocks and her blackjack winnings and her new scientific numbers methods.

"Yes," I say, "they made some giblet stuffing, but don't worry. There's raw ingredients for a whole new batch."

I cradle the pan to myself while Cecille walks around to the side door and hands down Zosie, who hits the ground in a skid and laughs. They walk up to the door, in their excitement leaving me behind with the pan, which is when it happens. I begin to slide, the pan in my hands. In a panic of self-protection I nearly jettison the casserole but at the last second with a skater's twirl, I divert the energy of the fall into my balancing feet. Cecille turns just as I regain my stance, puts her arm around my shoulder, draws me along.

In a whirl of relief, dizzy, I cling to her. And then in my thoughts there is a sudden almost frightening break.

It is as though I am on two channels all at once, flipping back and forth between us walking up the sidewalk together and me hearing an Ojibwa word, over and over, as the ice shifts, as the snow cracks, as the odd Christmas sun fades. I don't understand why at all, but the word affixes me. Adheres. It is taped to the sides of my temples and it swings from my ears so that I repeat it, under my breath, all the way up the walk.

Daashkikaa, daashkikaa, daashkikaa. I don't know what it means. Then Cecille takes over.

"Cally, your Mama ready for us all? You're a brave girl. Where's my-baby? Where's my baby? Oh, there!"

Cecille shakes both arms in the air and jumps on booted tiptoe up the rest of the walk. From just inside the door, my cousin Chook's spindly six-year-old daughter, Elena, hops and shouts. The two collide in a loud commotion and the grandmas and I barge in behind, pushing their excitement back through the entrance into warmth.

The twins are the only surviving children of a family of six who died in the flu epidemic. And they remain unconquered, too, by tuberculosis, fleas, dogbites, wormy rabbit meat, and the bitter cold of the winters of their childhood. They seem, in fact, to have relished living through the worst of what was thrown their way, even Zosie's tragic marriage. This very excitement is one of their charms. This relishing of hard luck. This gratitude for all that isn't. They are, of course, difficult to deal with in so many respects that this grateful side is what I try first to cultivate when they show up at Mama's.

Into all of our lives there comes a great uncertainty to foil us. Either, as is the case so often, we retreat in fear to guard what we know, or we shrug off those worn skins and go forward. For instance, Mary and Zosie, the two powerful twins, have the complex history of having loved the same vanished man. They march straight into the kitchen. Chook, my cousin and the nephew of my dad, is tempestuously divorced and has his daughter for the day. The place seems small not because it is, especially, or even that we have so many people, but because of the colliding histories and destinies. Loss, darkness. An inquisitive Roy energy. The air is close and hard to breathe. Then Chook grabs me around the shoulders—a boyish, cousinly sweetness to him.

He is tall and too lean with a fine brown ponytail, an inward and thoughtful face, and an almost painfully eager smile. Of us all, he looks most like Richard, only more vivid like a new inked stamp. Through the years of his drinking Richard's voice softened to a whisper, his eyes took on a filmy cast, his brown hair went a dimmer and dimmer indeterminate color. His hand grip, only, remained to the end amazingly resilient. It was difficult to wrest the bottle from his grasp. It was difficult to get anything away from him at all.

You know how they say sometimes a lot of water has passed underneath the bridge—you can be standing there a long time or standing there a short time: It just depends on how fast your life is moving underneath. I was standing there only a short time after my father killed himself. It seemed like a year had passed but it was only the flood run of the current, pulling time all along and away, so that when I got to the other side it could have been a week, it could have been a year, it could have been the rest of my life.

Mary and Zosie call the city Mishimin Odaynang, in Ojibwa Apple Town, because of the sound of the word—Minneapolis. They spend most summers on the reservation homestead, the old allotment that belonged to their mother, a farmed patch of earth and woods and mashkeeg from which they gather their teas and cut bark for baskets. Mary can fold and sew a ricing tray or a makuk without looking at her hands, but both she and Zosie prefer to construct and quill fancy boxes bearing animal icons—bear, loon, deer, and bear. They are hard-packed women with wise nimble fingers, heavy ankles, and legs that run straight down like fence posts into their shoes. Their faces have the same wide, plain soft beauty, but as twins will they have grown into their differences. Two cookie sheets, I think. Mary's is the newer sheet, relatively unmarred, while Zosie's is a pan baked on, burnt, shaded into character by her difficult marriage to the man her sister loved.

WINDIGO STORY

I

His name was Augustus Roy and he had loved the two of them as well. Asking for Zosie's hand in marriage, he told their ancient great-grandmother, Midass, that he would take care of Mary, too, should anything happen. For a woman with no teeth in her smile, her look was strangely ferocious. And a thing soon happened. The old woman died, leaving Mary alone in their old cabin, which was when Zosie and Augustus moved in with her and set their things within the back room once occupied by their grandmother. Took the creaky mattress ticking bed with sagging springs. Put themselves next to the oak bureau and the best window. Made the kitchen table a place where they all sat now, every night, Augustus with his papers and round silver eyeglasses and library books, Mary and Zosie with their trays and tins of seed beads of every color, their smoke-tanned deerhides, barbed quills.

Frank's kitchen is a long, sunny galley with three windows over the sink and a chopping board built into the side opposite the stove, underneath the cupboards of dishes. Out in the other room Cecille sets the table with Mama's holiday cloth—poinsettias and golden-eyed deer—and plates with the border of twined green leaves. She's brought her own special water glasses, sale cut glass of an elemental blue that does not match anything.

Just like her, I think, annoyed but also obscurely pleased. Everything else on the table is red, green, or gold. I've set it carefully, Mama collected the components on sales in mid-January, and here comes Cecille insisting on her blue water goblets. Yet, I've never wanted to be the sort of woman who sets a perfect table. I like to think of myself as less predictable, as more like Cecille.

She has the compact Shawano body, only slender as a dancer. She shows off her breasts and shoulders by wearing leotard tops. Her eyes are wide, deer-brown, caramel-cream, and she has grown her hair longer, thicker, wilder. She likes to streak it with henna. I am proud of her. Sometimes her earnest and pedantic air as she discusses her martial arts annoys me, but she helps me fill that empty space left by my sister, my first memory. Deanna. My other childhood mind and body. Still, I've absorbed the shape of Deanna's shoulder blade wings underneath my scratching hands and every expression on her face, and sometimes I run on her slender calves or mistake the shapes of the nails I am painting for her nails that I so often painted red.

I sugar the rhubarb Mary brought, frozen from last June. Following Frank's recipe, I spread it on the bottom of a baking pan with strawberries and then mix the butter, oatmeal, brown sugar, and crushed walnuts for the topping. Spread the sweet stuff evenly across. I slide the pan into the space below the turkey, almost ready, its small red-plastic timer button half extended. As I stand back from the oven, Mama is all of a sudden behind me, holding out a spoon to baste the tender, crackling skin. The heat fans our faces and breasts, and her hip brushes against mine. She turns. I feel the hush of her breath.

Family stories repeat themselves in patterns and waves generation to generation, across bloods and time. Once the pattern is set we go on replicating it. Here on the handle the vines and leaves of infidelities. There, a suicidal tendency, a fatal wish. On this side drinking. On the other a repression of guilt that finally explodes. I study it now in my classes, work the meaning of it out at home. From way back our destinies form. I'm trying to see the old patterns in myself and the people I love. Frank meets my mother's gaze as she turns from the stove. As though the flush of oven heat has followed her, I move carefully away. She takes his hand, walks with him into the room with the plates and the gold leaves and vines and the festive patterned cups.

"He was stubborn to the last and if you think I'm going to stop talking about him just because he killed himself, forget it."

Chook hands Frank the gravy pitcher, pretending not to hear Cecille talk about his favorite uncle, like a father to him. Chook's face is pained, he is searching for the right tone, stalling. Frank takes the pitcher in two hands and leans over to Mama.

"Give it a rest," Chook says to Cecille. She pauses, then turns away. Even with no marriageable male attention, she preens in her short skirt, folds her arms against her young breasts. Her eyes are perfectly lined and shadowed and her neck is sultry with a thick gardenia perfume. She bends her mouth into a seesaw smile of irony and does not give any satisfaction. Does not back off her subject either.

"I know. It's not in the family, maybe our culture even, to speak out, to mention these sad, hard topics. I know that. But how much better if we all accepted truth and spoke with honesty, from the heart! For instance, now Chook here is at a higher risk for suicide because his role model goes and shoots himself. I'm saying it. Because I want Chook to realize!"

"I'm not depressed," says Chook, "only temporarily deranged."

Chook stands before us gripping a salad bowl of honey-colored wood. He stares back at us and slowly, imperceptibly at first, then with increasing force he trembles, mildly jittering, from the feet up, from the ground, then with more vigor until his arms flap, his head tips to the side, his eyes roll back to the whites. The mass of dark leaves jumps. He grips the bowl even tighter until he is shaking all over in explosive starts and jerks.

"Chook! Chook!"

Mama starts forward, we all do. Chook stops. Looks around at us, blank. "Where am I?"

"Chook?"

Cecille's voice is instantly suspicious. "What was that?"

Zosie, from behind my mother, shakes the serrated knife she's using on the bread. "Get out of here, you windigo boy, or I'm gonna take this to you!"

Chook's taunting laughter rings from the next room, and Elena's excited shout, "Windigo, don't eat me. Don't!"

Mama unfolds her arms and goes back to fluffing her rice, puts the lid back on the pot, carries it in to the table with two dish towels wrapped around her hands as mitts.

"You egg him on," she says pointedly to Frank, in passing. He gives a pleased shrug. I walk out into the living room, stand in the doorway, and look at the table. The golden deer race along the borders of the tablecloth, horned, jeweled, and belled. Red candles. Ivy plants. Green paper napkins. The unexpected blue glass.

The table is long, with boards to add and with extra wings at the end. A table made for big gatherings and doings. It's a good thing, because the topics of conversation at the table tend to polarize us all. Especially the things my grandmas say. Past a certain age the Roy and Shawano women believe that they have earned the right to talk about sex, birth, blood, the size and shape of men's equipment, the state of their own, even at the Christmas dinner table. Frank never knew what he was in for, with these mothers. He made the table himself, planed and joined like a long prayer, hand-sanded and finished with coat after coat of clear varnish until the surface was wheat-grained and butter smooth. He bought Rozin a long wildly treed candelabra. The branches are different animals. A fish. An otter. A bear. Now, as I light the candles, the radiance from each pottery creature sputters but the flames hold true.

"There should be no salt on this table!" cries Grandma Mary. "In the early days we had no salt. We didn't know of it. We had no taste for it."

"Now look at us," says Zosie, whose high blood pressure medication keeps her dizzily alert.

"I can eat as much salt as I want—" This is to be the only statement I will even start.

"If you're pregnant—"

"I'm not."

"Eat the head of a skunk," advises Mary. "In the old days, that was the way to make sure the baby's head would be a little head, easy to push."

"Did you two have morning sickness with Rozin?" Chook with his tongue in his cheek asks both Mary and Zosie. His mouth stitches together in anxious amusement. "That skunk head might not sit too well."

Mary continues on with implacable deliberation.

"I knew a woman with that morning sickness. She ended up in labor for two weeks!"

Helping herself to mashed potatoes, Zosie takes up the theme in a darkly relishing tone of voice. "The pain was constant, too, hard labor for a total of twenty-four times fourteen hours. Plus, all the while she screamed. No, it was more a yodel. So pitiful. And people heard her—

this was before they set up the soundproof room in the hospital."

"A big baby?" Mary purses her lips in knowing fashion.

"They couldn't stitch her back together, yet she somehow lived."

"Only to die the next time, probably."

Zosie shrugs.

"On that note," says Chook, his face sunk and paled, his voice catching, "shall we toast an easy labor and healthy outcome? Toast!"

"I'm not pregnant," I say uselessly. "I don't even have a boyfriend."

But Chook desperately raises his mug of apple cider and downs it like a pirate tossing back hot grog. Still, the grandmas are not finished.

"That's a bad way to go. And they had to bury the baby in a little shoe box. Me, when I go," brags Zosie with a long slow wave of her hand across the heaping plate, "you won't have to take up a collection. My funeral is all paid up."

"Whose isn't?" Mary shrugs her sister's boast down. "Those vultures. They come around the reservation with those sales handouts . . . "

"Brochures."

"Catalogs. They make the rounds and you sit paging through those pictures of the caskets . . . "

"Mine!" Zosie says loudly. "Mine is frosted, I tell you, frosted!"

"Oh, that sure is wonderful." Mary rolls her eyes. "Like a cake."

"Please," says Chook, "do we have to—"

"If you must know," Mary loudly interposes.

"We don't need to know," says Chook.

But she ignores him. "I am paid up, too, with money from my checks. I put a small amount away each month. I got the cardinals, red cardinals painted on my casket and it's made of real oak, not cheap pine board. A cheerful woodsy scene on front. Spared no amount of big expense! I even got the dinner paid for and no jelly and no peanut butter—oh you bet, no commodity funeral dinner for me!"

"Ticking. Mattress ticking. Railroad cloth. I like that on the inside of a casket, though," Zosie reflects.

"Homey-looking."

"Like you were really going to sleep or something. And then the sheets."

"Mine are satin."

"Don't you think," Mama breaks in again from her corner place, where she's filled and refilled her plate, picking through her food with furious dispatch, "if you're going to spend for satin sheets you could at least get enjoyment out of them in life?"

"You would," says Zosie sternly, but her attempt at embarrassing my mother falls flat, for Mama just nods and as though struck by some ecstatic thought smiles openly and suddenly at Frank, right across the table. Everyone can see her and notice that smile, too, which is the sort of curious and gloating smile a teenage girl turns on the first boy she's shown her breasts to in a parking lot. Returning her look, Frank's face is grave and intent. Their look holds, and then, with quiet attention, tenderly, he dips some small morsel of dark meat into the scarlet of cranberries. Placing the tart, reddened flesh into his mouth, he casts his eyes down and chews.

"I suppose that brings us back to the topic of suicide once more."

Cecille, again. She's working all this out, I know, but I despair at her insistence that we talk about it in a healthy way.

"Cecille, that does not necessarily bring us back to suicide." I use my most moderate voice, twisting the words only slightly.

Frank, more direct, tries to plant a drumstick in her mouth. She bats his hand away.

"Turn up the volume on the radio!"

Nothing stops Cecille, though. She keeps talking and analyzing, fills her plate three or four times, and devours her food with the slow assurance of a woman of bottomless depth.

"Prosecute, persecute, what's the difference," she says. "They found where he dumped toxic waste way back when. Took the payoff. Used the money."

"But only for purposes that directly related to the tribe."

"Like a beachfront lake cabin."

Cecille speaks reproachfully. "That was a long, long time ago. Before he slid into the gutter. We all know it was where he held his meetings. His most high-level meetings."

"High is the operative word there," says Chook. "They used to go out and get drunk in the, quote, tribal motorboat. Decide things. Bring back a stringer of crappies."

Chook speaks lightly, but everyone knows he took Richard's long fall from grace and eventual death so hard that he himself got drunk and sped off in the tribal motorboat, spinning it in circles, and his wife had sat onshore watching, watching, until he ran out of gas and paddled back to the cabin still weeping.

"The men fish," says Zosie very quietly. "The women end up cleaning the damn things."

"Women should be in charge. That would be better," says Cecille. "Every tribe with a woman in charge is more stable. That should make the rest of us think to let the mothers run things!"

"Interesting to see," says Zosie, "how few crooked women in office."

"Just wait. Once we're equal, we will be equal enough to steal."

Grandma Mary gathers up her words and speaks forcefully, as though at an elders' conference: "But wait. Look. How many fewer women in prison? I say women have better morals, or just less of that male hormone. As a species, we're less apt to commit a crime."

"Women aren't a species, Grandma Mary, we're a gender," says Cecille.

"No," says Zosie. "My sister is right. Women are a separate species."

"I agree with that statement," says Frank.

"Politics. Politics."

"That's all we ever talk at the table and all we ever will." Chook hands himself the bowl of potatoes. "It's about time I get used to it, run for some office. But my heart's not in it. I'm the artistic type, I think." He looks slyly at Cecille and she makes a face at him.

"You can't draw a straight line."

"You can't walk one."

"Oh, ho, weee, Chook's getting out his BB gun."

"Chook's verbal slingshot."

"I'd like another helping of those Juneberries, please," says Frank to my mother. Her hand trembles on the lip of the plate as she passes him the bowl of berries, so hard the spoon rattles.

"Rozin's in love," Chook notices. "Rozin is bashful with Frank." All of a sudden, we notice that is still true.

WINDIGO STORY

II

Nights, winter nights, northern and slow. The lamp shone a peach golden circle at the table where Mary and Zosie arranged their saucers of beads—white for the background, Czech cut glass, delicate size 13, tiny loops of old greasy yellows and blues, a hank of mauves, a collection of glittering heart reds. Mary worked on moccasins already bought and half paid for by a summer-visiting chimookoman lady who would get them in the mail. While she worked across from Zosie, her sister's husband sat next to her. She breathed in the tobacco flavor of his hard skin, his once-a-week cigar, the very slight undertone of whiskey—Augustus was not a drunk but now and then tolerated a shot—and his clean sweat, for he bathed in the lake each morning, even breaking the ice sheaves for weeks once November came around. He had an old-time Indian's cleanly habits. And wore suspenders. But he was nonetheless an educated man and aware of the world. Read aloud to them from the newspapers. His low, vibrant voice sank down the front of Mary's dress. They were furtive. They hid their secret meetings. It was delicious.

Sitting across from each other at the table every night, the sisters beaded expertly, swiftly. Protected by his books and pens and envelopes and bills, Augustus couldn't know that it was as though the two sisters had licked, threaded, and waxed either end of a long piece of thread and began to sew with it, adding to their own peculiar pattern bead by bead until one night, after some involuntary response between Mary and Augustus, the thread pulled taut, the space shortened, Zosie and Mary's needles halted, and they looked each other in the eye.

"Give me the wishbone," orders Mary, "that goes to Elena. That wishbone should go to a little girl."

"I don't want it," says Elena.

"We still have the Thanksgiving bone," Chook says, "drying on the windowsill over the sink."

"Give it to Cecille," says Elena, who is sitting in the lap of her auntie.

"That custom," says Frank Shawano suddenly. "Where does it come from, I wonder?"

"From Ireland, where you fight over everything," says Zosie, referring to the Shawano mixture of bloods. "Even skinny little chicken bones."

Mary has removed the slender forked bone from the breast meat already and stripped it clean, handing it to Elena, who gives it back to Grandma Mary and has the presence of mind to say, "Share it." Pointing at Zosie. Mary holds out the wishbone, unwilling, and Zosie touches it. The bone is cool and faintly slippery in her fingers. The tiny strips of meat cling to it tenaciously. Looking into each other's brown, sorrowful eyes they seem lost, unguarded. The bone is fragile between them. They know from childhood that to break a wishbone to your advantage you must hold your thumb higher than that of your opponent, your sister.

And so Zosie does.

Now the men are talking. They have outlasted the women's hold on the conversation and they are talking about their cars. They are discussing the insides of their cars the way women discuss their own insides. Prelabor. Post-labor. Just the same except instead of doctors the men talk about their mechanics. Opinions, prognoses, prescriptions, and probabilities are exchanged as we clear the table for pie and rhubarb crisp. Everyone rambles to a task to let their dinner settle. Dishes clatter. Coffee scents the air. The house is too warm, though, so I decide to cool myself at the back door. I step out onto the tiny porch and stare from the steps out at the frozen gray yard and garage.

There are times in the city, rare times, when the baffle of sound parts. Through it a transitory silence rides. No cars. No planes' roar. No buses or distant traffic. No spatter of television noise, even people talking. Then just as you define the moment by what it is, not by the absence of all it isn't, someone laughs, a car door slams, there is a screech of tires, and it is gone, your moment of baseless peace.

The noise that brings me back is the muted plastic thump of a city garbage dumpster and then crisp, slow steps. Mama and Frank round the corner of the garage but they don't notice me because their eyes rest upon each other. I can see my mother's warm three-quarters profile as she gazes seriously up into her husband's face. He is turned from me, but although I cannot view his expression I know it. They are staring at each other not with moon-glow or sitcom eyes, not stupidly or foolishly, but with the true and sad authority of mortal love. I know it, recognize it, even though I've never had it. As they turn away and walk back to the alley, finding with a gentle start that Mama has forgotten to ditch the parcel of bones I handed her fifteen minutes ago, they have no idea I am a witness. They haven't seen me at all.

"I will not be hushed! I will not be hushed!"

Cecille at the table with the coffee and the pies. I know the time has arrived when either Frank or one of the grandmas or maybe Chook has challenged the trajectory of her bloodthirsty conversation. It is my usual task to step in and deflect, but as I sit down a golden veil drops before my eyes and I seem in my stupor isolated, as though I still stand in that oddment of the great inhuman quiet that existed here before the city. Silence. In it, what I see and know. Deep in concentration, I simply let Cecille go on saying what she's always wanted to say to the grandmas Zosie and Mary.

"You two stop. Stop right now! You purse-lips, stop looking at Frank and Rozin like you never had love thoughts! Of all people, you two, and Augustus Roy. What happened to him? *What did you do?*"

WINDIGO STORY

III

A woman used to deception knows how to hide her stitches. Zosie's beadwork was tight and true. No visible beginning or end to the design. Impossible to find the starting knot, the final tie. Unseeable the place where the needle went in or out. Her wild leaf or prairie rose or vines twisting skeletal on black velvet were done with invisible thread. She used those threads, too, on Mary and Augustus Roy. The two never saw the stitch work that kept them sewed to her side. They never saw the fabric upon which their passion was marked out in chalk. Or the inlay, one bead to the next, the remarkable interpenetration of colors.

For one thing, after she learned about those two, Zosie made Augustus Roy sleep alone in their parents' bed. Went back to the bed she'd shared all her life with her sister. Slept there. Made Mary sneak away. Watched the wall, eyes open, while the two were next door. Back then, the twins were still so much alike that no one could tell them apart except to check on the whirlwinds at the crown of their heads. One swirled to the left, the other swirled to the right.

Augustus had fallen in love with the enigma of his wife's duplication. The confusion of sameness between the twins made him tremble like an animal caught in a field of tension. Sitting at the table, he'd feel the current of their likeness. Things even they did not notice. Mary pricked herself. Zosie muttered *owah*! Zosie started a legging and Mary without even trying to copy constructed another of an identical design.

They got hungry at exactly the same time, ate precisely the same amount of the same food. Started humming one tune suddenly, no sign having passed between them.

When making love, there was barely anything one did differently from the other. He could tell them apart only with the greatest difficulty, even in their nakedness beneath his hands, but this exploration, rather than daunting, excited him. He could always make certain which was which by touching the whirlwinds at the crowns of their heads—that is, until suddenly it seemed they started combing their hair new ways. This way, that. Messing with his one sure proof.

In truth, the twins had simply begun taking turns with Augustus Roy. After the first flush of secrecy, Mary missed the communion of twinship and in a fit of resentment at Augustus for parting them, she told Zosie everything. They were together in their childhood bed, holding hands as they talked. Zosie nodded very slowly into the darkness and said she already knew. She had been hiding her knots for some time. By the next morning she saw exactly the course of her pattern. The twins worked calmly together in the kitchen. Augustus was stacking the wood he'd chopped. By the time he blew back through the door the configuration had changed. He noticed nothing. Only, the confusion between the two that so attracted him at first became a series of increasingly fine distinctions.

After they messed up the hair on their whirlwinds he searched and searched for another way to identify them. For a time, as they beaded, he surreptitiously examined their fingers. Curled around the needles, each nail just that slightest bit different from the next, he marked out the degree of growth, fixed in his mind a nick or a tatter. At night, he touched their fingers first and for a time was assured in that way of sighing the correct name into the proper twin's ear. For Zosie had always demanded her name, and now Mary did as well. And if he were to give the wrong name to Zosie she would know the truth immediately. And if he were to ask her name, she would also know. And if he were to believe her when she teasingly said she was her twin, his perfidy would stand revealed. One day he went so far as to buy, for Zosie, a thing she had always wanted. A golden wedding band. A marker. When she saw it, her face shaded. She gazed full into his stare until his flickered. She thanked him. Put the band on her finger. Slept with him for one night with it on. Then never wore the ring again.

He was driven to noticing the tiniest things. Became a devotee of nicks and scratches. Sometimes, in his desperation, he tried placing a mark on one of them himself.

You could say he started what happened next.

The accident occurred as a stroke of luck. Augustus knocked a hot fry pan over and grease splattered Zosie's wrist. For several weeks Augustus had a certain sign of Zosie's identity and this quieted him. He even gained a few pounds, for the anxiety had thinned him terribly. But Zosie's scar faded, finally disappeared, and when he could no longer find the mark he tipped the hot fry pan over once again, this time onto Mary, whose painfully burned foot had to be bandaged and unbandaged twice a day. Yet in time, she, too, recovered and her skin stayed unmarred.

How to leave a more permanent mark? He took a knife one day. Cutting a rope, he sliced through the air and nearly took off the tip of Mary's right ear. She ducked in time, but it gave him an idea and that night when Zosie came to him he worked himself into a heat and climaxed with the lobe of her ear between his teeth.

"So what did you do with him? Who took the first bite? I've heard it. Heard it all."

Cecille waves the tines of her fork side to side at the sisters. "They say, after you two started wearing the same kind of dresses, it was obvious. Something was strange, wrong. You never did that before. You were always determined to dress different from each other. To the people, it was clear what you were doing to Augustus. I can see the poor man sitting between you two, never knowing who was who while you sewed him to the sides of his chair, to your beds, to your hearts, fixed him in the science of your design! He disappeared, foul play, but the body was never discovered. What did you do? Boil him? Eat him? Grind up his bones to sprinkle on your rhubarb plants? What? Who took the first bite?"

Cecille slumps into her chair now and digs into her pie, breathless with triumph at the conclusion of her diatribe. Watching her eat, a subterranean thought surfaces, an odd thought, a vision almost of Cecille as my mother's twin, of my mother herself, a five-year-old holding in her arms her dead sister and both mourning and absorbing her life, thereby explaining some of the fearless, headstrong double powers she displays. The twins take in her accusations with looks of almost admiring interior humor, and I think it is Mary who whispers, turning to speak two words into her sister's mutilated ear, "He did." When they attend to the table, the rest of us watching in wary dismay, they take on an aura of demure excitement. They do not react to Cecille, or if so, it is only to spoon the dark juices of the pies into their mouths, eat daintily, and smile their slightly windigo smiles.

Everyone but me and Auntie Klaus is in the living room. I'm doing dishes, hands deep in soapy hot water, mind traveling. She's sitting in the shadowy corner looking at nothing in particular. Daashkikaa. Daashkikaa, I keep thinking. I place an invisible wall around us and I take comfort from the clean scent of dish soap and the steam that fogs the windows. Still, I am troubled. I see my father's bloody forehead as he lies in the hallway; his tears come up under my hands. I see Augustus at the end of the long isosceles of steel in my grandmothers' kitchen drawer. The one they use for boning chicken. Raw bites score his neck. I see Cecille talking fast, her lips moving, running, moving, her tongue grabbing words from the air and throwing them with invisible hands into a current that flows everywhere. Love pulls us, implacable, from under the skin, I see that. Auntie Klaus sits quiet against the wall. I throw a question over my shoulder, knowing she won't answer—Is it an old thing or a new thing? Is every love an ancient love born from that ancestral base of our mute brains? Is every love like the love I see within m[illegible] and Frank Shawano's faces? You have been to the other side of the earth, Sweetheart Calico. There, you have seen my namesake. So tell me. Tell me.

Grandma Zosie enters the room grumbling for cake. Knowing her habit, her love of sweets, I am already pouring her a coffee, already cutting into a twelve-layer chocolate raspberry cake that Frank has nearly pulled off his ponytail in frustration to get right, before she sits down at the table. I pour myself a coffee, too, and I pour one for Sweetheart Calico.

Grandma looks at me quizzically, with a slow and doggy quiet of regard that I find unsettling. I take a burning sip of hot coffee.

"Grandma," I say, "Daashkikaa. What does it mean?"

"Cracked apart," she says, looking at me strangely. "How do you know that old name?"

"It came into my head."

All of a sudden, she shows great interest. "Magizha it is you," she says, "who gets the names."

"What do you mean?" I ask.

"Do they come to you? Do they sit in your mind? Do they come in dreams? Perhaps you are the namer. Keep on listening."

I remain still, but there is only the sound of her chewing.

"I'm disappointed in my peers," she says after a while, teeth gritted in disgust.

"How come?" I ask.

"They do nothing."

"You mean they're lazy?"

"No, more like chicken. Afraid to be alive. There was this science tank at school," she goes on, "I remember it from the old days. My boarding school. I had a teacher who showed me that down on the bottom there was a fish that ate the ka-ka. Yesterday, my girl, you know I had this awful thought—us Indians are turning into the bottom-feeders of white culture. Too much television sports. Eating all the fake puffed-up flavors and watching all the cranked-up images and out of our mouth no real humor only laugh tracks." She shakes her head.

Then she takes a big bite of unhealthy raspberry chocolate sugar cake, chews it, and enjoys the taste. Her smile appears, and it is like a sunny moment of startling peace. Right in that sunny light, then, I ask her.

"Which of you twins is my grandmother?"

"The one you most take after."

Her answer is immediate and I sigh, knowing I will not get any farther than that.

"About my name, then?"

"What about it?" she answers.

"Where is it from? Who? Where did you get it?"

In answer, she puts down her fork. Folds her hands on top of her little old lady belly, cocks her head sideways, and stares at Sweetheart Calico, then at me. Thinking. Considering. Breathing. Baiting. Like a dog deciding whom to trust.

"Okay," she says.

But she eats her cake first, every crumb. Licks her fork clean. Folds her napkin. Picks her teeth. Polishes her glasses. Just when she starts plucking balls of fluff from her sleeves, causing me to resist jumping out of my chair to scream, she begins.

"There are these beads I love," she starts. "Deep ones, made of special glass. Czech beads called northwest trader blue. In them, you see the depth of the spirit life. See sky as through a hole in your body. Water. Life. See into the skin of the coming world."

I nod, let a long breath out, impatient to see how this bead talk connects with my name.

"You just wait," she says, "I'm getting it all fixed in my mind. My brain is soaking up the sugar. I have to let the cells energize before I go on telling you."

So we wait, drinking our coffee together, until she draws a deep breath and continues.

"When I was a child," says Zosie Roy, "I wanted beads of that northwest trader blue, and I would do anything to get them. I first glimpsed this blue on the breast of a Pembina woman passing swiftly. I saw her hand rise to the beads and then touch the blue reflection on her throat. Ever after, I knew I must have that certain blueness which was like no other blue. I scored my fingers making quill baskets and when they were finished I went to the trader and sold them. I looked behind his glass and wood counter at the hanks of beads hanging there on nails. I saw beads the ripe silk red of prairie roses. Silver beads, black, cut-glass white. Beads the tan of pony hide and green, every green there is on earth. There were blues there, sky blue and water blue, the blue of the eyes of those people we called the Agongos, Swedes, the gopher people, because they love to dig dirt. The blue of old pants and the blue of mean thoughts. The blue of simple distant heat rising off the end of a road. I put my fingers to the blue and I touched the blue. I searched for the blue of those beads I had seen on the Pembina woman, but that blue was different from all the other blues on earth. Disappointed at the trader's cache, I spent my money on sweet candy. There would come a time I would see the beads I needed, but I already knew they could not be bought."

Grandma Zosie stares at me, looking through me, figuring.

"During my motherhood, when I was rocking or nursing my baby," she went on, softly, knowing what she revealed, "I had a lot of time to think about this blueness. I could see it before me, how it appeared and disappeared, the blue at the base of a flame, the blue in a fading line when I shut my eyes, the blue in one moment at the edge of the sky at dusk. There. Gone. That blue of my beads, I understood, was the blueness of time. Perhaps you don't know that time has a color. You've seen that color but you were not watching, you were not aware. Time is blue. Or time is the blue in things. I came to understand that my search for the blueness called northwest trader blue was the search to hold time.

"Only twice in my life did I see that blue altogether clear. I saw that blue when my daughters were born—as their lives emerged from my life, that color flooded my mind. The other time, my girl, was the day I found your sister's name. Or dreamed it. Or gambled for it. Here's how it happened.

OTHER SIDE OF THE EARTH

I was a new mother-to-be, pregnant. Picking berries, I felt sleepy and lay on the ground. It was so soft underneath the tree, the grass long and fine as hair. I put down my bucket to rest and curled in the comfort. While sleeping, I saw the Pembina again—she came to me. I saw her as a tiny speck first, then bigger and bigger until she was down the road and standing right in front of me. Had those beads on. Still hanging from around her neck. They were made of that same blue I have described to you and I still wanted them with all my heart.

"Will you gamble for them?" the Pembina asked me, gently.

I told her that I wanted those beads but had nothing I could use to put down. No money. No jewelry. Just berries. She took Sioux marked plum pits out of her pocket, smiled, and right there in the road we sat down together to gamble.

"You have your life," she said gently, "and ones inside of you as well. Would you bet me three lives in return for my blue beads?"

I didn't even think twice but answered her yes—can you believe that? Three lives for that blueness. That madness. I bet easily. And then we started playing the game, throwing down the plum stones and gathering them up in our hands, taking our turn after turn until the sweat broke out on my forehead. I beat her the first of three games. She took the second. I took the third and gestured at her beads. Slow, careful, she lifted the strand over her neck and then she handed them over, looking into my eyes with a sharp humor that disturbed me.

"Now," she said, "you have the only possession important to me. Now you have my beads called northwest trader blue. The only other thing I own of value are my names, Other Side of the Earth, Blue Prairie Woman before that. You have put your life up. I'll put my names. Let us gamble again to see who keeps the beads."

"No," I said. "I've waited too long for these. Now that I've got them, why risk them?"

She gazed at me with her still, sad eyes, touched her quiet fingers to the back of my hand, and carefully explained.

"Our spirit names, they are like hand-me-downs which have once fit other owners. They still bear the marks and puckers. The shape of the other life."

I waited. "Why should I take the chance?" I asked, stubborn. "So what?"

"The name goes with the beads, you see," she said, "because without the name those beads will kill you."

"Of what?"

"Longing."

Which did not frighten me.

"I have already died of that," I said slowly, thinking of the nights and mornings I woke wishing for Augustus, for the light in his arms, for that blue. "I'm not afraid."

And so, in my lack of fear, I played her another game and yet another. That is how I won her names from her. Other Side of the Earth. Deanna's name. I went where Deanna's name brought me. Came back with more. And so, my girl, that was my naming dream. That is the name I gave to your sister. The other name I saved for you is a stubborn and eraseless long-lasting name. One that won't disappear.

I wanted her to say it, the old name, the original.

"Blue Prairie Woman." I heard, but I wasn't satisfied.

"And the beads?"

I am surprised to hear the sharpness in my voice. I haven't even thanked her, yet already the need is on me. I have got to know what the necklace of beads looks like, that blue. I can imagine it at the edge of my vision. Like a mist, like an essence, a blueness that is a hook of feeling in the heart.

"The beads." Zosie's whole face wrinkles, her thin lips slowly spread in an innocent smile. "Already, you want them, I know. But you will have to trade for them with their owner, your uncle's wife, Sweetheart Calico."

Who stands behind me, her gaze on my back like a cape of quills.

I have always been afraid of her. She is not just any woman. She is something created out there where the distances turn words to air and thoughts to stone. The blue beads, now, she wiggles the first from the broken place in her smile and then she pulls bead after strung bead from her dark mouth out into the open space between us. They gleam off her wrist, blueness of an unnatural dusk. That's where she was keeping them all of this time, I understand. Beneath her tongue. No wonder she was silent. And sure enough, as she holds them forward to barter, now, she speaks. Her voice is lilting and flutelike on the vowels and sibilant between the jag ends of her teeth.

"Let me go."

She offers me their blue sentence in exchange.

I take the beads, and then I walk out the bakery shop door with her, into the city. I don't know where we'll end up or where she wants to go. We walk up the streets and back. As we go, sitting on the park benches, rambling to the river, she never stops her long ramble but keeps on talking until my brain spins. All the words she's stored up. The impressions. The things that amazed her. What she's seen. She says:

"They're selling Christ's coffin at Pier 1. I had a vision of it, deep in the heart of the night, a fragile loaded vision like old, long-buried socks. It was a basket coffin with a woven lid. And it was made of raw teak strips deep in a third world jungle and made of sharp bamboo by children in China in a stinking backwater polluted by coal fumes and in Borneo from delicate and ancient barks of trees that never will again grow on earth and it was made by young virgins and their hands are scabbed raw and bleeding so an American has to hose those coffins down when they are shipped over here before they are displayed and he, Christ, was short, it appears, so the coffins are short, too, and just in time for Christmas!

"Or should it be Easter with hand-painted Easter chairs and spongy ass pillows and pastel eggs? I'm drowning in stuff here in Gakahbekong. In so many acres of fruit. In warehouse upon warehouse of tools, Sheetrock nails, air conditioners, and implements of every type and domestic and imported fabrics, and in the supermarkets and fish from the seven seas and slabs of fat-marbled flesh of warm-eyed cows who love and nuzzle their young. And Klaus, and Klaus. I'm drowning in Klaus."

And we keep on walking, walking north, past the river, where the lost always congregate. It is in the district where urban gardeners can claim land and farm a patch of cindery, glass-studded, nail-rich, irony dirt. Still listening as she raves on, I fall in and out of sleep until morning comes on at last, weary as old coins.

She is gone when I awake.

Before the first birds, then fresh as the light grows strong from inside my tent of sumac, I hear the voices of the Hmong grandmas outside and the rustle of their steps and clothes, their shuffling melody in dirt and then the smaller sounds of their hands among the vines and the leaves. I hear the snapping of stems, the dry little smack of rooted weeds pulled from dirt. I turn over and I watch them so comfortable and easy in what they do, poised in loose black and mud-brown clothes, intent, nodding back and forth so I know in their language they are teasing and talking grandma talk, of children and their accomplishments. Every time their hands go to the dirt, I feel better. More peaceful with each movement they make in their cages of tomatoes, at their bean rows, their eggplants and chilies and the unfurnished life. As they move and as the sun grows hot on the dirt, so the scent of it rises, same even in the city, that dirt smell, I know they are digging for me. This feeling comes up in me of how much and what I miss, my birth holder, indis mashkimodenz, little turtle connecting me back to my mother, her mother, all the mothers before her who dug in the dirt.

One grandma calls out hau! laughing, excited, and I know that part of my life where I have to wander and pray is done. When they did their fasting in the old days they saw their people's whole future. My Mama, she once blackened her face with charcoal around when she was my age. She went out in the woods for six days. There, she had a vision of a huge thing, strange, inconceivable. All her life she told me she wondered what it was. It came out of the sky, pierced far into the ground, seethed and trembled. I see this: I was sent here to understand and to report. What she saw was the shape of the world itself. Rising in a trance and eroding downward and destroying what it is. Moment through moment until the end of time if ever there is an end to this. Gakahbekong. That's what she saw. Gakahbekong. The city. Where we are scattered like beads off a necklace and put back together in new patterns, new strings.

19

Sweetheart Calico

A tiny boat with a windup rubber-band propeller—that's what the first sensations of her freedom are like. She feels the whir of that little rubber band undoing. Then the band slowly winds tighter. It clenches at the base of her stomach. Lets go. She breathes and waits with her eyes shut. Through the tight cracks of glass, the little panes of her window, the sun pours in with a serene warmth. The light sinks through her like warm honey, a vibrating sensuousness, as of tiny bees hiving in her veins. A swarm of ecstasy pulls her deeper, gently and in waves, into the softness, until she is curved against a great fur belly of mothering sunlight.

There, she feels the world breathing, the air, the turning order. It is all alive, arrayed carefully around her, and she is safe in the hollow of the mattress. When she was nine years old, a car going seventy miles an hour grazed her, and she was flung clear, landing just before barbed wire on the edge of a horse pasture. She can't remember getting there. Flying or tossed. What she does remember is the comforting smell of horses—their grassy dung, sweat, and dust.

There is a lull and the sun is sucked behind a cloud so the gray light intrudes. How did he bind her, and leave no mark? How did he take away her freedom, when her sense of it was so strong? It was so powerful, her traverse of boundless space. Time is endless in the heart, where sky meets earth. Always, in his eyes, that ungated fence. Always, in hers, that silence.

20

Windigo Dog

So there was this big canine rabies outbreak in the state of Minnesota. Here's what happened. The state sent three dogcatchers to work day and night rounding up the dogs. The first dogcatcher was from a crack Norwegian dog-catching school, the second was Swedish, the third was an Indian dogcatcher. Each had a truck. They traveled together in a squad. They worked hard all morning and by noon each of the dog-catchers had a pretty-fair-sized truck full of dogs. About then, they were getting hungry, so they chained up the back of the trucks. But they forgot to lock the doors themselves, see, so by pushing and wiggling the dogs could open the doors behind the loose chain just enough to squeeze out, carefully, one at a time.

When the dogcatchers came back from lunch, then, first thing they looked into the back of their trucks. The crack Norwegian dogcatcher's truck was totally empty and so was the Swedish truck. But the Ojibwa dogcatcher's truck, though unlatched the same and only chained, was still full of dogs.

"This is something, though," said the Swede and Norwegian to the Ojibwa. "How do you account for the fact all our dogs are gone and yours are still there?"

"Oh," said the Ojibwa, "mine are Indian dogs. Wherever they are, that's their rez. Every time one of them tries to sneak off, the others pull him back."

"I don't like that joke," said Klaus. "My rez is very special to me. It is my place of authority."

"Geget, you filthy piece of guts," said the Windigo Dog. "I like it there, too. Don't get spiritual on me."

"Why do you like it?" asked Klaus. "You have no spirituality whatsoever. What's there for you?"

"On the rez," said the windigo, "the ladies, they roam. Bye now. Gotta maaj."

"Good riddance." Klaus turned over and slept.

While he was sleeping he remembered that he was really someone else with a life and a toothbrush and a paycheck. He lived a normal day in his sleep, rising in the morning to do a hundred crunches and fifty push-ups, then pouring himself a bowl of cereal before he showered. That felt good! Next, he was shaving, just those few whiskers on the blunt end of his chin. He was walking away from his actual house. Locking his door. Getting into his car.

Car! Once upon a time far away and long ago. These things had been his. He had earned them with work and money. His mouth watered. Coins and bills. He remembered the solid pack of his wallet in his left jeans pocket. He was left-handed, a lefty. What did that matter now? He was totally ambidextrous with the bottle.

Klaus was sleeping with his head sticking out of the bushes in the park, and he was wearing a green baseball cap. A young black man wearing thick earphones and chewing a piece of bread-tie plastic whipped around the bushes, expertly mowing grass for the city park system. He rode the mower with sloppy assurance—the big red machine itself encouraged reckless driving with its fat cushy seat and wide cramping whine of protest. That's what his lawn mower was—one long scream of protest—the world of grass was never meant to be shortened to a carpet so that the outdoors is like one big wall-to-wall room. The young man rounded the corner and ran over Klaus's head.

There was no warning, of course. No chance to prepare himself in his dream for getting his head run over by a lawn mower. Only the jagged ear-splitting raucous blade shrieks, only the helmet of metallic motor sound, only the fact, lucky Klaus, that a powerful stray dog bolted toward the machine and got hit, slammed into the air. Bounced off a tree and vanished. The impact jarred the machine to a giant skip so that the accident left no more than a neat bloody crease down the exact middle of Klaus's face.

Seemed to Klaus that he had dreamed himself a drum struck violently and rapidly. In his dream, his drum face wore the sacred center stripe. Klaus blinked up into the sky. Sun shot and pearly. Leaves gleaming and tossing. His ears were suddenly unpacked of cotton and his thoughts ran pure between his temples, open and sparkling. In the extraordinary light Klaus made a thousand decisions. Two of them mattered. Number one, he would finally stop. Just stop. And he knew, the way he had known so many times before, right down to his aching big toe, center of his soul, that he was done drinking. He could do that.

The other of his important decisions was not so consciously settled. It was just that he knew, in vague detail but with overriding certainty, the next thing to do.

Bring her back. Bring her back to us, you fool.

Getting sober. Letting her go. The idea of it hurt so bad he momentarily wished that the lawn mower had struck him full on, taken off his head, his thoughts.

21

Sweetheart Calico

Klaus folded and unfolded the strip of cloth that was his headband, traced the small buds and sprigs of pink unbudding roses and white roses, the sweetheart calico. Sweat and dirt and drunken sleeps, railroad bed, underpass and overpass, dust of the inner-city volleyball courts and frozen snirt and river water were all pressed into the piece of cloth that held the story of his miserableness and which was still—though grit scored, dirt changed, and sun faded—tensile, woven of the same toughness as the old longing.

We all have it in us. Or if we don't, we're half dead or lucky. It is longing makes us do the things that we should not. Even longing for the good, for love.

Longing is the bliss of thieves that getting kills.

Klaus wrapped the strip of calico around his wrist like a bandage and he waited, as he had waited near the church parking lot for over a week, until he became part of the scenery, a tree or anyway a stump. It looked to him, because the sun was out shining, that he was waiting for something to happen that would not happen. And then, just as he grew bitter and upset and his stomach set itself on fire, he saw her.

Red flashed. A curtain dropped away. She walked across the old carpet of the bedroom but it was downtown concrete. His wife, his *we'ew*, his Blue Fairy, his torture, his merwoman, mercy and love. She was careful, walking along very slow and hesitant, waiting for lights to change before she crossed, reaching for her own hand. Her dark fall of hair hung tatty and lifeless. She breathed in clear air and blew smoke out her nose, mouth, eyes, ears. Looking over her shoulder at him, sensing his presence, her eyes were no longer living agates but had turned to the dead gray underfoot.

Klaus stepped from the alleyway.

"Boozhoo," he said to her.

She started nervously, but then shrugged, lighted a cigarette from off the one she was smoking already, and didn't run away. Quietly, she looked at him, through and through, weary. His dear love's face was thin and tight, the bones still showing pure and stark, pressing just the right places under her skin. How he used to trace them was still locked in his hands, and his fingers began to move across the rips in his T-shirt.

She stepped closer and he reached out and took her hand. He held her long-fingered delicate hand in his own. Then, pulling the band around their wrists, he tied her hand to his hand gently with the sweetheart calico. He had no plan to do this either. No plan for what happened next, but it was simple. They started out. Started walking.

North and west, along the river until the herringbone brick path with decorative plantings became a common sidewalk and then turned to tar black as licorice at first and then lighter, lighter, showing stones in the aggregate and thinning, rubbing out, erasing, absorbed back slowly into the earth and then the earth itself under their feet, a worn path for joggers and for bicyclists, clear at first and then less so, grassier, fainter, grown over, traversing backyards or parkland or back lots of tire stores or warehouses and a few developments, wild mustard, polleny green-gold, a farm, then another one farther along and then far into the day, but still, all of a sudden undergrowth so thick along the banks they could not enter.

They turned from the water flowing off the edge of the world and started walking due west.

They walked all evening, rested. Fell asleep in a grassy old yard just beside an abandoned shed that still sheltered a hulk of metal that once was a car. Against the shed, still chained to the door, there was a cracked leather collar. Strung through it bones of a dog vertebrae. Scattered beside more bones and baked hide.

Kept walking. Next morning, kept walking. Drank from a clean pothole lake and walked on until, over a slight rise, the sky suddenly and immensely opened up before them in a blast of space.

"Ninimoshe," he said softly.

He felt her start, tense, breathe the air in deeper gulps. When like a flowing fawn material her grace came over her, he understood: If he looked at her he wouldn't be able to do it. So he did not look at her face. Slowly, reluctantly, fighting his own need, dizzily, Klaus pulled at the loop of dirty gray sweetheart calico, undid the knot that bound her to him. At first, she didn't seem to know what her freedom meant. She gazed at the distance until it filled her eyes. Then she shook her hand and saw that she was no longer bound to Klaus. She stretched her arm out before her, turned her fingers over curiously, examined her blank brown palms.

"Go," he whispered. His voice was terrible and he sat suddenly down like a baby dropping to its seat, sprawled in the grass, addled, tears slowly pumping from the inside of him deep and far away as the call of hoot owls. He threw down the strip of cloth that had tied her to him and then tied him to the bottle. "Gewhen," he said. "Gewhen!"

When he did that, he imagined that she would bound forward in the lyric of motion that only her people have. But she did not spring from his shadow, only walked forward a weary step. Confused, broken inside, shaking her head, she stumbled over the uneven ground. She began her way west. Klaus watched her going. The land was so flat. She was perfectly in focus. He could see her slender back, quick legs, once or twice a staggered leap, a fall, an attempt to run. Klaus thought that she might turn around but she kept going, kept moving, until she was a white needle, quivering, then a dark fleck on the western band.

22

The Surprise Party

The bruised pods of cardamom. Sweet cake flour fine as powder. Scent of vanilla easing up the stairwell. Frank was browning tart crusts. Made his own lemon curd to fill them. Juiced the lemons, shredded the peel, stirred the pudding in a thick-bottomed kettle with the timeless assurance of a man whose beloved wife is just upstairs. Rozin was at her desk organizing, studying, taking notes, all with the relieved intensity of a born-again student. She breathed the vanilla and felt on her skin the slow increasing tension of the baking crusts below her, and vaguely anticipated the moment of piercing sweetness, the first bite, the taste he would bring her at noon.

She shuffled her note cards and let the screen saver—silver bolts of lightning touching purple, magenta, pale yellow, silver again—streak and snag across the humming face of her computer. Almost a full year had passed since the wedding, and she wanted to do something special for Frank, something memorable, something even a little outrageous so that, in the future, when thinking back to their wedding, they would remember instead of the bloody tragedy of that event the excess and pleasure of their first anniversary.

Frank was bored by gestures of storybook romance. Flowers and music left him blank, even fancy wines. Those things were too predictable anyway. She needed something more, something that reached toward Frank in a way that touched some essence of who he was, and it would be private, and it would be just the two of them, which would surprise him, because Frank had heard her speak wistfully of gathering together the very people who had come to their wedding. But she would instead do as he'd rather and create some sexy private moment, some personal ritual that would be known only to them.

To this end, she set her mind.

In a how-to-get-him magazine article, she had once read about a woman who greeted her man at the door wearing only plastic wrap. It was, she considered, a sort of miracle substance to Frank—he used it all the time when he baked. She thought of getting a roll from the kitchen and making of herself the surprise. But then, the stuff itself was so clingy, so staticky, so dry and unwieldy and easily ripped that she doubted it would feel that good to make love dragging in its folds. She thought of wearing only chocolate, of homemade raspberry jam, of sugar frosting, and of peach. She thought of lemon curd and cheesecake filling. Considered buttering herself and rolling in a bath of cinnamon. Or fluff, she thought, go cheap maybe. Marshmallow fluff. Marshmallows. A tiny bikini of tiny multicolored marshmallows. Frank could take his time eating them, but then, once she was naked, he would be stuffed full of awful, stale, sugary, sweet marshmallows, Rozin thought. Her mind drifted. Whatever they are. Are they made of marsh? Or mallow? From long ago, when Cally and Deanna were young, she remembered being fed invisibly and fully, a kind of spirit food that her daughters made, touching her lips, seaweed marshmallows.

And then suddenly she imagined that she prepared the cake, the thing itself, the cake from the recipe he had perfected. The blitzkuchen. Theirs. But then what? How would she wear it? How would they eat it? What if she made a mistake? In her imagined dream she saw them grind the cake to crumbs between them. Yes, and no. She would wear something else, or some lack of something. She came full circle to the plastic wrap. Thought, almost obsessively, about the way to devise her dress.

Frank was well aware and the knowledge was a stitch in his side—this was the time of year, the depth of the year. The full run of the first year of their marriage was approaching. He did not like the sense of eerie violation that came with the anniversary. He wanted to look forward to the week and the day and especially the security of the first evening of their fully acknowledged togetherness. There was some sense in him that just to have that treasure was to reexperience his own creation on this earth—and he wanted to, wanted the everyday stroke of the unerring hammer. Wanted to experience the sometimes boredom of their powerful, exquisite, ordinary love. For each day he was with her was a day less of their future, and he wanted every hour of it, every solid, aching minute.

So he thought to himself, What shall I give her? On a bit of cash register paper he made a list of gifts and possibilities. Expensive jewelry. Luxuries. A private, exquisite dinner. A night of solitude in some remote vacation place or just a camp-out on the kitchen floor. He thought of her, what she would like, however, and then he thought of her again, understanding what she'd really wanted, though he understood the need, took pleasure, imagined it now with her transferred enthusiasm. After all, he'd heard her mention the party with longing, out loud.

Everyone who'd been at the wedding. Friends, family, reunited enemies, survivors of that year. They'd meet. They'd have a party—where . . . here. Frank looked around him. Here! In his bakery shop and in his place of business. Right below the rambling darkness and light of their apartment. Out back, where the locust trees shed that fluttering shade, he'd string lights. Speakers. He sighed, resigned to it. There would be music. Dancing. Kool-Aid. Pastries. Cake and barbecue. He'd make the cake of cakes once more, again, from the refined recipe. They'd all be there. It would be generous, big, loud, and best of all, a smile slowly dawned in him, exquisite, he would make it a surprise.

The week before their anniversary, she panicked. Thought of buying him a watch. A name bracelet. Shoes. Something he would look at every day. Neither one of them could mention the anniversary, however, and its avoided bulk grew between them—bigger and bigger like a twice-risen bread, and then a vast wild-yeasted dough. It doubled and redoubled itself—and the tipping load of it grew flimsy and the two grew shy. They couldn't touch, retreated after work; isolated in their plans they neglected each other's company and brooded. Made secret phone calls. Each cultivated a convincing memory loss. They mentioned little as the date approached, then less, then nothing. It was as though they were both secretly adulterous.

Their anniversary day.

So far, no frost. Most of the trees were still leafed out to their fullest and blowsy in their end-of-summer leaves. The air was dusty and faintly golden, too warm, perhaps, for autumn, but the morning had been cold so that the scent of the trees and the fugitive fall blossoms of roses hung here and there in pockets of sweetness. All day, at class, Rozin glanced at the index card that held her plan—after the store closed he would be downstairs finishing the cleanup. She would be upstairs setting flowers in vases. Unwrapping candles. Sautéing mushrooms. Changing the sheets on their saggy double-bed mattress. As he neared the predictable end of his routine she'd light the candles in the bedroom. Doff her clothes. Apply perfume. She would cover, or rather decorate, herself strategically with stick-on bows. Two bright pink ones on her tawny nipples. One below.

That evening, she did all exactly as she had envisioned. Last thing, she peeled the waxy paper off the stick-on rectangle and applied the bows. The two pink. Below her navel, she stuck on a frilly expensive bow, white and silver, bought at a Hallmark shop. She pinned her hair up and stuck another tiny hot pink one over her ear, a white one on her shoulder. A tiny spice-brown bow on each earlobe. She wedged her feet into silver high-heeled pumps. Picked up a match, a sparkler, a cupcake. Nothing else. Her heart drummed as she smoothed on her lipstick and touched an extra dab of perfume to each temple.

Downstairs in the store, sliding through the front door from which Frank had removed the bell, and from the back alley through the bakery, the wedding party guests came whispering, tiptoeing, sneaking childishly, huddling together. In the big room below, where the staircase from the upstairs apartment gave out into the bakery, there was a wider step, almost a landing, next to which Frank stood with his hand on the light switch. He had informed them all of the routine. When Rozin came down the stairs and reached the landing, placed almost like a small stage at the entrance to the kitchen, when she paused in the gloom, he'd hit the switch. They'd all yell . . .

Walking down the staircase through the hush of the evening toward Frank's voice, hollow at the bottom of the steps, Rozin was preoccupied with balance and timing. The heels were higher than she was used to. Naked but for the bows, she shivered. She came down slowly so as not to stumble. That would ruin it all. She planned that she would stand at the bottom of the stairs, where light would catch the satin in the ribbons of the stick-on bows. In one hand, the cupcake with the sparkler in it. In the other hand, the match she would strike on the rough wood of the door frame . . .

The scrape of the match, the flame, and her uncertain voice. Frank flipped on the lights. The packed crowd shouted on cue. Surprise!

And everybody was surprised.

Rozin blinked. The sparkler sparked on the cupcake she held. Naked, but for the motionless bows, heels together, her mouth opened in shock too deep for screaming. For an endless moment, the party of friends and family, just as stunned, stood paralyzed, gaping. Then Rozin stumbled backward, gasping, as Frank with extraordinary presence of mind whipped a starched white apron off the hook behind him and draped it over her. He bent close in concern and horror. Face working, she waved him off. Tears stung his eyes to witness her humiliated loveliness. Nobody had the presence of mind to speak. The silence held until it was broken by one solitary hiccup from Rozin. Huddled over the apron, the cupcake smoldering and smashed at the silver tip of her shoe, she hiccuped again.

The party waited. The hiccups sounded like the prelude to a bout of hysteria. Though she was no weeper, Frank nonetheless expected her to cry. Her shoulders shook. Her forehead was red in her hands. But when she lifted her face to his, a great bold crack of laughter sizzled out of her and lit like a string of firecrackers all the other laughter in the room, so that his own scratchy, hoarse, unfamiliar, first laughing croak was part of the general roar.

23

Scranton Roy

The first time he stumbled in his deerhide boots, the old woman he'd killed came to visit him, dragging a sledge of skulls and bones. She passed by at some distance. He was still certain it was her. Scranton Roy had fallen sick in the mud of spring. His body seemed to want to turn itself inside out. His body would endure anything to get rid of the soul riding in it, Scranton thought, violently dreaming. His fever built and Scranton saw her again. The old woman came to stand beside his bed this time and gestured flat-handed at the bloody hole his bayonet had made in her stomach. Her voice was oddly young, high and lilting, and she spoke to him in her language for a long time. He did not understand the words, but knew the meaning.

Who knows whose blood sins we are paying for? What murder committed in another country, another time? The black-robe priests believe that Christ allowed himself to be nailed high on the cross in order to pay. Shawanos think different. Why should an innocent god, a manitou spirit, have to settle for our bad drunks, our rage, our heart-sown angers and mistakes?

Those things should come down on us.

Yet, though he heard her out, he still thought that he could make amends. Scranton Roy began to plot in a fever. Plans came to him in swollen dreams. She was there, the old woman, stumbling toward him with a grandmotherly anxiety, her face not ferocious but pleading, hopeless, satisfied to divert his attention, shot, pistol, from the running children. She threw herself toward him, a sacrifice. With shame, he saw again her sight rush inward to meet her death.

Where were her people now? he wondered, at last. Where did her bones lie? How had she found him?

On the hundredth night that she visited him, exhausted and fearful, Scranton Roy made a promise to the now familiar old woman. He would find the village and the people he had wronged. He would bring along the son of the boy nursed on Father's milk. His grandson, Augustus. With them two packhorses loaded with everything he could spare and not spare of his possessions. She seemed to accept this. When he woke, he found his strength improved. Clouds had disappeared from his eyes. The excruciating knots in his bones untied. His fever dropped and Augustus no longer had to hold his grandfather down, forcing the spoon between his teeth, during rough seizures.

They set out over the bleak farmland, leading their packhorses laden with grain, with strings of trade beads, hatchets, kettles, string, salt, hominy, wool, molasses, and dried mushrooms. Augustus had no more than six fine brown hairs growing on his chin. Young and shy, he went stark red and silent at the sight of any woman. All of his life, he had lived alone with his grandfather. Learned to read, write, do passionate games of arithmetic, play cards at the table by the deep sills and pots of blooming acid red flowers. Now, his feet big, step gloomy, his forehead raw from the cold spring wind, he trudged east leading the horse toward a place he'd never been and a destiny set into motion by his grandfather's guilt and an old woman's ghost.

The world was poker-table flat underneath a low green sky. They stopped and camped beside a lightning-scored oak at the edge of a series of regular hummocks of land that seemed patted into place by the hands of a giant child. From there, they looked into an earthscape of sloughs and lakes, potholes, woods of delicate yellow-green lace, undulant hills. Into that perfectly made land they wandered, searching out the people now confined to treaty areas, reservations, or as they called them ishkonigan, the leftovers. Seeking town to town, following the lumber crews and then the miners, the Indian agents and at last the missionaries, Scranton and his grandson came to the remnants of the village and the unmended families, the sick, the bitter, the restored.

Everything is all knotted up in a tangle. Pull one string of this family and the whole web will tremble. There stood Augustus with the hanks of red beads in his hands, the old ones of highbush red, white centers, glowing glass. The ruby red whiteheart beads all the women loved. These were the beads he traded to Ten Stripe Woman, Midass, relative of the woman his grandfather killed. Augustus traded the beads and all he owned for the silent young girl his eye fell upon when his grandfather and he entered the camp. He could not stop looking at her, watched her every move. He became uncharacteristically stubborn and declared that he would not leave the bashful one whose hands were in the water, the skillful one scraping the hide with a deer's white scapula, the good one, the bad one, half of the set of ravenous gentle-eyed twins whom he would live with, who would start out thin and then grow fetchingly plump. Whose eyeteeth gleamed and who were modest and yet sly. Who had every reason on this earth to hate his grandfather. From whose cabin he would disappear.

The beads Augustus Roy traded to Midass for her great-granddaughter were sewn onto a blanket she was making for a woman expecting a child. Still later, before the favorite blanket was snagged to pieces, the child was named for the decoration it loved, Whiteheart Beads. That name went on until Richard ended up with it. Long after the beads were scattered and the blanket turned to rags, Richard Whiteheart Beads married the daughter of a Roy. He would have died in his sleep on his eighty-fifth birthday, sober, of a massive stroke, had his self-directed pistol shot glanced a centimeter higher.

All that followed, all that happened, all is as I have told. Did these occurrences have a paradigm in the settlement of the old scores and pains and betrayals that went back in time? Or are we working out the minor details of a strictly random pattern? Who is beading us? Who is setting flower upon flower and cut-glass vine? Who are you and who am I, the beader or the bit of colored glass sewn onto the fabric of this earth? All these questions, they tug at the brain. We stand on tiptoe, trying to see over the edge, and only catch a glimpse of the next bead on the string, and the woman's hand moving, one day, the next, and the needle flashing over the horizon.

The Johnny B. Good Foundation

The Johnny B. Good Foundation is about personal empowerment and spiritual growth. The general purpose of the Foundation is to foster the creation, development, and implementation of services and programs that will help individuals learn about personal empowerment and spiritual growth. Participants in these services and programs will learn how to take responsibility to improve the quality of their lives for the benefit of themselves, their families and friends, and their community.

The Johnny B. Good Foundation
1107 Hazeltine Boulevard, Suite 200
Chaska, MN 55318
612/361-8900